To Mia & Otto

GW00792212

Busbeater's Magnificent Adventures In Time

Big Trouble In The Court Of King John

Stephen Price

Here's to a billion magnificent adventures

Stephen x

28 April 2016

For Olwyn

Without her inspiration, cajoling and all round 'Get On With It',
Busbeater would have had no adventures, magnificent or
otherwise and Gerald would have had no days to save.

Table of Contents

CHAPTER ONE

A Moon Landing And Seeing A Wardrobe

Gerald Jones, the Most Excited Boy In The World, woke early. For today was the day that astronauts Neil Armstrong and Buzz Aldrin aboard their space ship Apollo 11 would land on the moon. Ever since he was a small boy he had been waiting for this day. And now, finally, when he was twelve years, two months, four days, fourteen minutes and twelve seconds, no thirteen, no fourteen, no fifteen seconds old the day had finally, finally come. He lay as still as he could staring up to his bedroom ceiling. Dangling from it were models of the Saturn Rocket, the Apollo landing module and globes of the moon. He was even wearing his special Astronaut Pyjamas.

'It's the moon landing,' he whispered to himself, barely able to believe it. 'Today,' he added, as if he hadn't been lying in wait for July 20 1969 for ever.

There was a light knock on his bedroom door.

'Hello sweetheart,' his mum called as she pushed open the door holding a breakfast tray.

Gerald's mum woke him pretty much every morning but he was a bit surprised at having his breakfast delivered. Normally, even on a Sunday, he was woken up and practically frog-marched bleary eyed in to the kitchen to have breakfast at the table with his dad grunting and usually swearing behind the sports pages of the papers. This was a special treat.

'It's a special day Gerald. It's the moon landing!'

Gerald's mum was just as excited as he was. She had cried when the

Saturn rocket took off four days ago and had been in a state of high emotion ever since. Now, on the day astronauts would land on the moon she had made a Special Moon Landing Day Breakfast for Gerald to mark the occasion. His mum was a trier but she wasn't a very good cook. More often than not small fires broke out during the preparation. Last year's attempt at coq au vin to this day remains a legend in the family and beyond.

But she'd done an exceptional job today. Before him Gerald marvelled at a Saturn Rocket shaped sausage, toast with the outline of the Apollo landing craft burnt on it and a scotch egg designed to look like the Moon.

'Crikey Mum, this is brilliant. Look, I am eating the moon.' He dived in to his scotch egg.

From outside on the landing Gerald heard the coughing and swearing of his dad as he wheezed into life. Smoking an early morning fag, he shuffled past Gerald's room on his way to the bathroom. He was dressed in an old, stained vest and scruffy trousers. His greying hair was unwashed and he hadn't shaved for many days making him look like a vagrant. He bumbled past without even saying hello to his excited son. Gerald knew his dad wasn't and had never been even remotely interested in the moon landing. Or much else really; he was just a fat useless layabout as far as Gerald was concerned. Life would be a whole lot more fun if he just cleared off.

'Bloody waste of money. What's the point of going to the moon? It's nothing but a big ball of rock. Pointless and stupid,' had been Gerald's dad's not very well thought out response to the whole thing.

Unknown to Gerald, his dad, Arnold Jones was once full of beans and ideas and fun. Indeed right up until just after Gerald was born he was a nice, kind and thoughtful chap with a mischievous glint in his eye. He'd been introduced to Linda, Gerald's mum in the autumn of 1956. For him it was love at first sight; Linda was recovering from a broken heart and he made her laugh easily. They married very quickly and soon Gerald arrived. Arnold settled in to a job and was happy to provide Linda and his son with a nice, safe home even though he knew something was missing for both him and Linda. But he had had his adventures and now it was time to settle down and give Linda's heart time to heal. Then things went a bit wrong. Whilst digging up turnips one Sunday afternoon when Gerald was only three, Arnold badly sprained his back and he couldn't work. After six months he still wasn't better and was laid off from his job; he hadn't worked since. His pride was shattered and the overwhelming feeling of despair was made worse because he knew Linda's family was paying the mortgage that he couldn't; he was humiliated.

He loved Gerald with all the fibre of his being, but with confidence at rock bottom and self pity clawing at him, he had lost the ability to show it. Then just a few days ago and completely out of the blue something fantastical happened which instantly reignited Arnold's spirit. It was then that he hatched the idea to send Gerald to Busbeater Mansions for the summer. Maybe this way he could show his son that he wasn't the dead beat Gerald thought he was. He dug out an old book, a diary, in which he wrote an inscription, a comic and a tee shirt and placed them in a big brown envelope. He hid the envelope in the knapsack he had bought Gerald for the journey. With disguised excitement he then retreated to his normal farting and belching self. He so much wanted to tell his son everything, but he knew he'd never believe him. All Gerald saw was a sad, pathetic man who snuffed the life out of his beloved mum. Gerald would have to find out on his own.

Gerald's mum, Linda Jones was gentle and softly spoken with a distant look in her eyes, but absolutely no pushover. She had banished Gerald to his room with no supper on more than one occasion. The worst time was that incident with next door's budgie, a washing up bottle and some glue. But usually they got on famously and were always laughing and joking. Growing up, Linda Busbeater had wanted to be an explorer, an adventurer. She had read tales of derring-do by Jules Verne; H Rider Haggard; Arthur Conan Doyle; Rudyard Kipling. Linda was always climbing trees and hills and scrambling down banks into streams searching for treasures or lost civilisations. She was a Busbeater; it's what Busbeaters did. Then when she was 19 she met the man who would be her king; they would get married and like the heroes in her books they would travel the world seeking adventure. But then one day inexplicably he vanished and Linda's heart broke in to a thousand pieces. Her spirit of adventure withered that day. Not long afterwards she met Arnold, a decent, funny man and she fell for him; they married within weeks and very soon had a son. A son who would love adventure.

Gerald did indeed love adventure. From an early age he had shown an independent spirit always doings things his way in much the same way his mum had done when she was little. As soon as he could walk he would spend as much time outside as he could. Gerald had some friends at school but was happiest alone in his own world building forts, lurking in bushes and fighting imaginary enemies. Gerald's imagination ran riot almost all the time he was awake; when he learnt about space exploration and that men were going to land on the moon, his heart leapt like a salmon. This was The Greatest Adventure Of All.

'Gerald,' his mum spoke quietly, 'you know you ought to think about packing. Think about what you want to take' her voice was sad but she was trying not to let it show.

Gerald's useless deadbeat dad had insisted he be sent away for the summer to his aunt and uncle at Busbeater Mansions. He'd never even met them before but he knew they were old and probably smelled and they lived in the middle of nowhere with no other kids there or pets or anything to do and it would be really, really boring and he just wanted to stay here at home with his comics and endlessly re-enact the moon landing. But his dad had insisted and his mum had reluctantly agreed. Gerald thought it the worst idea in the very world.

Gerald had lain awake the night his mum told him he must go. He would be away for the whole of the summer holidays; SIX weeks. It would be horrible, beastly and most of all extremely boring; where would he find adventure at his million year old uncle's smelly old house?

Normally the summer holiday was the best time ever. With no rubbishy annoying school to go to he could be an adventurer. Stalking imaginary prey across the local fields Gerald, armed with his toy rifle pretended one day to be a great hunter; the next a pirate; then an intrepid explorer of distant lands in the pay of a rich but power crazed Queen. Other times he'd be an Indian or a Cowboy or an ancient King defending his land from invaders. When his mum came along as she sometimes did he made her be a damsel in distress. Although only after some initial confusion about damsons (the variety of plum) and damsels (long haired young ladies in mediaeval towers needing to be rescued) had been cleared up.

'It's not quite the same thing Gerald, saving a fruit in distress,' pointed out his mum.

'I am a bold knight and I will save whatever needs saving,' said the intrepid and determined Gerald.

'That's very noble of you kind Sir Gerald, but I don't fancy being a plum, so shall we say damsel and not damson?'

'OK Mum. I will save you from the dragon my damson in distress.'

'Damsel!'

On rainy days when he was smaller his mum would read stories to him from her adventures books. He had been captivated by the adventures of Captain Nemo, Allan Quatermain and Sherlock Holmes. The idea of having to go away from his mum to stay with boring old people was one that brought him to the brink of tears. He would wonder what Allan Quatermain or Neil Armstrong would do. They wouldn't cry, so neither would he. But sometimes when he was being Gerald Jones and not an explorer and he remembered he had to go away for the summer, his heart would feel heavy and sink; his eyes would well up and he would dive under his pillow. Why did he have to go? He didn't understand …

'I want to take my comics and the lunar module. Do I have to go Mum?'

'It's for the best, it'll give your father some time to-'

'Fart and burp like a train even more …?'

Gerald's mum smiled to herself.

'Give him time to make sure his back gets better so he can get a job.'

'I don't see how me being away at stupid smelly old Busbeater Mansions is going to help his back heal.'

'Careful Gerald. That's my family you're talking about. They don't smell. Probably.'

They both burst out laughing before his mum conceded, 'Well, OK maybe old Uncle Busbeater does pong of cigars a bit, but it's not that bad. And Auntie Marjorie's bound to have a new perfume she and Major General Loosehorn will have tried which will disguise the whiff a bit.'

Gerald smiled but he still wanted to stay put. He knew though that if he whined on it would just upset his mum even more so he decided to be all twelve years, two months, four days, twenty two minutes and seven seconds, no eight, no nine, no ten seconds about it and go along with the whole stupid thing.

With some slightly false cheeriness Gerald's mum stood up as he finished the last morsels of his Moon Landing Day Breakfast and announced, 'It's a special day Gerald, but it's Sunday and that means some chores so chop chop, let's get those teeth cleaned and some clothes on.'

As he brushed his teeth and pulled on his trousers, socks and Apollo 11 tee-shirt - which was actually a plain white tee shirt with Apollo 11 written on it in varying and fading shades of green felt tip with '11' in blue as the green pen ran dry - his mum was playing Fly Me To the Moon on the record player at full blast downstairs to the increasing irritation of his dad who bellowed 'Turn that bloody racket off. I'm not well you know' over and over until eventually he managed to haul himself out of bed and slam the bedroom door shut.

His sandy hair wild but brushed, proudly wearing his tee shirt and with shoe laces not quite tied Gerald stood in the kitchen doorway and watched his mum. She was tall and slim and the fringe of her dark brown hair was held back by a band. She was wearing a flowery summer dress and an equally flowery pinny. She seemed full of life. An image helped enormously by the dancing at the sink and the singing; 'Fly me to the moon, let me sing among those stars, let me see what spring is like on Jupiter and Mars ...' she warbled happily.

'Mum'

She didn't hear him

'Mum!'

still no

'Muuuuuuum!'

'Oh sorry sweetheart, I was ...'

'Singing.'

'Singing. Right. You look a picture. Now, help me with the drying up.'

Gerald hated doing the drying up but knew in the same way it was Neil Armstrong's mission to land on the moon (today!) it was his mission to do the washing up as quickly as he could. So bravely he hitched his up trousers; but then he had a sudden and bright idea and ran back out of the kitchen.

'Gerald, you've still got drying up to do!' called his mum, slightly irritated.

'Yes Mum, haven't forgotten back in a sec' he called as he hurtled upstairs.

'Keep the noise down; I'm not well you know.'

'Sorry Dad' croaked Gerald as he crept in to his room and straight over to his goldfish named after the Apollo Astronauts Neil Armstrong and Buzz Aldrin.

'Crikey dad is boring and dull,' muttered Gerald. His dad was always so ill and never seemed to do anything to try to get better while his effervescent mum was always so full of beans and kind to him. His dad with his stupid bad back just lay there the whole time moaning and groaning and telling him off. Although sometimes he actually got out of bed to go to the toilet; and to tell him off.

Gerald returned to the kitchen via the bathroom five minutes later sporting a very realistic spaceman's helmet which was actually a gold fish bowl. As he got to the kitchen door he slowed down to walk as he imagined Neil Armstrong will do after he lands on the moon.

'Houston, the ground is tiled like a kitchen floor; over.'

'We copy that Commander Gerald. Is there a sink in there with dishes that need drying up? Over.'

'That's affirmative Houston; over.'

'Your mission Commander Gerald is to dry them in record time, over.'

Gerald's mum watched her odd son moonwalk over to the sink and start drying the dishes in super-fast time

'Er Gerald?'

'Yes Houston … er I mean Mum' said Gerald from inside his helmet/goldfish bowl.

'Where are the goldfish?'

'Neil and Buzz are in the bathroom.'

At that moment the bathroom door slammed shut.

'Gerald, did you put them in the sink?'

'Er, well not the sink exactly. I couldn't find the plug; over.'

'Or the bath?' Gerald's mum's voice began to squeak

'Er, nooooo …' Filling up the bath would have taken ages.

With washing up gloves still on Gerald's mum ran out of the kitchen and was half way up the stairs when the inevitable happened …

'Aiiiiiieeeeeee. There are goldfish in the toilet! I told you I wasn't well!' Gerald's dad had found Neil and Buzz.

The bedroom door slammed shut.

'We won't see Dad much today. He'll be in shock for hours.'

Linda felt Gerald had done enough chores for this day of days so let him off the hook early.

'Gerald, off you go. You've helped enough.'

'Brilliant, thank you Mum. Over.'

'But take the bowl off your head. Neil and Buzz might want it back after having your father's bottom loom down on them like that.'

'Yes Mum.'

Gerald swiftly filled the goldfish bowl and with the sieve he poured Neil and Buzz back in. If fish could look startled Neil and Buzz looked very startled indeed.

Gerald sat on the floor in front of the telly. He watched captivated as the TV presenter James Burke explained how the landing would take place with models just like Gerald's. The hours trudged by while Apollo 11 zoomed ever nearer the moon. And then suddenly the next best thing happened.

'Gerald. Lunch is ready. It's a Special Moon Day Landing Roast.' His mum announced proudly.

Crikey thought Gerald. This whole day seems to be just an excuse for mum to make big meals and give each one of them a special name. In front of him was a slice of beef with three or four mutant carrot astronauts walking across them. The Yorkshire Pudding or The Sea of Tranquility was in the middle of the plate. The sausage was a surprise but like breakfast, it was the Saturn Rocket. There was something else on the plate which may have been a vegetable or something but it was scorched black, bullet hard and Gerald was worried that if he moved it, it might ignite. That had happened before with his porridge one very cold morning. Gerald wondered if other families were on first name terms with everyone in the fire brigade.

Finally Gerald was released from dinner and he hurtled back in to the living room, making large ripples in the rug as he slid to a halt right in front of the TV again brilliantly balancing his rhubarb crumble (he was guessing, it had gone a bit wrong but at least it was purple. And that was definitely custard. Probably).

Gerald was glued to James Burke on the TV. The landing was still hours away but the excitement was gradually building. All at once time was zooming by and yet going painfully slowly. After what seemed like several lifetimes, the lunar module was now at very last approaching the moon. Gerald was, officially, really very, very excited now.

'Gerald, get away from the TV.'

'I'll damage my eyes, I know, I know' he said shuffling back.

'No, I just can't see a thing with your head in the way' replied his mum.

The clock ticked its way to just before twenty past nine and as it did so the moon raced in to view ever closer on their small black and white TV.

Linda Jones shuddered and looked around. What was that? She thought she felt something on her shoulder …

Simultaneously upstairs Arnold Jones sat bolt upright and shivering slightly rubbed his shoulder 'what the ...?'

Gerald clutched his lunar module and glued to the TV held his breath as he saw the moon get closer and closer listening to Mission Control Houston and Commander Neil Armstrong talk urgently but with infuriating calm.

Houston 'You're go for landing over.'

Beep.

Neil Armstrong 'Go for landing, 3,000 feet.'

Houston 'You're looking great.'

Beep.

The flickering black and white pictures showed the surface of the moon getting ever closer. Gerald gripped his lunar module even tighter. They were nearly there.

Houston 'thirty seconds.'

Beep.

Armstrong 'contact light? OK engine stopped.'

Beep.

Houston: 'we copy you down eagle.'

Beep.

Armstrong: 'Houston er, Tranquility Base here. The eagle has landed.'

Gerald hadn't moved; his mouth hadn't closed; his eyes hadn't blinked in case he missed something. As he watched the misty pictures from 200,000 miles away he saw a flash of something. What was that? Weirdly and improbably it looked like a wardrobe! Had he imagined it? He scoured the TV screen, but it wasn't there. But he was sure. Then he became aware of a muffled noise behind him. Dragging himself away from the black and white flickering images of the Most Important Thing That Has Ever Happened In The World Ever and maybe some item of furniture, he turned to his mum. Her face had turned in to a cushion from which the muffled noises were coming. Gerald was suddenly worried. What had happened?

'Oh Gerald' his mum sobbed as she removed the cushion from her face 'they've landed on the moon! They've landed.' She leapt up and put the record player on. Before he knew what was happening Gerald and his mum were dancing around the room; 'Fly me to the moon let me sing

among those stars, let me see what spring is like on Jupiter and Mars …'
sang his mum heartily.

'What's all this bloody racket about?' Ruining the mood completely,
Gerald's dad stood in the doorway of the living room in his vest and
pants sucking hard on a cigarette. They had both been so gripped by the
TV that they hadn't put any lights on. Gerald's dad stood in the doorway
bathed in the flickering grey light of the television.

Suits him, grey, thought Gerald.

He saw the TV.

'Is this still bloody on? Haven't they crashed it or something
interesting?'

'They have just landed. It was beautiful' retorted Gerald's mum.

Arnold mumbled something about idiots and slumped in front of the
telly. He made Gerald get him a beer and lit another fag. In the darkness
of the room Arnold Jones watched, gripped at the grainy images coming
from the moon. He had been secretly been listening to it all day on the
radio under the covers. This was without any shadow of a doubt a great
day. 'One day Gerald, one day very, very soon my boy' he whispered to
himself.

'What Dad?' asked Gerald as he came back with his dad's beer.

'Er, I er, I … was wondering where the heck you were with my beer.'

'Here it is' said Gerald and sat with a thump on the floor.

Arnold took it and opened it immediately as a fizz of liquid bubbled
out of the top. From the shadows he watched his little boy grow wide-
eyed with excitement at the TV.

He looked on and silently in his head whispered,

'Soon Gerald, I promise you - soon.'

Then, back to his self-afflicted role of burping and farting and twenty further minutes of moaning on, he fell asleep. Loudly.

Gerald's mum looked on sadly at her husband. And then at her overexcited boy. Despite the racket from Arnold's every orifice, Gerald had completely conked out. He was exhausted after the excitement of the day and had fallen asleep lying in front of the TV clutching his Apollo Models. It was school tomorrow, she'd better get him to bed. It was no use asking Arnold. He was dead to the world. Linda picked him up as best she could and slowly took him upstairs.

She dressed him in his astronaut pyjamas and settled him in. He was asleep but his grip on the lunar module remained as tight as a vice. She left it with him and tucked him in to bed. Gerald sleepily murmured something.

'Mum, did you see The Wardrobe?'

'Pardon? The what? Where?'

'The Wardrobe. On the moon. I saw a Wardrobe.'

'No Gerald, I think your weary brain just imagined it. There are no wardrobes on the moon. In your bedroom maybe, but not the moon.'

Before he drifted off Gerald managed to mutter

'What a fantastic day Mum. The best of my life.'

She kissed him on the forehead and said, 'Yes, mine too. Good night my little astronaut' she whispered as she turned the light out and closed the door quietly behind her.

3.30 a.m.

Gerald's mum crept in and knelt by her son's bed. She whispered next to his ear, 'Gerald, sweetheart. They are walking on the moon in half an hour. Do you want to watch it?'

Gerald sat bolt upright.

'Do I want to watch it? You bet your scorched porridge I do.' He leapt out of bed nearly knocking his mum over in the process and zoomed downstairs.

His mum had followed him down at a more sedate pace but was now sitting next to him on the sofa. They were both motionless, gripped by the hazy pictures of history being made. They could just make out the shape of a spacesuit. It made its cumbersome way out of the landing module and down the steps. The world stopped as this lone figure made his way to the surface of the moon. What would Neil Armstrong say? What would he do? Gerald had waited for this moment for weeks.

Armstrong: 'I am at the foot of the ladder. I am stepping off the LAM. It's one small step for man one giant leap for mankind.'

And that was it. Man was on the Moon and he Gerald Jones had seen all of it. And then suddenly he conked out and was fast asleep dreaming an awful lot; he was in a wardrobe hurtling through time waving at Neil Armstrong as he raced by them as they headed toward the moon while he was on his way to another magnificent adventure.

CHAPTER TWO

A Strange Present And A Magnificent Secret

The next morning Gerald dragged his weary self to St Cuthbert's Comprehensive school. At least he thought, they had promised to show the moon landing on Mr Phillips' new-fangled recorder for those who had missed it. Missed it? 'What sort of wimps are they?' thought Gerald, if a little sleepily.

The prospect of watching it all again however perked him up and as he got to school he headed straight for the gym where the huge TV was set up to make sure he got a good seat in the kids section right behind the front row where the teachers had rudely reserved their seats. From behind the TV came the unmistakable and bad tempered swearing of Physics teacher Mr Phillips. After a sudden and loud electrical bang that sent Mr Phillips' swearing to an incredibly high pitch, the TV monitor came on and the big box of wires and lights glowed and whirred.

Mr Phillips emerged, flustered, smouldering and with a split in his trousers but he was triumphant. He'd volunteered his new recording device which he had built in his shed but wasn't entirely confident it would work. Now, however, here it was, working. This will show them that Kevin Phillips isn't a dullard just because he still lives with his mother aged thirty seven.

Eventually the Headmaster, the nervous Mr Fitzsimmons, arrived along with the other teachers and tried to get the gathering children to listen.

'Right you lot. Today we are going to watch history being made.'

'Wasn't it yesterday sir?'

'Yes alright Jenkins, very good. Yes it was yesterday but since ALL of you would have been asleep in readiness for the school day then I am assuming you missed it.'

After Jenkins' hilarious joke about history being on yesterday bedlam broke out once more. Chief amongst the anarchists was Gerald's arch nemesis Nicholas Johnson; Gerald made sure he was well away from Nicholas. Well, so he thought, the hard flick on the right ear proved him wrong.

'Interested in a bunch of divvies prancing about on the moon are you Jones?' he sneered.

'Oh shut up Johnson' retorted Gerald just at the moment when Fitzsimmons had got everyone quiet.

'Care to share Jones?'

'No sir.'

'Shut up then. As I was saying … oh, just be quiet and watch this.'

Mr Phillips proudly flicked a switch and after an anxious few moments the screen flickered in to life. Gerald recognised the smell coming from Mr Phillip's machine; the same burning smell that came from the kitchen when mum was making a salad. The TV seemed to be working for now anyway and Gerald concentrated hard to recapture each moment. Soon despite Nicholas Johnson's best efforts to distract him with threats of using his henchmen the Butcher Twins on him at break, Gerald was once again lost in the drama of the moon landing.

It was just as magnificent the second time around. But wait, there it was again. This time he was definitely sure it was a wardrobe. He saw it more clearly on the big screen. All the other kids were mucking around throwing paper airplanes and occasionally Peter 'Wimpy' Clipstone about the place. The teachers were trying in vain to regain control and all the while the burning smell from Mr Phillips' machine was getting stronger and stronger. Gerald ran up to the big monitor and scoured the picture. Then it went blank. Headmaster Mr Fitzsimmons was exasperatedly trying to control the excitable mob.

'Alright everyone, calm down now. Sit down everyone. That includes YOU Jones'

Wimpy Clipstone slid at high speed across the gym floor for the fourth time. The Butcher twins, how appropriate Gerald had always thought, being the flingers-in-chief.

'Pat and Frank Butcher stop that; Clipstone, stand up for yourself man. Sharon Good, what are you doing? It most certainly is not nothing young lady, now sit down and put whatever that is away.'

Then suddenly … KABLAM.

Mr Phillips had disappeared behind a plume of smoke while flames leapt out of his recording machine and on to the crash mats which soon began to burn brightly. Mr Fitzsimmons tried to get everyone to leave in an orderly fashion but led by the unpleasantly insane PE teacher Mr Burke there was a charge for the exits.

'Somebody call the fire brigade …' screamed Burke as he sprinted for the door, elbowing many a first year out of the way in the process.

Holding his screwdriver Mr Phillips emerged from the smoke looking startled with his face scorched, shirt ripped, smouldering hair standing on end and his eyebrows and moustache burnt off.

'I think I know what went wrong …'

'Hello Gerald mate. Not your mum's coq au vin this time then?'

It was Charlie the fireman who had been so nice a couple of weeks ago when he'd been round to put out one of mum's small cooking related fires.

'Hello Charlie. No, Mr Phillips' recording machine blew up'

'Yes. We have recovered what's left of it.'

Charlie handed Gerald a bright shiny disc. It was rather heavy.

'A flywheel. Want it?'

'Er, thank you Charlie.' He briefly inspected it. Considering it had been in a fire and an explosion, it was in very good condition, but what was he supposed to do with it? He liked Charlie and didn't want to hurt his feelings so slipped it in to his pocket. He also got the impression that Charlie was gently but firmly insistent; that 'no thank you' wasn't an option.

'Good lad.'

'Hello Mum.'

'Gerald. You're home early.'

'Yes, Mr Phillips blew up the school.'

'All of it?'

'Well, no just the gym, but Mr Fitzsimmons sent us home early anyway. He said something about wanting to get shot of us. I think he was crying ...'

'Ahh well, you're just in time for lunch'

Which reminded Gerald, 'Charlie came to put the fire out.'

'Did he? That was nice.'

'He gave me this.'

Gerald showed his mum the flywheel.

'What is it Mum?'

'Er, it's er, it's ... I don't know what it is. Part of an engine?'

'Charlie said it was what was left of Mr Phillips' recording machine. But it looks in awfully good condition for something that was on fire for a while. What should I do with it?'

'I don't know, but I'd keep it with you in case you, er, need it one day.'

'Mum' said Gerald matter-of-factly, 'lunch is on fire'

'Oh bum, bum, bumwaldo …'

Gerald was in his room re-enacting the Moon landing for the umpteenth time when his mum knocked on the door and came in.

'The school's been on the phone. Mr Fitzsimmons has decided to close the school early for the summer holidays after the explosion. He has been ordered to have complete rest. So that's you done for the year my boy.'

'Brilliant. Hoorah. Hot diggity dog'

'Hot diggity dog?' Gerald's mum frowned. 'You mustn't watch so much TV young man.'

Anyway, you know you're going to Uncle Busbeater's on Friday, well, er, how do you fancy going a day or two early.'

At that moment his dad emerged in the doorway behind his mum. He put his greasy arms around her waist. Gerald felt a pang of anger.

'Yes son. I think it would be for the best. You'll have a great time.' He didn't once look at him and without waiting for a response he left again. As he walked away he glanced discretely over his shoulder taking one last look at his son before he left; he knew the next time he saw him everything would be utterly changed.

Some things Gerald never understood. Why did his mum put up with him? And why did she let him tell her what to do the whole time? Why was she was letting him send him away for the summer? He didn't want to go and was only not making a fuss to avoid upsetting her. So he was stuck. He would have to go.

'When am I going?'

'How does Wednesday sound?'

Terrible.

'OK'

Gerald's mum left trying to hide the tears, but not doing a terribly good job. Gerald crash landed his lunar module in to a cardboard box immediately renamed Planet Dad and jumped up and down on it for good measure.

On the platform Gerald's mum went through the inventory;

'Ticket?'

'Yes Mum.'

'Suitcase?'

'Yes Mum.'

'Fifteen pairs of pants?'

'Yes Mum.'

'Fifteen pairs of socks?'

'Yes Mum.'

'Fifteen shirts?'

'Yes Mum.'

'Fifteen pairs of trousers?'

'Yes Mum.'

'Comics?'

'Yes Mum.'

'Knapsack with your packed lunch, apollo souvenir, lunar module, comics and general boy stuff in?'

This could have gone on for a while but the train was pulling in.

'Now on you get. Get a nice seat for yourself, by the window.'

'Yes Mum.'

Gerald gave his mum a big hug and could feel her laughing heartily. Except she wasn't laughing.

'Come on, chop, chop, get on the train or it'll go without you.' she sniffed.

'Will it. Really?' Gerald brightened.

'No. Get on the train.'

After dragging his unfeasibly heavy suitcase on to the train and asking the ticket collector to put it on the rack for him, Gerald settled himself in by the window just as the train began moving away. His mum was waving him off with her hanky running after the train as it accelerated. He leaned out of the window, waving heartily … then frantically … disaster was looming.

'Mum, Mum watch out for the -'

Too late; Linda Jones was so intent on waving goodbye to her son that she clattered in to Phil Phillips, the station manager and brother of teacher and school recording device inventor Kevin. Phil Phillips went flying head first in to the thorny hedgerow behind the platform swallowing his whistle on impact. In the collision Gerald's mum's hat had ripped so that the brim dangled across her face and the heel of one shoe had come off. But she recovered her poise, straightened her flowery dress, retrieved her handbag and listing slightly got ready to wave off her son. As she waved that last goodbye with both arms the emerging station master, bruised and bloodied from the hedgerow and the initial assault got a smack across the face from her handbag and whistling frantically went stumbling back in to a pillar whereupon a hanging basket, loosened by the vibrations fell, landing right on his head. He slid dozily to the floor. What with nearly blowing up the school and being knocked out by a bunch of flowers, Kevin and Phil Phillips were having a bad week.

Linda Smith waved her son off.

Life, thought Gerald, was about to become seriously boring.

The journey had already lasted around two hours and he had been on his own for most of the time. He had half an hour to go according to his Apollo 11 watch. Which was a normal watch with some badly drawn astronauts stuck on the strap. The ticket inspector who was oddly familiar had been nice enough though. He'd stayed and chatted for a while about how fantastic the moon landing had been and was interested in Gerald's models. At one point Charlie's flywheel had fallen out of Gerald's knapsack as he was rummaging around for his corned beef sandwich; quickly the inspector picked it up.

'Don't want to be losing that …' he said earnestly, suddenly becoming quite serious.

No, thought Gerald; although he didn't actually remember packing it in the first place.

Slowly the train wound round mile after mile of dull countryside. Gerald thought about his immediate future; probably bed by 7 o'clock; lots of cabbage for lunch and tea; absolutely nothing to do all day, every day in the middle of nowhere surrounded by old codgers who will go on about the olden days all the time. It seemed to Gerald a very bleak future and a very, very long summer. He sighed and as the window steamed up from his breath he drew a frowning face with an arrow pointing to his name - Gerald. Eventually the train slowed down even more until it shuddered to a stop at Little Piddlington. The ticket inspector walked past and stopped where Gerald was sitting.

'Your stop old son.'

'Thank you.'

The inspector hauled his suitcase off the rack above him and dragged it on to the platform before re-boarding the train. It pulled away very soon afterwards leaving Gerald standing all alone wondering what to do next.

'Welcome to Little Piddlington' said a voice. 'I am Sheepshanks, Lieutenant Colonel Busbeater's batman.'

Sheepshanks was a tall thin man but with a large round and quite wrinkly face framed by wild white hair and big, grey slightly sad eyes. It was a warm summer's day so obviously he was wearing a long black jacket over a white shirt, black trousers that were slightly too short and, oddly, enormously long brown walking boots. He smiled warmly at Gerald who thought he must be at least 100 years old. Or sixty at any rate. Gerald looked at this beanpole of an old man. Blimey he thought, I hope Auntie and Uncle aren't this ancient. This is going to be a dull enough summer as it is without having to be some kind of nurse maid to a bunch of old folk.

'Ah, hello. I am Gerald.'

'I know. We have been expecting you. A pleasure to make your acquaintance Master Gerald.' He began to bow a low, slow extravagant bow. Then as Sheepshanks was almost bent in half it stopped. For quite some time. Gerald wondered what to do …

'Er, Mr Sheepshanks, are you OK?'

Gerald bent over a little to see if he could see his face. Sheepshanks turned to him and smiled weakly, 'It's just Sheepshanks. No need for the Mr part' he wheezed with some difficulty. 'Just give me a moment. All will be well …'

In sudden jerking movements as if trying to generate momentum the whole of Sheepshanks' body shook until finally and rather suddenly he was upright again. 'There, all ship shape and Bristol fashion Master Gerald.'

'Does that happen often?'

'What?'

'Getting stuck like that?'

'Oh yes. Every time.'

'Why do you do it then?'

'Well, er,' actually that was quite a good question and one Sheepshanks had never thought about before. 'Well, I er, erm, I well ... is this your bag Master Gerald?'

Gerald followed Sheepshanks out in to the car park toward a big very old fashioned car.

'I think this is it' remarked Sheepshanks. Looking around Gerald could see no others anywhere in the car park so he was rather assuming it was. For a moment Sheepshanks looked puzzled as if trying to remember something; anything. Gerald waited patiently until he could stand it no more.

'Mr Sheepshanks ...?'

'Ahh yes, Master Gerald, Sheepshanks is indeed my name and this is our car.'

'Is everything alright Mr Sheepshanks?'

'Yes, all is fine and splendid. I just drifted off there for a moment. It happens occasionally. And please, it's Sheepshanks only. No Mister; not been called that since back in the day when I was a young buck about town.'

Gerald tried hard to imagine Sheepshanks as a young chap. It seemed impossible. Sheepshanks had the manner about him of someone who had always been quite old.

Gerald threw his knapsack ahead of him and clambered in to the back of the big, black 1946 Lanchester LD10. Sheepshanks closed the passenger door behind him and loaded his suitcase in to the boot. The seat was enormous and Gerald's feet barely touched the ground. The leather was very shiny and soft and Gerald decided to slide about a little bit. He'd never been in a car this big before. His dad's small and rubbishy old Vauxhall Viva rarely left the drive these days, much to mum's irritation. It was, Gerald decided, just like his dad; useless, broken and doesn't go anywhere.

Sheepshanks slid in to the front seat and put on his chauffeur's cap.

Why is he sitting there? wondered Gerald. The steering wheel was on the other side. A moment passed and Sheepshanks got out, walked slowly around the car and clambered in to the driver's seat.

'Aha' he announced as if he'd found what he was looking for for the first time.

Gerald began to feel slightly alarmed. His mum had gone on about these new-fangled seat belts quite a bit as a way of stopping you rolling about dangerously in the car as it was moving. Gerald looked around in vain. The big old Lanchester had nothing of the kind anywhere. So he felt for the leather strap handle on the passenger door and gripped it firmly instead. At that very moment the car let off a loud bang and lurched forward to the sound of crunching metal as Sheepshanks fought with the gear box. The car rumbled forward toward the fence. Sheepshank had both hands and eyes on the gear lever cursing its very existence trying to force it in to first. All the while the big old Lanchester rolled ever more quickly toward to the rather flimsy fence, beyond which was the railway line at the bottom of a cutting. In the not too distant distance Gerald could see a train coming.

'Er, Mr … I mean, Sheepshanks, we are going to crash in to the fe …'

'Aha, that's got it' cried Sheepshanks as the gear lever finally engaged and he returned to looking at the road; or in this case the looming fence. Without a murmur he turned the car to the left and it kangarooed its way out of the car park alongside and very close to the fence as the express train to London raced by. Gerald clung on to the door handle very tightly now. It was his only protection in what he just knew would be quite a journey.

Once on the road Sheepshanks seemed to relax, although paying only scant attention to where he was actually going. There always seemed to be knobs and dials to attend to and mirrors to adjust all of which took precedence over watching the road. Combine harvesters are big, often red and slow moving, but still Sheepshanks conspired only to see it at the last minute; jolted in to evasive action by Gerald's loud shouting and thumping on the front seat which had been going on with increasing urgency ever since the combine harvester was a mere dot in the valley road below.

Further along, a man on a bicycle wobbled in front of the ill-attentive Sheepshanks and swerved dramatically; his only escape route was the ditch from which he had just extracted himself after Sheepshanks clanked him in there when weaving toward the station earlier on. Gerald watched the man out of the back window as they lurched obliviously away. The man on the bike, currently without his bicycle which remained in the ditch, stood waving his fist at the retreating Lanchester.

Gerald thought if he really wanted to the man on the bike could probably have caught Gerald and Sheepshanks up. A swift stroll would have had him zooming past. For all that Sheepshanks' driving was utterly calamitous it had the one advantage of being terribly slow. As snails speeded by and the hours passed, the big old Lanchester crawled up the endless incline eventually reaching the top of Precipitous Hill. Here Gerald assumed the cautious Sheepshanks would slow to a crawl to negotiate this quite steep decline. But no. He rammed it in to a higher gear and slammed his foot on the accelerator. The Lanchester lurched back then violently forward shooting off down the hill at a frightening speed. Gerald had been thrown to the floor but was hanging on grimly to the door handle.

The engine of the Lanchester was screaming in agony as the car accelerated ever more until eventually at the bottom everything began to slow down a bit. Gerald started to haul himself back on to the seat. At that very moment the car swerved violently to the left hurling Gerald back on to the floor, and accelerated across what sounded like gravel.

Then it suddenly and certainly stopped.

Gerald lay on the floor still hanging on to the strap on the door. Except it was no longer attached to the door. Just his hand.

Sheepshanks opened the door and in a matter-of-fact manner and as if Gerald was not lying on the floor of the car clutching the now detached leather strap unable to say much at all, Sheepshanks announced their safe arrival.

'Welcome Master Gerald to Busbeater Mansions in the ancient county of Rutland in the village of Lower Piddlington.'

Gerald struggled to his feet, practically crawling out of the car in fact. He thanked Sheepshanks for what he wasn't sure, and turned to look at where he had been deposited.

Busbeater Mansions was unfeasibly massive or so it seemed to Gerald. In all his twelve years, two months, seven days, twenty two minutes, eleven no, twelve, no thirteen, no fourteen seconds he'd never seen anything quite like it. He thought you could probably get his parents' house inside the place six or seven times.

As Sheepshanks manhandled his suitcase out of the boot Gerald looked about him. The tyre marks of the Lanchester drew swerved lines up the long gravel driveway to the front door. On three sides he was surrounded by the house made out of a pale stone; in front of him was an enormous black front door with several brass fittings which made it look rather forbidding. On either side jutting out at right angles to the front of the house were two square wings each with very tall ground floor and first floor windows. Some sort of red foliage grew up the walls and round and to a large extent over the windows. Running along the edge of the roof was a balustrade beyond which was a cupola, a small dome made of arches in the centre of the roof from where Gerald thought he could see someone holding a shotgun. The garden was a large affair but pretty untidy having had no gardener to tend to it for some twenty years. Gerald's spirits lifted a bit as he imagined playing cowboys and Indians and hunters and adventurers in the tall grass.

BLAM!

They sank again pretty swiftly as whoever was on the roof blasted their shotgun at some movement in the grasses yonder. Gerald quickly changed his mind about playing cowboys and indians out there; it was incredibly dangerous. What the heck was going on?

'Never mind master Gerald' said Sheepshanks from under his suitcase – the manhandling hadn't gone well – 'That's just the Major General letting one of the rabbits have it with his trusty shotgun Sheba. One day he might even hit one.'

Gerald sighed to himself. This place was clearly mad. So far he'd encountered a lunatic butler with all the driving skills of a short sighted badger and a Major General on the roof blasting away at rabbits which were more likely to suffer deafness from the misdirected booming gun than actually being shot. Gerald mused that on the upside the summer might be a bit more interesting than he had thought; always assuming of course that he survived it. He looked about him; sure enough the house was in the middle of nowhere. What would he do? Where would he go? He shuddered and missed the cosiness of his home and even, surprisingly, his dad's moaning on. And of course his mum. He missed her terribly. But he wanted her to be proud of him and so he hitched his trousers up, stood as tall as he could, squirrelled up his bravest expression and looked at Sheepshanks for instructions.

'Let's go in Master Gerald. The Lieutenant Colonel and the Mrs L Lieutenant Colonel are just finishing breakfast.'

Breakfast thought Gerald; at 3 o'clock in the afternoon? He shook his head slowly, wearily. No amount of bravery was going to be enough for this crazy house he thought.

At that moment in the far distance at the end of the drive the man on the bicycle appeared. Even from this far away Gerald could tell he had serious and miffed intent about him.

BLAM!

'Did I get one Sheepshanks?' called Major General Loosehorn.

Sheepshanks leaned in to the Lanchester and from the glove compartment retrieved an ancient looking telescope. He put it to his left eye. Then his right. Eventually he settled on his left.

'Not a rabbit sir, no sir, sorry sir.'

'What then? I got something.'

'Mr Cheesecake sir. You got Mr Cheesecake. In much the same way as I might have clonked him with the Lanchester on the way to and from the station.'

'What the blinkin doodah is he doing here?'

'Well at the moment sir he appears to be lying down and shouting.'

'I would have hit that rabbit if that blitherin' fool hadn't cycled in the way.'

Through his telescope Sheepshanks reported that Mr Cheesecake had picked himself up off the floor and was riding his bicycle which had actually taken the shot and was looking even more battered now, in the wobbliest way you could imagine. He appeared to be shouting something.

'What's the fellow saying Sheepshanks?'

'I can't quite hear sir.'

Gerald's ears had a better range. 'He said "I'll get you lot. I will make sure you lot pay. I'll get you lot."'

'What does he mean Sheepshanks?' hollered the Major General.

'I am presuming sir that he means to Get Us Lot. Sir.'

'Oh.' replied Loosehorn.

From where Gerald was standing the Major General seemed quite a large figure. He had wavy grey hair and a goatee-style beard and a large slightly hooked nose. At school Gerald had studied General Custer at the Battle Of Little Big Horn and Loosehorn looked rather spookily just like him. That is apart from what he was wearing; it was bright pink and looked, well, it looked awfully like a dress.

From the rooftop of what Gerald was to discover in alarming circumstances soon enough was The West Wing, Loosehorn less bellow-y this time called out

'And who is this young chap then?'

'This is young Master Gerald Jones sir, the Lieutenant Colonel's nephew. He is staying with us for the summer.'

Loosehorn leaned further forward to see Gerald a bit more clearly.

'Ahh, young Linda's boy eh? Spiffing to make your acquaintance young fellow-me-lad.' He bawled waving Sheba above his head. 'We'll be seeing you for dinner I hope.'

'Er, I hope so too sir' said Gerald who wasn't altogether sure he was THAT hopeful.

'Sheepshanks?'

'Yes Master Gerald?'

' Was the Major General wearing a dress?'

'Oh yes' replied Sheepshanks quite matter-of-factly, 'that's his rather fetching pink taffeta number. He usually wears it when he's blasting away at rabbits of an afternoon.'

'I see' said Gerald not seeing even remotely.

'Now, come on, let's go in and introduce you to Mr and Mrs The Lieutenant Colonel.'

CHAPTER THREE

Introductions And Too Many Geralds

Inside the absolutely massive hall, Sheepshanks put Gerald's suitcase down and asked him to wait there. Gerald did. The hall was oak panelled with a giant staircase in the middle of it. To the left and right of the staircase were two long corridors with doors at the end of each. Both were closed. Under the stairs was a large-ish door leading, Gerald presumed, to some kind of cupboard. To Gerald's right was The West Wing the roof of which was where the Major General had been blasting away at rabbits but hitting Mr Cheesecake instead; to his left was the East Wing which is where Sheepshanks was heading. At least he would in a moment. He appeared to have lost concentration again and stopped. Gerald helped out.

'Sheepshanks? Hello. Erm, I think you were going to announce me to the Lieutenant Colonel and Mrs Lieutenant Colonel.'

'Pardon? I was what? Ah yes, I was, what. Thank you Master Gerald. Sort of drifted … yes, off there yes. OK. Drifted off. Indeed. Right.'

Sedately and with measured purpose once again Sheepshanks set off for the breakfast room to announce Gerald to the Lieutenant Colonel and the Mrs Lieutenant Colonel.

The East Wing formed quite a substantial part of Busbeater Mansions and it took Sheepshanks with his deliberate gait some time to get to the breakfast room where the Lieutenant Colonel and the Mrs Lieutenant Colonel were still eating breakfast even though as Gerald's Apollo 11 watch had earlier confirmed, it was actually by now 3 o'clock in the afternoon.

The breakfast room was a vast place and occupying almost the entire length of it was the breakfast table. At one end sat Marjorie Busbeater, or the Mrs Lieutenant Colonel as Sheepshanks called her. After all he couldn't possibly call his employer's wife by her first name. Marjorie Busbeater had shoulder length curly auburn hair, ruddy cheeks and kind green eyes. Even though she was sitting down it was clear she was a tall lady who wasn't terribly worried about weight watcher diets. Her voice boomed rather and despite her permanent smile held a very determined air.

At the other end of this huge table sat Lieutenant Colonel Busbeater. He had a mop of silver hair to match his splendid handlebar moustache. He had warm, grey eyes and he shared the ruddy-cheeked complexion of his wife. He was very tall even sitting down and very slim despite the amount of full fat cream, meat, wine, sherry and what not he put away regularly.

Across the vast expanse of the table Marjorie called, 'Butter Gerald?'

Lieutenant Colonel Busbeater hollered by way of reply 'yes please.'

Seeing Sheepshanks walk in at that very moment Marjorie asked, 'Take this to the Lieutenant Colonel will you Sheepshanks?'

Sheepshanks' slowly and deliberately set off along the length of the table.

He eventually arrived armed with the butter.

'Butter sir?'

'Not now Sheepshanks. Toast gone; on to coffee. Get me the milk would you?'

Sheepshanks set off back to the other end of the table

'The Lieutenant Colonel wants the milk Ma'am.'

'Full fat or semi-skimmed?'

Sheepshanks sighed slightly and set off back to the Lieutenant Colonel, 'Full fat or semi-skimmed sir?'

'Full fat please Sheepshanks.'

Sheepshanks returned, picked up the milk and took it back to the Lieutenant Colonel and poured it in to the Colonel's coffee. Except there was no coffee. He trundled back the length of the table and returned with the coffee.

'Tea please' asked Busbeater contrarily.

This went on for some time but by 4 o'clock, earlier than usual, breakfast had finished.

Then Sheepshanks suddenly remembered Gerald.

'Yikes' he muttered under his breath 'Master Gerald has been in the hall for an hour.'

Marjorie saw that Sheepshanks was looking anxious, 'What's up Sheepshanks? You look anxious. Have you forgotten something?'

'I have Mrs Lieutenant Colonel.'

'Well, what is it?'

'Master Gerald, Mrs Lieutenant Colonel ma'am.'

'No-one's called old Busbeater master for some time Sheepshanks'

Lieutenant Colonel Gerald Fitzherbert Shoeberryness Busbeater perked up at the mention of his name.

'What's going on Sheepshanks, Marjorie?'

'Sheepshanks here says he's forgotten you.'

'What are you on about man? Here I am full of life as ever right in front of you. How can you have forgotten me you sentimental old fool?'

'No sir, Mrs Lieutenant Colonel ma'am not you sir.'

'Well don't beat about the geraniums Sheepshanks what do you mean? Do you see any other Gerald's standing around here?'

'Not here sir. But there is one in the hallway.'

'One what?'

'A Gerald.'

'A Gerald? In the hallway? You mean … er, what do you mean Sheepshanks?'

'Master Gerald Jones is in the hallway.'

Busbeater was struggling a bit, 'Master Gerald … er?'

'Your nephew sir.'

Marjorie suddenly got it, 'Linda's boy? He's here?'

'Yes ma'm Mrs Lieutenant Colonel ma'am' said Sheepshanks, relieved. He knew there'd be confusion. Although he had expected Master Gerald to actually be in the room when it occurred.

'How long has he been there?' asked Marjorie.

'About an hour.'

'An hour?' exclaimed Busbeater. 'For goodness sake man, go and get him and let's introduce ourselves.'

Sheepshanks set off.

'Sheepshanks, we'll be in the drawing room when you eventually find him.' declared Marjorie.

Upon returning to the Hallway Sheepshanks noticed with some horror that Gerald was no longer there. 'Yikes and crikey, where could he be? Master Gerald!' Sheepshanks called out expectantly and yet slightly desperately over and over.

There was a loud crash followed by an echoey 'oooomph' as Master Gerald tumbled out of the cupboard under the stairs wearing a bucket on his head.

Whilst waiting for Sheepshanks to return and after he began to wonder if he ever would actually come back at all, Gerald had got a bit bored. After some aimless mooching about he'd ventured over to the staircase and gingerly checked out the cupboard door. What's in here? he wondered. After one or two careful tugs, and then a more vigorous third heave the door flew open. Inside all neatly tidied away was a bucket and a mop and a bunch of cloths, each unsullied by evidence of the use for which each had been made; cleaning. And a stuffed owl. Gerald crept in and looked about him. He turned in the tiny cupboard/lunar module, knocked Commander Owl off his perch, clattered in to Commander Mop, fell against the door of the cupboard/lunar module and tumbled out wearing the special NASA designed tin helmet, or bucket.

'The Eagle has landed' Gerald guffawed lying flat on his back.

It was then that Loosehorn, disturbed by Sheepshanks' hollerin', sashayed in to the hall brandishing Sheba only to be confronted by a bucketed oik proclaiming the landing of an eagle.

Sheepshanks first moved to reassure Loosehorn that not since that owl incident some years back had there been a bird of prey in the hallway and maybe it was time to dress for dinner.

'Good thinking Sheepshanks. It'll take me a couple of hours to find the right outfit. Want to look me best for Linda's boy. Do something with that guffawing bucket first though eh?'

Sheepshanks sighed a little, said he would and after ushering Loosehorn back upstairs went over to Gerald who by now had stopped laughing and was gamely trying to put the bucket, mop and owl back in the cupboard.

Eventually the two of them managed it. For some reason getting all the stuff back in and closing the door was fiendishly difficult.

'Has it shrunk in there?' asked Gerald

'Quite possibly Master Gerald. Quite possibly.'

After much huffing and puffing the cupboard door closed shut, but not very tightly.

'This way Master Gerald' said Sheepshanks as he began the long walk to the drawing room.

At that moment the cupboard door burst open and everything spilled out once more making an infernal racket.

'Is that that bally eagle again? I'll get him I will,' bellowed the Major General from his bedroom 'once I am out of this corset I will … any moment …'

Sheepshanks and Gerald left the floor strewn with little-used cleaning utensils and the Major General's bird of prey/corset rant which, Sheepshanks knew from experience, would eventually peter out.

Sheepshanks and Gerald walked slowly, obviously, along the long corridor that led to the East Wing and past the dining room which until recently had hosted breakfast.

'Afternoon Mrs Bunyon' called Sheepshanks to the cook/maid/non-user of cleaning utensils as she swept, literally, the breakfast things in to what to Gerald's untrained eye looked very much like a wheelbarrow.

'Gets through a lot of crockery that way' mused Sheepshanks. 'Saves on the washing up apparently.'

On they meandered along pictures of past Busbeaters in varying uniforms but all posing victoriously over some defeated foe or other. Gerald was impressed. Maybe old Busbeater wasn't such an old bore after all. Not if these brave ancestors of his were anything to go by. In the middle was an empty space where a picture should be. A plaque underneath read 'Frederick Alfred Busbeater; went missing in 1857 on an expedition to Central Africa.'

Eventually they reached the drawing room. There Lieutenant Colonel Busbeater was handing Marjorie a drink as she sat in one of the two huge red leather arm chairs. Neither had noticed that Gerald or Sheepshanks had arrived.

Sheepshanks' cleared his throat; 'Ahem, Lieutenant Colonel and Mrs Lieutenant Colonel ma'am, may I introduce Young Master Gerald.'

'Master Gerald' cooed Marjorie. 'How unspeakably spiffing to have you here at Busbeater Mansions. You are most, most welcome.'

She hugged Gerald to her really quite ample bosom before Gerald could say anything. Cocooned in Marjorie's chest he was speechless for quite some time. Eventually freed he reeled back slightly only to be hauled forward again by Lieutenant Colonel Busbeater's firm handshake.

'Good to see you me young cock-sparrow. How the devil are you?'

The Lieutenant Colonel's handshake was vigorous and virtually lifted Gerald off the ground on each stroke; it was like a rag doll was having its hand shaken by a gorilla. Eventually the greetings were over and after one more mini Marjorie hug, Gerald was ushered over to the magnificently enormous sofa. Feeling like the incredible shrinking boy he scrambled on and sat there, feet many inches from the floor wondering what on earth to say. Lieutenant Colonel Busbeater broke the silence.

'Crème de menthe young fellow?'

'Gerald!' exclaimed Marjorie.

'Yes?!' replied Gerald and Gerald simultaneously.

'Ah' said Marjorie. 'This might not work terribly well. We need a system.'

'Why not say call ME Gerald Fitzherbert Shoeberryness Busbeater' said Busbeater.

'What? Every time?'

'It'll work.'

'It won't. Everyone will be exhausted. I think we call Gerald, Gerald.'

'That's settled then, I am Gerald' said Busbeater.

'No. I mean darling that young Gerald here should be called Gerald. You we will just call Busbeater.' Marjorie was beginning to get slightly exasperated. Since childhood Marjorie had had a bit of a wonky left eye, but most of the time everything worked well and both eyes looked generally in the same direction at the same time. When things got a bit stressy however, the left one went walkabout. This was one of those times. Not unreasonably then Sheepshanks, standing to the left, thought she was looking at him.

'As you please Mrs Lieutenant Colonel ma'am.'

'What? No, not YOU Sheepshanks.'

'I thought he was Busbeater now' grumbled Busbeater

'No, no, nooo. For goodness sake.' Marjorie slurped her luminous green drink and fanned herself with her free hand.

Gerald remained still on the massive sofa. What on earth, he wondered, was going on? And what was his name, currently?

Marjorie drained the rest of her crème de menthe and taking a deep breath began again. Pointing at Sheepshanks she said, '*You* are Sheepshanks.'

'Thank you ma'am Mrs Lieutenant Colonel ma'am sir.'

Then at Busbeater, 'You darling will be Busbeater for the length of Gerald's stay.'

Her tone softened as she turned to Gerald. 'And you my patient wee fellow will always be just Gerald.'

Turning to Busbeater and Sheepshanks and in slightly more robust tones said 'Understand that?'

'Yes Marjorie/ma'am Mrs Lieutenant Colonel ma'am' they muttered simultaneously and sheepishly, looking down at their shoes.

'Good. Now, Sheepshanks fetch Gerald a ginger beer and lets have dinner in half an hour shall we?'

'But I don't want a ginger beer' said Busbeater.

'Busbeater!' wailed Marjorie her left eye crazily out of control.

Gerald sat in the middle of the massive dinner table opposite the Major General who had scrubbed up rather well. He had trimmed his beard and his hair was combed and Brylcreamed back. He was resplendent in a 1930s evening gown of a striking cobalt blue finished off with a mink stole, which Gerald was sure he saw move.

'Evening Loosehorn,' declared Busbeater, 'fine outfit.'

'Thanks old man. It's in honour of young Gerald here.'

'That's nice Loosehorn. Very thoughtful' said Marjorie gently.

Gerald felt honoured and at the same time rather perplexed. This bunch of eccentric friends and relations he had been sent to spend the summer with were clearly all round the bend but despite his initial impressions he had never felt so welcome; well, except by his mum which was every day. Suddenly Gerald's heart sank and a small tear began to well up. He felt much warmer toward his crazy relatives but he was terribly tired and would quite like to have had a cup of cocoa, a bit of a chat with his mum about the day's adventuring and a long sleep. He missed his mum a lot. But also thought about how much she'd like it here. He began to fantasise about them all living together at Busbeater Mansions. Maybe his dad could stay at home and wait for the cat to come back … He sighed silently and his shoulders sagged. He missed his mum.

'Would you like some fizzy pop Master Gerald?'

Suddenly from absolutely nowhere Sheepshanks was at his side. His big old face was beaming at him as his sad but clear eyes bathed Gerald in warmth and affection.

Slightly wobbly but as firm as he could manage Gerald replied, 'Yes please Mr ... er, Sheepshanks.'

Sheepshanks withdrew to fetch the pop. Marjorie was looking across at Gerald who seemed so small at this enormous table.

'Gerald. Why don't you come over here and sit next to me. You look a little lost over there on your own' she suggested.

'Yes good idea' boomed Loosehorn, 'it's a bit like looking at a tiny pea in a massive pod from over here.'

Gerald smiled.

'Off you go me young sparrow' joined in Busbeater.

Gerald began to pick up his dinner setting.

'I'll do that Master Gerald,' Sheepshanks was there again from nowhere. For a fellow who moved so slowly generally he didn't half get about fast.

'Thank you' replied Gerald who was recovering his vim but still hadn't relished carrying so many knives and forks and plates across this aircraft carrier sized table. What could they all be for?

He sat next to Marjorie who put her arm around him and squeezed. Gerald spluttered a bit.

'He's not an accordion dear, let him breathe a bit at least' called Busbeater.

'Sorry Gerald' said Marjorie a bit sheepishly. She had wanted a son of her own but it had never happened so she was going to make the most of young Gerald's stay with them. Her enthusiasm had got the better of her; she let a slightly wheezy Gerald go.

The door to the dining room swung open and in staggered a huge pile of silver serving plates with lids on balanced delicately on top of one another. Underneath, the plates' thin legs with huge boots tottered this way and that. Marjorie, Loosehorn, Busbeater and Gerald all swayed in unison with each totter with their arms half out stretched as if ready to leap forth should one of the plates fall. Miraculously they didn't. Instead Sheepshanks, for the legs were his, managed to get them to the table and then perhaps relaxing a bit too soon let them clatter on to the shiny surface in time to watch them career all over the place until finally coming to a rest on various parts of the table top. The biggest of all was right on the edge nearest Loosehorn. As everyone held their breath Sheepshanks walked carefully over to the plate which was by now beginning its inexorable slide off the table and toward the floor. As it left the table, Sheepshanks made a diving grab for it and they both vanished. Silence. Emerging triumphantly Sheepshanks returned the still intact and full plate to the table and began serving dinner as if absolutely nothing had happened.

Dinner of roast hog, two hundredweight of potatoes and general vegetables followed by sticky toffee pudding, especially for Gerald, took about two or three hours to consume. Sheepshanks who never seemed to have time to eat thought Gerald, was on the go the whole time; on the go slowly though.

By the time the dessert plates had been cleared away it was well past 11pm and Gerald was struggling to stay awake, which Marjorie spotted.

'Time this young chap went to bed', said Marjorie, 'Sheepshanks, take him up to his room would you?'

'Yes Ma'am Mrs Lieutenant Colonel Ma'am. Come on Master Gerald.'

Sheepshanks led the way. Gerald was practically asleep on his feet. As Sheepshanks entered the hallway he turned around. He could see Gerald was about to fall over from fatigue so scooped him up and carried the sleeping boy to his room.

'Master Gerald' said Sheepshanks softly 'wake up.'

'Mum? I er … oh sorry Sheepshanks I was … er, where am I?'

'In your room Master Gerald.'

'This is MY room?'

'Yes.'

Gerald's eyes, so sleepy a moment ago, were now wide open. This was his room? The ceiling was painted like the night sky full of stars and galaxies and all around him were models of the Apollo 11 spacecraft. His bed had been made in to the shape of the Saturn rocket; the blanket was decorated with spaceships and planets; all the parts of the spaceship were hanging from the ceiling heading for the moon which incredibly was right there outside the widow, for real.

'How? Er … '

There was a light knock on the door; Marjorie, Busbeater and Loosehorn all stood in the doorway looking faintly embarrassed.

'Er, do you like it young fellow?' muttered Busbeater.

'Like it? Like it?' spluttered Gerald. 'Do I like it? It's the best thing in the world ever, ever.' He could barely believe it.

Busbeater went on 'Your mum rang and told us you were interested in the Moon landing …'

Interested!?

'So we thought, you know, to make you feel at home … we, er, we … anyway. Here it is. Sheepshanks worked very hard.'

'You did this Sheepshanks?' asked Gerald full of admiration.

Sheepshanks stood looking bashful.

'Well, yes I er, yes with a little help from … well, er no-one as it happens.'

'I'm an absolute duffer at this sort of thing' confessed Busbeater.

Loosehorn agreed before going on,

'And I can't even shoot rabbits let alone build anything.'

Marjorie stepped forward and placed the enormous scarf she'd been knitting around Gerald's neck.

'It's a special Moon Day Landing Scarf.'

At this Gerald burst in to tears and hugged Marjorie. 'Poor lamb, he's worn out.'

Busbeater and Loosehorn slowly retreated as Sheepshanks helped Marjorie put Gerald to bed.

Busbeater turned to Loosehorn 'I think he liked it though?'

'He did. Just as well *you* didn't try to build anything mind you. Remember the garden shed?'

'The instructions were wrong.'

'It exploded.'

'That's what's wrong with you Loosehorn, always Mr Picky.'

'I lost a good twin set and pearls in that blast.'

'I never liked you in puce' said Busbeater reflectively.

'Night, night Gerald' whispered Marjorie.

'Night, night Auntie Marjorie' Gerald mumbled.

'Good night Master Gerald' murmured Sheepshanks.

'Good night Mr Sheepshanks. Thank you so, so much.'

'It's just Sheepshanks Master Gerald', but Gerald was completely asleep.

Sheepshanks turned the light out, and as Marjorie left, quietly closed the door. Marjorie paused for a moment outside Gerald's room and sighed.

'Time for an aperitif I think please Sheepshanks.'

'Certainly ma'm Mrs Lieutenant Colonel ma'am.'

The next morning. About 8 o'clock in the morning. Breakfast.

'Have some breakfast dear' said Marjorie pointing to the huge buffet on the side of eggs, bread, sausages, bacon, more eggs this time scrambled in to an egg mountain, fruit juice and more cheese than you could imagine even at a cheese fair on Cheese City's World Cheese Day.

After having loaded his plate as high as he could Gerald sat at the table next to Marjorie and tucked in.

With the morning sun pouring through the giant windows Gerald stuffed his face, Marjorie sipped her coffee, Loosehorn read Particle Physics for Duffers and Busbeater, The Times. The Lieutenant Colonel harrumphed a cheery harrumph, folded the paper and decisively placed it on the table. He had an announcement and one he was pleased about.

'First day of The Test Match and its a glorious sunny day. Marjorie, I shall be in the study listening on the radio all day.'

At that very moment a massive window-rattling clap of thunder heralded the start of a gigantic downpour. Busbeater sat down again immediately and sorrowfully.

'Or not' he said gloomily.

'Let's retire to the drawing room' declared Marjorie as cheerfully as she could.

Gerald just wanted to go and sit in his magnificent bedroom but Marjorie was rather insistent that he played canasta with her.

'Canasta? What's that?' he asked, a bit fearful of the reply.

'It's a card game' explained Marjorie.

'Oh. Not Spanish instruments then?' asked Gerald.

'No dear. That's a guitar.' said Marjorie patiently.

'He means Castanets' interrupted Busbeater.

'Oh did you dear? Not guitar?' Marjorie turned apologetically to Gerald.

'Probably not Auntie Marjorie,' sighed Gerald. Another confusing conversation ending up in a cul de sac. This was clearly going to be a long day.

Marjorie then had a better idea.

'Why don't you write to your Mother? She'd be so excited to get a letter from you.'

Gerald rather liked writing. He liked to be expansive in his descriptions. When handing in essays his fellow pupils only gave in one or two pages; Gerald regularly handed in seventeen or eighteen. Each with tightly written script. Mrs Carter, his English teacher and the only one in Gerald's view with any sense or imagination always smiled as he handed over his bundle. She usually set aside a single evening and a large glass of wine just for Gerald's stories.

Marjorie found a pen and paper and gave them to Gerald who had clambered on to the enormous sofa in the drawing room. He chewed his pen wondering what to write. In her equally enormous chair Marjorie had started a new knitting project while in his Uncle Busbeater was reading a large novel entitled 'Don't Look Down' by Eileen Dover.

After a few minutes of searching the cosmos for inspiration, Gerald began.

Dear Mum,

I arrived safely at Busbeater Mansions and so far it isn't too smelly but it is huge. It takes poor old Sheepshanks ages and ages to get from one end to the other. Uncle and Auntie are very nice and are looking after me. They both say hello and send their love. Major General Loosehorn is interesting. He wears dresses all the time but no-one seems to notice or mind very much. He's a bit grumpy but he is kind to me.

Sheepshanks is very mysterious. He is very slow all the time and yet somehow gets so much done. And you should see how he decorated my room. It's amazing! It's like my very own Space Station. I love it.

Meals are massive and go on for ever, so I don't think I'll starve. I am a bit bored. There isn't much to do here. I shall explore a bit today to see if I can find something interesting. But I doubt I will.

I miss you Mum but I am OK. I will write as often as I can. Say hello to Dad for me.

Lots and lots and lots of love,

Gerald

xx

Gerald put his pen and paper down.

'Finished dear?'

'Yes, I have.'

'That was quick.'

Nothing much to say thought Gerald.

'I'll get Sheepshanks to post it for you.'

'Thank you.'

Marjorie went back to her knitting.

Gerald was bored. He puffed out his cheeks; then tried to see how long he could hold his breath - forty seven seconds apparently. Next he lay on his back with his feet in the air until the blood drained from them making them tingle. None of this entertained him for long. He then counted his nose; 'one.' He then tried to see how far back he could bend his fingers; 'ouch.' Not very far was the answer.

He looked around him for inspiration. Maybe given a decent amount of time to be polite he could sneak off back to his room and play Apollo Moon Landings. At the back of the room by the door and all along the wall was a large bookcase crammed untidily full of books and magazines. He scrambled off the huge sofa and went over to it thinking a cursory glance would be enough before some sneaking out could begin. He scanned the spines of the books on display;

'Pride and Not Liking People Very Much' by June Morris,

'A Lot Of Fuss About Nothing' by Bill Wobblestick,

'Dr Yes' by Jan Phlegming,

'Jane Air' by Honor Geestring,

'Scoop' by Evelyn Waugh. Gerald picked it out wondering if it might be about ice cream. On the back was a picture of the author who looked exactly like a middle aged man. Gerald stared hard 'Poor woman', he thought. 'Called Evelyn but looks like a bloke. Tough time at school I'd imagine.' He put it back uninspired.

Crammed in between the books were many magazines, which looked more promising. After a bit of a struggle Gerald freed a bunch.

They all slithered across the floor like a glossy avalanche. Quickly Gerald dropped to his knees to gather them up before his aunt and uncle noticed. As he collated them he noticed the titles were mostly pretty dull. Like 'Looming Today; everything an amateur loomer needs to know about looms and looming' and 'Duck Monthly: a magazine for tall people and the things they walk in to.' Then, rather more intriguingly Gerald noticed one entitled 'Fantastic Machines Of Ancient and Modern Times.' Maybe the Apollo Spacecraft would be in here. He shoved the other magazines back on the shelf and leant back against the bookcase to read Fantastic Machines. At first he was disappointed as there was nothing about the Space Missions at all. He checked the date '4 August 1953.' Crikey, no wonder - it's ancient he thought. Still, in the absence of much else to do he flicked through it slightly less interestedly now.

Then, on page sixteen he recognised something. There was a technical drawing of a flywheel. Below it was a description: 'The Flywheel as Illustrated here was thought to be the key to the time machine.'

Gerald stared at the picture. The illustrated flywheel was flat and round, slightly raised in the middle with four notches taken out of the rim at what looked like, but weren't, random intervals. The article next to it explained this might be the actual size of the flywheel; if it existed. After centuries of searching by eminent scholars and adventurers however no-one had found any evidence of it or the time machine's existence. The article went on to explain the myth; *'Ancient legend suggested that the Chinese Scientist and Philosopher Zhu Zhi, who lived at the time of the founding of the Three Kingdoms around 169AD, had invented a time machine.'* The story went that Zhu Zhi had built four machines and maybe even a fifth, more powerful one before he vanished, presumed dead. *'The latter machine, it was said, could be used to change historical events but its whereabouts, like the others has never been verified. Zhu Zhi was championed by the boastful Emperor of the North Kingdom Ts'ao Ts'ao. However, soon after the Three Kingdoms was established following Ts'ao Ts'ao's defeat by the emperors of the south and south east at the Battle Of Red Cliff all traces of Zhu Zhi vanish. Over the centuries various ancient documents have surfaced purporting to be diagrams and schematics of the machines but mostly they turned out to be fakes. This diagram of the flywheel however has been proven to be from the right period by the watermark on the paper. It was the only thing left that might yet prove the existence of these machines.'* The article concluded however that no-one had ever actually seen let alone held the flywheel in real life.

Gerald's eyes were as wide as Auntie Marjorie's dinner plates; 'I have' he thought, astonished. He stood up, tucked the magazine in to the waistband of his trousers and without saying a word stole out of the drawing room. Once out of earshot he accelerated like a mad thing scampering up the stairs to his room. After a couple of minutes of rummaging and making a right mess of Sheepshanks nicely folded and stored everything, Gerald found what he was looking for; the silver flywheel. Carefully he placed it on the picture of the ancient diagram; it matched exactly. Gerald gasped.

'Crikey mikey!' He sat back and leant against his bed. He knew this must mean something but what? What on earth did it mean? At that moment the front door bell rang, urgently at first then frantically accompanied by some shouting and hammering on the very door itself.

CHAPTER FOUR

A Stranger Comes Calling

'Get the blasted door will you Sheepshanks?' cried out Busbeater from the drawing room. 'What an infernal racket. What could be so urgent?'

'Maybe it's Mr Cheesecake. He was pretty miffed yesterday after Sheepshanks ran him over; twice,' offered Marjorie.

'On my way Lieutenant Colonel sir' replied Sheepshanks as he made his deliberate way to the door. Slowly he unlocked the very many bolts that secured the door – mostly there at Loosehorn's insistence in case the rabbits got any ideas – and hauled the massive ancient door open.

Standing in the pouring rain the man at the door was in his forties with short black hair. He was powerfully built with very strong forearms but a slender neck all of which made him look taller than the five feet ten he actually was. He was wearing a black leather jacket over a dark green waistcoat. His black trousers were neatly tucked into his laced up boots which were also black but shiny with metal plates in the heel. His blue eyes were ablaze starring wildly about him as Sheepshanks opened the door.

'Can I help …?' Sheepshanks had no time to finish. The stranger barged past him and dived inside, slamming the door shut behind him.

'No time to explain. Where's The Wardrobe?' gasped the stranger, his back pressed against the door. He then moved forward and got uncomfortably close to Sheepshanks who was slowly backing away not understanding anything that was going on; but the stranger kept coming.

'C'mon man, The Wardrobe. Where is it?' By now the gasping had turned in to full on shouting.

Busbeater and Marjorie had come to see what all the hollerin' was in their hallway. The stranger turned to them. He was frantic.

'The Wardrobe? Where is The Wardrobe?!' he cried

'Calm down man' blustered Busbeater. 'Who the devil are you, you soggy fellow and what are you doing shouting about wardrobes in my hallway?'

The soaked stranger stopped for a moment and realised that maybe shouting and looking half crazed wasn't going to get him anywhere. He closed his eyes and took a deep breath.

'My apologies sir. It was rude of me to arrive a bit shouty and unannounced. But this is a matter of Great Urgency and Importance.'

Busbeater could see the stranger was serious. But still there was decorum to follow; introductions were required.

'Apology accepted. But before you go on to explain just what the captain pyjamas is going on, who are you, precisely?' asked Busbeater.

'My name is Cornelius Golightly sir' replied Cornelius.

Busbeater shook his hand.

'I am Lieutenant Colonel Gerald Busbeater' said Busbeater and turning to Marjorie said 'this is my wife Marjorie Busbeater and this' he gestured toward Sheepshanks 'is my batman Sheepshanks.'

'Pleasure sir' said Cornelius taking Sheepshanks hand.

He turned to Marjorie and Busbeater.

'Charmed ma'am, and good to meet you Lieutenant Colonel.'

'Busbeater will do. Now what is the cause of all this kerfuffle and soggy commotion?'

The general hullabaloo had brought Mrs Bunyon from her kitchen. She was standing next to Sheepshanks rubbing flour off her hands on to a towel. Some of it was sprinkling on the floor. Marjorie tutted. Cornelius continued unaware of the tiny domestic irritation that was going on behind him.

'Lieutenant Colonel sir, I wish to see The Wardrobe.'

Busbeater was slightly irritated. He knew that already.

'I know that. But what wardrobe?'

Mrs Bunyon then chipped in, 'Is this The Wardrobe the two gentlemen came to see at the weekend?'

Busbeater and Marjorie looked at one another; very puzzled now.

'How come so much goes on in this house that I don't know about?' complained Busbeater.

Cornelius turned to the floury cook

'Yes, that's it.'

'What gentlemen, what wardrobe?' wailed an exasperated Busbeater.

Silence.

'Well Mrs Bunyon, you seem terribly well informed?' demanded Marjorie.

'Last Saturday two very tweedy older gentlemen came calling.'

'Cartwright and Carruthers …' interrupted Cornelius.

'Yes, that was them. A bit excitable and slightly round the bend it seemed to me. Anyway, Sheepshanks was out, taking the Major General for a fitting, so I answered the door. It's not as if I haven't enough to do round here you know …'

'Get to the point please Mrs Bunyon' exhaled Busbeater.

'They were babbling about some Chinese wardrobe in the Major General's room.'

'In Loosehorn's room?' asked Marjorie.

'They were very specific' continued Mrs Bunyon 'and were very keen to see it. So I showed them upstairs.'

Mrs Bunyon left out the part where they said they would buy it for a substantial sum if it proved to be genuine. She'd quickly planned to pocket the cash and then claim it was stolen or something. She worked hard at this madhouse and they owed her. She continued her story, 'Once they saw The Wardrobe they almost squealed. Then they clambered inside and got even more excited going on about it most definitely being it and the one. Then rude as you like they just left. Ran out like I wasn't there. I was appalled at the way they had treated your home.' Mrs Bunyon looked at Marjorie in mock horror at this invasion of Busbeater and Loosehorn's privacy. She was a greedy and resentful woman and her real irritation was entirely because they had left without giving her the substantial sum of money they promised.

'Would you take me to the Major General's room Mrs er ... Mrs' asked Cornelius urgently.

'Bunyon' said Mrs Bunyon.

'Carbuncle, Mrs Carbuncle ... would you?' continued Cornelius more impatiently this time.

At that moment Gerald came careening along the landing and down the stairs. He saw the stranger with his aunt and uncle and Sheepshanks and the cook/cleaner. He stopped.

'Charlie. What are you doing here? Is there a fire?'

Busbeater was on the point of exploding with confusion

'Zounds; what the ...? You know this chap Gerald?'

Unclear himself what exactly was going on Gerald stuttered slightly

'Er, erm, yes. This is Charlie; he's a Fireman. He puts out my mum's coq au vin.'

'Your mother's what?' sighed Busbeater, now unutterably bewildered.

'It's a French dish dear' interjected Marjorie. Mrs Bunyon the cook had, ironically, never heard of it.

Charlie turned to Gerald.

'Little time for explanations Gerald, but my name isn't Charlie. It's Cornelius Golightly.' In front of Gerald he crouched on his haunches and looked him right in the eye.

'Do you trust me Gerald?' Cornelius asked slowly and seriously.

'I er, think so' said Gerald.

'Good man. Now, do you have the flywheel I gave you?'

'Yes I do. It's in my room.' Cornelius gently rubbed his forehead and closed his eyes from relief. 'It's part of a time machine' Gerald went on.

Cornelius whispered, 'I know Gerald. I really, really know.'

Busbeater still behind the curve spluttered more desperately now, 'Will someone please if it's not too much trouble tell me just what the blue trousers is going on?!'

Cornelius turned to him, 'There is no time; I have wasted too much already. Gerald go and get the flywheel we'll meet you in Loosehorn's room.'

Gerald looked confused. Suddenly as if from nowhere Sheepshanks was at his side. Matter-of-factly he said 'Young Master Gerald doesn't know where the Major General's room is sir. I do. I will go with him and bring him to you.'

Gerald was relieved for the help but he was also alarmed. For with Sheepshank being so slow it might take ages and Charlie, er, Cornelius was clearly in a hurry.

Cornelius looked at Sheepshanks, 'Thank you. Now we need to move fast. The Baron is not far behind us.'

Busbeater purple with bafflement blustered, 'The Baron?! Who the half baked prunes is The Baron?!'

Then something really odd happened; Sheepshanks zoomed. Almost gliding across the floor he well, he sort of ran. 'Come on Master Gerald. Lets get that flywheel,' he said urgently.

Cornelius stood in front of the Major General's wardrobe. It was quite big; eight feet high, six feet wide and six feet deep. It was a deep, browny red with golden inlays depicting scenes from ancient Chinese life. At the front, just above the middle and set across the lacquered doors was a circular brass plate, matching the smaller circular hinges at the side. Through two solid hoops on each door a long brass rod held them closed. Cornelius withdrew the rod and opened The Wardrobe doors.

Major General Loosehorn stood there as everyone piled in to his room, 'What on earth is going on here? Is there some kind of general emergency? Some kind of owl related alarm?'

'You must be Major General Loosehorn' said Cornelius offering his hand.

'I am indeed. But who the big shiny spoons are you?' Loosehorn replied shaking Cornelius' hand absently looking around for clues.

'This is Cornelius Golightly' interrupted Marjorie 'He's got a thing about your wardrobe.'

'And there's some Baron involved somewhere' interjected Busbeater resigned now to his own confusion.

At that point Loosehorn caught a glimpse of something out of the corner of his eye. He turned and looked out of his window, 'Would this be him?' he asked seeing a big black vehicle driving slowly through the front gates.

Gerald and Sheepshanks hurtled in to his room to get the flywheel. At first in his blind haste Gerald couldn't see it.

'Is this it Master Gerald?'

Sheepshanks held up the shiny metal flywheel.

'Yes, brilliant, yes that's it, thank you …'

Sheepshanks dropped it in to Gerald's knapsack.

'It's safer this way and you never know if we'll need to keep it somewhere' he said as he handed the knapsack to Gerald.

On his way Gerald grabbed the copy of 'Fantastic Machines Of Ancient and Modern Times' and they both bolted for the door. Gerald reached the landing first and then suddenly stopped realising he had no idea where Loosehorn's room was. Sheepshanks had no time to stop and careened in to Gerald sending them both skittering across the floor on their bottoms. A small clattering sound told them both the flywheel had fallen out of the knapsack. It was resting on the very edge of the landing. Gerald carefully reached out, grabbed it and put it firmly back in his knapsack, noticing a fat padded envelope in there as he did so. What's that? There was no time to find out.

'I don't know exactly who this Baron fellow is Master Gerald' said Sheepshanks looking anxiously out of the landing window, 'but this might be him coming down the drive now.' Gerald ran to the window.

Outside an enormous black car was approaching. As it got nearer Gerald realised it wasn't a car at all; it was a tank with a gun turret revolving as it went. The tank was rolling across the lawn toward Loosehorn's wing.

BLAM

Clearly, Loosehorn had seen it. A small puff of soil and grass and scattering rabbits showed he had, as usual, missed.

'We had better get going Master Gerald' said Sheepshanks. Even his voice, usually so calm and measured now had an element of urgency to it.

Following the speeding ancient butler Gerald headed for Loosehorn's room where chaos reigned unabated.

Loosehorn was firing Sheba out of the window as fast as he could reload with Busbeater at his friend's side blasting away with his old blunderbuss. Not since that tricky situation in Ishmaelia when caught between The Patriots and The Traitors had Loosehorn and Busbeater joined together in combat; they were rather enjoying it.

'Take that you blighter; get off my land!' bellowed Loosehorn.

BLAM

'It's MY land technically' remarked Busbeater.

Loosehorn ignored his friends' hair-splitting.

'Coming here with your fancy tank contraptions all over the place' he continued as he reloaded.

BLAM. BLAM.

'Take that.'

Busbeater looked out, amazed. 'Strewth Loosehorn you've actually hit something you were aiming at for once' he said, aghast.

Loosehorn had indeed hit the tank square on. Which actually might not have been such a good idea. Clearly riled the machine stopped and slowly, menacingly turned it's gun turret toward Loosehorn and Busbeater's window.

A whistling sound was followed by cries of 'duck' from Busbeater and Loosehorn which in turn was followed by a howling and then an explosive thud. Luckily the aim of the tank gunner was Loosehorn-esque in the accuracy department and instead of hitting the window took out the copula on the roof where Gerald had first seen Loosehorn shooting at rabbits the day before.

Gerald and Sheepshanks arrived. Where were Cornelius and Marjorie?

'They are in The Wardrobe' wailed a terrified Mrs Bunyon from under the bed

'Ahh, Gerald at last, come here' cried Cornelius from inside

'I say, who is this fellow … this mountebank?' wondered Loosehorn as a tall, dramatic looking man clambered out of the tank and toward the front door.

Cornelius ran over to the window.

'That is The Baron; he's on his way up here. Come on everyone, in The Wardrobe now.'

'We can't all get in there!' cried Loosehorn. It was big, but not THAT big.

'We can, come on!' replied Cornelius.

'Anyway, what good is hiding in a wardrobe going to do? This fellow's got a tank' argued Loosehorn pointing out of the window at the blustering Baron.

'It'll become apparent' gasped Cornelius desperately. 'Now come on. Trust me.'

Loosehorn and Busbeater looked at each other, shrugged, nodded and dived in.

Meanwhile downstairs, The Baron was at the door and battering it with his gloved fists.

'Let me in. I know you are in zere Golightly. I know you haff ze vardrobe. It is mine I tell you. MINE!' The Baron was over six feet tall, powerfully built and was wearing a long grey overcoat, underneath of which poked large, shiny black boots. He had wavy black hair and a thin pencil moustache. His eyes sparkled green behind his thick rimmed spectacles. He reached in to his massive pockets and withdrew a large old fashioned pistol. He leant back, took aim and fired at the door lock. The bullet ricocheted around the doorway before flying out and clobbering a rabbit. They had become so used to being missed by a lunatic with a gun that the rabbit population of Busbeater Mansions thought nothing of another crazy fool wandering about the place blasting away. Cliff, the cockiest of all the rabbits had been watching the latest chaos from atop the bird bath, and paid the price for this hubris. He would, as the bullets bounced off the door, later become The Baron's only consolation on a bad day; his supper. For a moment The Baron stood fuming and cursing at the door which remained steadfastly un-open. He then ran back to the tank, clambered in and drove it toward the house at high speed.

Gerald carefully placed the flywheel in to the socket at the back of The Wardrobe.

Cornelius then withdrew the panel above the flywheel to reveal a blank display and a set of dials. He quickly turned them until the display read: 'Runnymede, June 14th 1215.'

'Now Gerald turn it slowly to the left until it clicks' advised Cornelius.

Busbeater and Loosehorn were standing guard just inside The Wardrobe doors.

'I say Golightly, I think this Baron fellow is breaking down my door' remarked Busbeater.

'Our lovely door' moaned Marjorie quietly.

Because of Loosehorn's many anti-rabbit locks and bars the door took some battering down but eventually …

CRUNCH

'Actually, I think he has now broken my door,' said Busbeater 'Hot trousers Golightly, he's in, hurry up doing whatever the heck it is you are supposed to be doing.'

Click

'Now again, to the right, quickly this time.'

Gerald did so.

Busbeater was getting nervous, 'Golightly, the bounder is clattering up the stairs, he's practically he …'

As he said that The Wardrobe shuddered and the doors slammed tightly shut.

The Baron with pistol to the fore ran in to Loosehorn's room. All he heard was Busbeater cry out ' … he's practically he …' as the doors shut. The Baron, inches away fell against The Wardrobe thumping his fists against it.

'Nein, nein …' sobbing now 'nein. Zo close. Zo very, very close …'

The Wardrobe shook violently, throwing The Baron off. Before his very eyes amid much wheezing, clattering and unfolding wooden panels it grew and grew until it was five times its original size. It crashed and broke the furniture around it sending splinters across the room, smashing glasses and ripping some of Loosehorn's finest ball gowns. And then silence. The Wardrobe was gone. Alone in the shattered room The Baron sat forlorn and very cross. Only moments before everywhere had hummed to the sound of violent excitement; now all was suddenly silent.

'Have they gone?' asked Mrs Bunyon as she crawled out from the wreckage of Loosehorn's bed.

'Yes. You stupid voman; vhy did you not ring me earlier?!'

'Golightly, the bounder is clattering up the stairs, he's practically here. Oh I say, what the heck has happened?'

Just as Gerald turned the flywheel to the right The Wardrobe shook, the doors slammed shut and … all went very quiet apart from a fading cry of 'neeeeeeeeeeeeeeeeeeein' from outside.

Lieutenant Colonel Busbeater, Major General Loosehorn, Marjorie Busbeater, Sheepshanks and Gerald all sat in the now much bigger wardrobe looking in silent, puzzled expectancy at Cornelius Golightly. Busbeater broke the silence.

'So Golightly. Just what the very heck is this all about?'

Loosehorn looked sharply at his old friend, 'You mean you don't know either? It was after all you lot who came bursting in to my room disturbing my morning reverie with outlandish and rather loud tales of time machines, barons, flywheels and what not. I thought you had all hit the crème de menthe a bit early. And now I find myself in my own wardrobe, which I notice is considerably bigger than it was …'

'Like the Doctor's Tardis?' interrupted Gerald.

Cornelius gave a contemptuous snort.

'The Doctor? He's not real, he's just an invention for TV. The idea for the Tardis came from The Wardrobes when I … oh never mind. Just never trust people in show business …' Golightly fumed. He shouldn't have had that second glass in that wine bar in Shepherds' Bush.

'As I was saying' re-interrupted Loosehorn irritably 'er, where was I?'

'If I can sum it up' rejoined Busbeater; 'Cornelius would you kindly explain to all of us just what the bally heck is going on?'

CHAPTER FIVE

Off To The Wrong Time

Everyone sat down as The Wardrobe slid sedately through time and space. They were surrounded by dresses, ladies shoes of many shapes and sizes, feather boas, mink stoles all of which swayed gently as if they were sailing on gently rolling seas rather than crossing the cosmos.

Gerald pondered his position for a moment. His short time at Busbeater Mansions had been full of more surprises than a massive box labelled 'Surprises In Here - Loads of Them.' Now he found himself, incredibly, in a time machine amongst Major General's Loosehorn's dresses hurtling through time and space on goodness knows what mission, although it did seem quite urgent, with a man who up until twenty minutes ago he thought was a fireman called Charlie. He gulped. 'Crumbs, this is a real adventure' he thought. He had a determined expression on his face, but inside his tummy butterflies were flapping away like they'd just invented flapping and were determined to do lots of it. What on earth had he got himself in to and what would Neil Armstrong do? Be brave and heroic that's what. He'd expected life at Busbeater Mansions to be boring. How wrong could a twelve year old boy be? This wrong he thought. He was nervous but terribly, terribly excited.

Everyone was looking expectantly at Cornelius who frankly owed them a bally explanation, as Busbeater was exclaiming.

Cornelius swatted a green evening dress out of his eyes and began. 'We are in a time machine.'

'We'd gathered' interrupted Busbeater irritably.

Marjorie threw him a fierce look, 'Let him explain dear.'

'A time machine invented by a Chinaman called ...'

'Zhu Zhi' interrupted Gerald.

'Yes! How did you know that?' Cornelius was puzzled.

'I read it in this magazine', Gerald held his copy of 'Fantastic Machines Of Ancient and Modern Times' up for everyone to see, 'I found it in Uncle's library.'

Cornelius opened it to page sixteen and read the article with widening eyes.

'They didn't probably know it but they were spot on' he gasped.

'Who were spot on about what?' Busbeater was fidgeting with massive annoyance.

Cornelius explained who Zhu Zhi was, about the four machines and the possible existence of a more powerful fifth one.

'In the magazine they say no-one has ever found them and they may not exist. But they do. All five of them. They very much exist.'

'Well, clearly. We're in one' said Loosehorn.

'This fifth machine Golightly', asked Busbeater, 'What's that about? And how do you know this isn't it?'

'It's the most important one and it's flywheel key is a five pointed star as opposed to the round one we are using; It's what we always look for. The fifth machine lets you change historical events. If you can do that to suit yourself, then you can rule the world. And that's what The Baron wants to do; it's my job to stop him' said Cornelius.

'So why was it so important he had this one?' asked Gerald.

'It's simple really,' Cornelius went on, 'if The Baron has all four machines he can set about looking for the fifth one without anyone interfering. As it is he already has two and this would have been a big prize for him. If he had three I'd be forced to rely on Carruthers' and Cartwright's machine putting me at a massive disadvantage while he and his henchman could be in three places at once looking for the fifth machine. But now its two each; the odds are even.'

'Did you have a machine?' asked Gerald.

'I did. But The Baron stole it in Casablanca in 1931. I went there because the rumour was that the fourth machine, missing for centuries was there somewhere.'

'Wait a minute' said Loosehorn 'Casablanca you say?'

'Yes, that's right? Wh …?' before Cornelius could ask why, Loosehorn interrupted.

'When?'

'1931,' Cornelius was getting a bit irritated having to repeat himself for what could be just a ridiculous anecdote. Sure enough it was ridiculous; but very interestingly so.

'I was in Casablanca in 1931. I bought this Wardrobe there' muttered Loosehorn staring at the floor in disbelief.

'I knew it,' said Cornelius, 'When did you bring it home? Precisely.'

Flustered by the thought of actual details, Loosehorn hesitated. His old friend came to the rescue.

'July 4th 1931' said Busbeater.

'Oh darling, you remembered' cooed Marjorie.

'The day I met my wife' said Busbeater looking faintly embarrassed.

Cornelius ignored the significance of the date and exclaimed, 'Two days. Two days!'

'Two days what?' asked Loosehorn.

'I arrived on July 6th 1931. I missed you by two days.'

'What happened to your machine?' asked Gerald.

Cornelius looked pained as he dragged up the memory, 'The Baron and his henchmen stole it …'

'Just who is this Baron Cornelius? He sounds like a bounder to me' asked Busbeater.

'Baron Friedrich Hohenzollern von Achtung is my arch enemy - and yours too now - who stumbled across his time machine in the Palace of Versailles in 1871. The Prussians had just beaten the French and while Count Otto von Bismarck was declaring a united Germany in the Hall of Mirrors, The Baron had nipped out the back to smoke his cigar and discovered King Louis XIV's wardrobe; except it wasn't King Louis' wardrobe …'

'It was a time machine?' chipped in Marjorie.

'Indeed it was. The Baron quickly realised this and stole it. He knew the story of Zhu Zhi's machines and the possible existence of the all important fifth machine and hatched a plan to use the machine to find it, change history to suit himself and so rule the world. He was always bitterly jealous of Bismarck and wanted him out. And ever since then he and I have jousted through time and space. He a blustering old fool but a cunning, ruthless and immensely strong blustering old fool. He is not to be underestimated.'

Everyone went a bit quiet. It was turning out to be quite a day.

Cornelius continued his North African story; 'anyway, back in Casablanca, The Baron and his henchmen kidnapped me and locked me in a basement near the souk in the centre of the city. I escaped from the basement soon after but without my machine I was stranded in Casablanca until 1934 when Carruthers and Cartwright turned up; late and slightly disorganised as usual. We've been looking for this machine ever since.'

'Well now you've found it, now what?' asked Busbeater.

'We have to find the fifth machine before The Baron does.'

'Well, clearly' snorted Busbeater 'So where are we going?'

'Carruthers and Cartwright got a tip off that it might be in the court of King John, so we are heading for the day he loses all his treasures in the Wash as he was fleeing the Dauphin, Louis of France.'

'Er,' Gerald interrupted 'Er …'

'What is it Gerald?' asked Marjorie seeing something was up 'Is something up?'

Gerald had been quiet all this time as he already knew the story of Zhu Zhi and so began rummaging about in his knapsack for that envelope he'd seen earlier. Inside he found a book entitled; 'The Big Book Of Facts For The Boy Adventurer', a copy of The Eagle comic featuring Dan Dare 'Pilot of The Future', a crumpled up Dan Dare tee shirt and a diary full of stories of traveling through time. Inside the front page was an inscription; *'For Gerald: My True Adventurer; be brave, be strong, be funny. Follow my adventures, learn from my mistakes, and find the fifth machine! I love you more than you'll ever understand. But come back to us. Your ever loving Dad.'*

Cornelius looked over and smiled.

'Ahh, I recognise this,' he slid across to Gerald who was holding the diary looking very confused.

'I, er, this is from my dad?' Gerald felt most peculiar. A mixture of excitement, puzzlement and worry.

Cornelius took the diary from Gerald and inspected it more closely, 'Yep, it surely is,' and gave it back to Gerald.

Gerald was utterly perplexed. What did this mean? His dad's diary of adventures? That can't be right; his dad was no adventurer. He was a fat and farty deadbeat in pants and vest who said the moon landing was just pointless. Then, wait a minute - he suddenly had a thought. A possibly life changing thought.

He looked up at Cornelius and haltingly said … 'Cornelius, are you …you … you my Dad?'

Cornelius looked genuinely shocked and surprised as Marjorie looked on anxiously, 'What? Crikey Gerald no. No, this is Arnold Jones' diary with his inscription. Arnold - my sidekick until he met your mother; my sidekick and your father.'

Marjorie could see this was getting fairly serious for the young chap. She moved to sit next to Gerald and put her arm around him squeezing him reassuringly and tightly.

Gerald's mind was whirring and blurring. He couldn't think straight or see straight. What was this about his father? An adventurer? How can this possibly be true? What was Cornelius going on about? Gerald fell in to Marjorie's arms. The only thing for certain right now was that he wanted his mum and she wasn't here.

Marjorie sensed this and squeezed Gerald tightly to give him some security.

'I think you should explain Cornelius.'

Cornelius nodded, 'Of course. Arnold and I travelled in my machine looking for the fourth and fifth machines from when Arnold was about twelve, your age Gerald. The Second World War had just ended and Arnold had lost his parents in a bombing raid and was wandering around London on his own. I landed looking for the machine but instead found Arnold. He had such an independent and adventurous spirit and we hit it off immediately. So we set off together. Then in 1957 we landed in Lincoln looking for The Wardrobe, this Wardrobe in fact, in the Cathedral. I met Linda, your mum, there, which wasn't the plan. I have a rule; never get involved with anyone. I can't stay long enough anywhere. But stupidly I went out with her a couple of times and things started to get serious. But I had to go …'

Gerald looked horrified. Cornelius/Charlie was his hero and now it turned out ... 'You left my mum? You made my mum sad?'

Cornelius pleaded, 'I had no choice.'

'Yes you did; you could have stayed.'

'I can't stay anywhere Gerald; I can't allow The Baron to find the fifth machine.'

'Oh stuff The Baron, stuff everything. You hurt my mum! You made her sad.'

Quietly and kindly Cornelius simply said, 'If I don't stop The Baron one day all of us, all of *us*,' he cast his arm around to encompass Marjorie, Busbeater, Loosehorn and Sheepshanks 'and your mum and dad too, will be no more. He will obliterate us all as he will all his enemies and their relatives.'

Gerald wiped away a tear as Marjorie hugged him tightly. She gave Cornelius a beseeching look as if to say give the lad some good news.

'So, the night before I went I made sure Linda and Arnold met. Arnold is a good, good man Gerald. Read his diary; you will see how brave and funny he is.'

Gerald was finding this all a bit too much and too weird; he remembered Neil Armstrong and how brave he was. He dried his eyes, sat up straight and said more firmly, 'So why did you give me the flywheel at school?'

'None of the machines work without their very own flywheel. When I was stranded in Casablanca I discovered the flywheel being sold in one of the stalls. I couldn't believe my luck. It meant whoever had the machine didn't know what it was ...'

'Quite right' interrupted Loosehorn. 'As far as I was concerned it was just Lady Spankhandle's wardrobe; the one that didn't make it on to The Titanic; unlike the unfortunate Lady Spankhandle.'

Everyone threw Loosehorn a look and Busbeater booted him in the shin; Cornelius continued 'otherwise they would have taken the flywheel. It also meant The Baron didn't have it or if he did he couldn't use it. By pure fluke I had gained some time. When Carruthers and Cartwright found me we hatched a plan that they would find the machine and only when they definitely had, unlike the unsavoury Austin Seven fiasco, would they call me. I thought if I kept the flywheel separate even if The Baron managed to get to the machine first it would be useless; just a wardrobe. Carruthers and Cartwright eventually tracked the machine down to Little Piddlington and Busbeater Mansions. I couldn't believe it; Busbeater Mansions? The place Linda had spoken so fondly of, had had so many adventures in. All the time the machine was there!'

'Why did you give Gerald the flywheel Cornelius?' asked Marjorie imagining only too clearly the danger this had put the boy in.

'When I realised where the machine was I tracked Arnold down and told him everything. I was so surprised to see him in such a low state.'

'He hurt his back,' said Gerald forlornly.

'I know Gerald, I am sorry. But we hatched a plan; it was like the old days. The Baron was hot on Carruthers, Cartwright and my tail; except he didn't know precisely where the machine was. Arnold saw an opportunity for you Gerald; he knew how much you loved adventure and knew this might be your chance. He also knew you'd never believe him if he told you what he once was. He loves you so much Gerald; he doesn't want you ending up like him, lazy and useless and unhappy; he wanted you to have your own adventure and maybe then you'd believe him. So he suggested that you go to Busbeater Mansions with the flywheel. He made sure it was in your knapsack the night before you left. The Baron didn't know about your connection with Busbeater Mansions and wouldn't suspect a boy.'

'Well he does now,' fretted Marjorie.

'Yes', agreed Cornelius, 'he does. But this way we knew that the flywheel would be delivered to the machine safely. I kept an eye on you as you went.'

'The ticket inspector?' asked Gerald.

'Yes that was me too.'

'Did you talk to my mum?' Gerald was still a bit cross with Cornelius.

Cornelius lowered his eyes thoughtfully, 'No, I didn't want to er …upset her any more.'

'She didn't recognise you when you put the fires out?' asked Marjorie.

'I always kept my helmet on.'

'Why didn't my dad go instead of me?' asked Gerald.

'He wanted to stay behind and look after Linda; he never felt he was good enough for her and wanted to prove himself to her somehow. He loves your mum so much; he wants to be worthy of her; and you.'

Gerald sat back and leant in to Auntie Marjorie exhausted from it all. He didn't know what to say. Then he remembered something; in his dad's 'Big Book Of Facts For The Boy Adventurer.'

'Cornelius?'

'Yes Gerald?'

'Where are we going?'

'To catch up with King John before his treasures sink in The Wash; Carruthers and Cartwright have a tip that The Wardrobe full of the king's riches might be the fifth machine.'

'But what date?'

'14th June 1215' replied Cornelius confidently.

'That's the wrong date' said Gerald holding out his 'Big Book Of Facts For the Boy Adventurer'; 14 June 1215 was the day before King John agreed Magna Carta; the treasure fell in to The Wash in October 1216.'

Cornelius looked stunned and read Gerald's dad's book; sure enough they were going to the wrong time. Carruthers and Cartwright had had another Austin Seven moment …

'Can't we just change it now?' asked Gerald.

'No, you can't change the date in mid-flight. We have to wait until we land …'

At that very moment The Wardrobe shuddered and with a heavy crash suddenly stopped.

' … and we have landed' confirmed Cornelius. He moved toward the dials to change the date. Too late; the doors flew open.

CHAPTER SIX

An Unfriendly Reception

Outside stood twenty or so men in leather tunics and metal helmets looking straight in. They lifted their massive lances and pointed them at The Wardrobe, blocking the way out.

One of them, presumably in charge, pushed his way to the front, folded his arms behind his back and peered inside, 'Well, what have we here?'

'We are ...' Cornelius began.

'You are under arrest, that's what you are,' interrupted the captain coolly.

With a dismissive wave of the hand he turned his back on Cornelius and addressed his sergeant; 'Take them, they are clearly French spies. And send for a ...' he looked at The Wardrobe over his shoulder 'a REALLY big cart to carry their contraption.'

Spies? thought Gerald. That didn't sound good. He clutched his knapsack to his chest. Gerald Jones, he thought to himself, you are right in the middle of an Adventure. A real life proper adventure, full of potential peril and opportunities for derring-do. Crikey trousers, he thought to himself; it wasn't what Neil Armstrong would do any more. It was now what would his dad do?

Standing next to him Cornelius whispered to Gerald to remove the flywheel that was just behind him. Quietly he said, 'We must keep it separate until we can get to 1216. That way if The Baron finds The Wardrobe he won't be able to use it.'

Gerald shuffled backwards as surreptitiously as he could and began to unlock the flywheel behind him.

The soldiers were busy ushering everyone, rather rudely Marjorie thought, out of The Wardrobe and on to a rickety cart. One of them noticed Gerald who was standing very still and in a slightly suspicious way. He stepped in to The Wardrobe and brushing aside a few ball-gowns moved toward him lowering his pike, 'Boy what are you …?'

Before he could get close to Gerald, Busbeater moved in between them, 'Leave the boy' he boomed.

The soldier was annoyed and bristling said, 'You are under arrest I can do what I want.'

Unfazed Busbeater loomed over the soldier and looking him right in the eye and with a masterly and sinister tone slowly said, 'You are a small man with a metal head surrounded by dresses; I'd be careful …'

Spooked the soldier felt something or someone behind him, 'er …'

It was Loosehorn, closing in on the soldier to further intimidate him. At that moment Gerald unlocked the flywheel and with a massive shudder The Wardrobe began to shrink violently. In the melee the soldier was spat out of The Wardrobe and landed with a dull thud on Loosehorn amidst a flurry of taffeta and pearls. The soldier, completely freaked out, got to his feet and spluttering embarrassedly as his colleagues guffawed, brushed himself down and said weakly but gesturing wildly, 'Well, don't do it again …' before scurrying back to shout at his still chortling and so-called brothers-in -arms.

Gerald squeezed Busbeater's hand and whispered 'Thank you Uncle.'

'You're a Busbeater Gerald; we look after our own.'

After all the commotion the captain bustled up to the now much smaller wardrobe, 'What the flippin' Eleanor-of-Aquitaine is going on here?!', he demanded, 'You men, be quiet or it'll be Jabberwocky hunting for you.'

Fearful, the soldiers immediately fell silent. The captain was about five feet six inches tall with blonde hair poking from under his metal helmet. He was stocky and with quite muscular arms; so muscular in fact that they didn't quite fold parallel to his body, which made him waddle like a duck a bit. He generally tried to disguise this by marching about with his hands behind his back. He glared at Marjorie, Sheepshanks, Loosehorn in a dress, Busbeater, the boy Gerald, Cornelius and a giant, but now mysteriously smaller wardrobe full of lady's ware. This was turning in to a perplexing day.

He addressed the motley looking gang generally; 'I am Captain Hieronymus Bott, your captor and intellectual superior. Which one of you is in charge of this … this … er' he was struggling to know how best to describe what he saw. He wasn't a stupid man he thought. He had been taught by the monks from four years old until he was six; he could even read the odd word or two. Hence he had always considered himself something of an intellectual although few others agreed. This situation however was beyond even his relatively fierce powers of description. But he was stubborn and refused to give up.

'This er, this …' he gave up. 'What the heck do you call yourselves?'

Cornelius stepped forward. Loosehorn was a bit miffed, 'Who elected you leader then Golightly?' he mumbled under his breath.

'Cease mumbling madam … sir … er' said the now ritually confused captain glaring at Loosehorn.

Cornelius had a moment of genius, 'I am Cornelius Golightly and we are but actors sir; come to play at the court of King John as he works tirelessly to end these civil wars, defeat the French and free our people.' He had read two lines of Gerald's dad's 'Big Book Of Facts For The Boy Adventurer' and guessed the rest. It worked.

Bott visibly relaxed. He hated actors so this ramshackle lot suddenly didn't seem so threatening. They might still be spies of course but very unsubtle ones dressed as garishly as they were with an enormous … er suddenly smaller wardrobe in tow. Still, he mustn't let on that he's rumbled these … these *actors*.

'I think he's relaxed a bit' hissed Loosehorn to Marjorie.

'Most definitely' replied Marjorie 'I bet he thinks were a ramshackle lot now.'

'He'd be right mind you' confessed Loosehorn.

'Well, yes, maybe ...' agreed Marjorie.

Bott, more confident now, rounded on Marjorie and Loosehorn.

'Be quiet harridans ... er, harridan ... er you two.' Turning back to Cornelius he began circling him. With his arms behind his back he tried out a wry grin as he went, hoping to look sinister and menacing.

'Has he got trapped wind?' whispered Marjorie to Loosehorn.

'It would explain that weird expression. I'm not standing near him in case there's some whiffy trouser fluttering going on.'

One of the soldiers behind Loosehorn stabbed him sharply in the leg with his pike. Loosehorn turned around ready to shout blue murder. The soldier was stifling a giggle.

'We call him windy-bots,' he whispered, 'but he doesn't know that.'

'Be quiet all of you,' squealed Bott as he continued to circumvent Cornelius. He confronted him again at the end of the third lap.

'So actors eh? What sort of acting? French acting? Acting as French spies?' Bott was pleased with himself and his clever word play. His two years of education would shine through now and that would show them. He awaited Cornelius' reply.

'No, just actors sir. We do all nationalities, but especially the Welsh.' The Welsh? thought Cornelius, why on earth did he say the Welsh? He knew nothing of the Welsh.

'Say something in Welsh then,' demanded Bott.

Cornelius was stumped. He was about to attempt some terrible impersonation when Gerald stepped in to Save The Day.

In a perfect Welsh accent Gerald announced rather dramatically, 'Bora da. Un, dau, tri, pedwar, pump.'

Everyone stood amazed. What on earth was that and what did it mean? Gerald translated; 'It means "We are honoured to be your guests and wish to entertain your king and your men so he can work for peace." Slightly amazed by himself Gerald bowed in front of the captain.

As he stood up Busbeater hissed, 'Good man Gerald. When did you learn to say all that in Welsh?'

'I didn't.'

'What? What did you say then?'

'Good morning. One, two, three, four, five.'

Busbeater beamed his approval. Gerald had pluck; no doubt about it – he was a Busbeater through and through.

Bott's self-regarding intellectual prowess had few flaws he thought but one of those flaws, if indeed there were any, might have included a lack of languages. He was very anxious however that no-one knew that. He was the educated one around here and he must show no signs of weakness.

'Of course, I knew that,' he blustered, 'but you remain under arrest. The king isn't terribly fond of the Welsh; they are troublesome. Now get in to this cart and we will send another to pick up your … what is it?'

'It is our props cabinet' replied Cornelius. Bott looked blankly.

'Costumes. For our plays' clarified Cornelius.

'Ahh, Yes, plays. Right.'

Cornelius had an idea, 'If it would please you we would very much like to have our props cabinet with us in case the king wishes us to perform.'

'It wouldn't please me and you'll be lucky if the king doesn't just boil you all in lard. He's not known for his love of the arts.' Bott had taken against this strange crew. They seemed a tricky lot; far too charming and quick witted to be anything but a threat. If the king didn't, he'd soon dispose of them once back at the castle.

Everyone fell silent as they were drawn away in a rickety old cart by two huge brown and white cart horses over the rough meadow floor. As they left the clearing where the time machine had landed and entered the surrounding wood, The Wardrobe disappeared from view. Gerald gripped the flywheel tightly through the knapsack. How the heck were they going to get back to the time machine? And does The Baron know where it is? He'll be on their tail if he does. This seemed a very troubling moment to Gerald.

'Cornelius?' whispered Gerald.

'Yes Gerald?'

'Does The Baron know where we are?'

'Good quest ...' but before he could answer Bott interrupted.

'Stop the cart!' he bellowed. He walked slowly toward the cart and his prisoners 'What do you know of the barons?' He pushed his face close up to Cornelius.

'I, er, didn't mention a baron,' said Cornelius hoping to bluff Bott.

'No but the boy did and you seemed to know.' Bott was not to be put off so lightly.

'The Baron?' snorted Busbeater coming to the rescue, 'he's just a ridiculous old buffoon we met once; claims to be German.'

'German you say?' Bott didn't know there were any German barons coming to the conference. The king would be most interested to hear this. If he delivered what sounded like significant information to the king he might get the promotion he so craved. He was desperate to get away from the numbskulls he had to deal with everyday and work with people on his own superior intellectual level. This might be his passport out of the intellectual-free swamp he had to wade about in all day. These actors could be useful to him after all. Maybe their immediate disposal could wait; just a few hours.

'Move on and be quick about it,' he commanded his men, 'I need to see the king.' It was now important they got to Windsor Castle quite quickly.

Gerald and Busbeater wondered what they had said to cause Bott to get in to such an agitated state. Gerald discretely turned to his Big Book Of Facts For The Boy Adventurer and read, 'King John had fought civil wars with his barons who were fed up with him stealing their money in order to fight more futile wars with the French. After a truce in May 1215, the king agreed to meet the barons at Runnymede the next month. Here the barons would put forward their demands to have their rights protected and for this protection to be enshrined in law which the king himself had to obey. It would form the basis of the World Famous Magna Carta. But each side still fiercely distrusted the other.'

Gerald caught on quickly; If Bott thought they had inside knowledge of the barons, as opposed to the nutcase Baron von Achtung who they were actually talking about, then he would look good if he delivered them all to the king, maybe getting a promotion or something. He explained his theory to Cornelius and Busbeater who both agreed.

'What are you doing boy?' asked Bott.

'Er, reading sir.'

Reading? He was *reading*? This put Bott in an awkward position. After years of bragging about his reading ability, confident that no-one amongst his troupe would ever challenge him since they were mostly illiterate, ignorant oafs, he now faced a situation where he might have to prove he can read something beyond 'ye cat sat on ye mat', which at six years old was pretty advanced. In subsequent years confident bluffing had got him through many a scrape and ultimately to captain; it would work now with these tedious actor fellows. He wouldn't be shown up by a mere boy.

'Hand it over' he demanded.

Gerald did so.

Guessing based on his knowledge of mats and their whereabouts and the sedentary activities of cats upon them, Bott held the book the right way up, luckily, and read it silently; well, stared at the bewildering symbols on the page silently; not a mat or cat or cat on a mat anywhere. After what he hoped was a convincing few moments of confident knowledgeable-looking nodding he guffawed loudly, pointing at the page; 'Ah, yes, very funny. Ha, ha, ha. Yes, very amusing.'

He felt he'd got away with it and handed the book back to Gerald, glaring at him and daring him to challenge him. Gerald was smart enough not to fall for that one. He thanked Bott and read what he had 'read.' It said a curious thing; 'Captain Hieronymus Bott is a short windy bottom liable to massive trouser trumps and isn't as clever as he thinks he is. And he can't read unless it involves felines and rugs and parking one's behind.' Gerald stared unbelievingly at the book before looking up quizzically to Cornelius who mouthed silently, 'I'll explain later.'

Crikey thought Gerald, more explaining.

He went back to the book which had now seemingly reverted to explanations of the history between the barons and King John. Whatever the heck was going on with his dad's book, and by now he was learning to expect the weird, one thing was clearly apparent; Bott couldn't read. That might be helpful. Oh and he can't speak Welsh. That might be less helpful.

The journey to Windsor was slow. The cart they were all crammed in to was old, rickety and its wooden wheels weren't smoothly round. Loosehorn leant across to Busbeater and muttered just as the cart clattered in to and out of a big hole in the road, 'This is one of those times when it might actually be useful to re-invent the wheel.'

'Quiet' yelled the Sergeant, Bott's number two.

Marjorie, not used to being pushed around like this was indignant,

'Where are you taking us?' she demanded of the Sergeant.

Sergeant Day, small, skinny with buck teeth and rough skin, was in a bad mood. He was supposed to have had a bit of time off this week. He'd been fighting non-stop for years and frankly he felt it was time he had a rest. But noooo; Captain Bott kept him on demanding he be part of King John's outliers looking for spies, either Frenchies or rebel sympathisers, in the run up to this conference thingy arrangement. In the past year he had hardly seen his wife Holly, although somehow she'd managed to deliver him a child, whom he'd never seen, and named him Wednes. Wednes! What sort of name was that? And now here he was being harangued by this old crone about something or other when he could have been at home bouncing young Wednes Day on his knee.

'What old lady? What could you possibly want?' he barked.

'Well,' replied Marjorie clinging on to the side of the rickety cart as it bounced along the rough track, ' I have never ... ooof,' she fell back but recovered quickly with the help of Busbeater's right arm, 'I have never been spoken to in such a manner. I asked you a perfectly civilised . . ouch, oooof!' A really big hole in the road sent her flying backwards again, landing on Loosehorn this time. Determined to give this oik a piece of her mind, she recovered again 'I er, I have ... er.'

'Never been spoken to in such a manner?' chipped in Busbeater helpfully.

'Ahh yes, thank you darling, yes' cooed Marjorie before turning on Sergeant Day again. 'I have never been spoken to in such a manner by such an oaf in all my days.'

'There have been a lot of days haven't there?' replied Day rudely.

Marjorie was speechless with rage 'I ... I ...'

Day continued, 'I mean normally if anyone reaches sixty they are pretty clapped out. I had an aunt who lived to sixty five once but she was a freak. But look at you lot. All of you are, well, ancient. The boy is practically middle aged and he's a babe in arms compared with you. I mean how old *are* you?'

Marjorie was gamely trying to get out of the cart, but Busbeater held her back, 'You … I … leg … I you, why I have never … ooof, let go Busbeater … I have never …'

'What is all this screaming and hullabaloo here?' demanded Bott. 'You, crone, sit down you are making the cart unsteady.'

'Because otherwise it's like a Rolls Royce' muttered Loosehorn. No-one heard.

'Now, Day, what is going on?'

'This woman was being insolent and so I gave her short shrift.'

Marjorie spluttered 'I merely asked where we were going and he, that chump, was very rude.'

At that moment something pinged loudly in to Day's helmet shooting it off his head and in to the grass; in the shock he fell backwards and with arms flailing landed in a very large pile of fresh cow dung. The soldiers guffawed loudly, bringing the rickety cart to a standstill. Even Bott giggled.

'What the hard boiled eggs was that?' spluttered Day, now covered entirely in poo.

Gerald looked at Sheepshanks to see him discretely return a catapult to his inside pocket followed by a wink. Sheepshanks. Super Hero. I must get him a cape thought Gerald.

Bott, impatient to get to the castle and deliver his hot news to the king ordered Day to apologise to Marjorie so they could get on.

'You may be a savage Day, but I am an intellectual. I order you to apologise to the crone …'

'Sorry crone …' said the reluctant Day.

'And please walk down wind of the rest of us will you Day? You smell like someone who's just fallen in a massive cow pat … oh, no wait …'

Marjorie fumed. Crone? *Crone?* She'd show them when she got the chance. No-one but no-one talked to Marjorie Busbeater this way and remained untarnished.

Crestfallen and covered in poo, Day retreated to the back of the line. He had never been more fed up in all of his life. He hoped this fiercely determined old woman would somehow confront Bott in a one-on-one then he'd see how scary an annoyed, looming crone could be. One day he vowed he would get Bott back for humiliating him.

'Bit further back Day', Bott waved with the back of his hand.

'Any further back and he'll be YesterDay' chortled Gerald.

The soldiers on either side of the cart thought this was hilarious and doubled over from their guffawing, with only their pikes stuck fast in the ground holding them up.

'Easy crowd' thought Gerald. He watched Day trudge behind everyone and instantly felt bad for making fun of him. He looked humiliated. Day had been rude to Marjorie and deserved a telling off, but Bott was being too mean; and he had joined in.

'Even more Day. You really are whiffy' Bott went on.

There's no need to keep on thought Gerald. He wanted to make it up to Day, but he'd not get a chance now.

Marjorie, never one to let anything go as Busbeater had found out many, many times, still demanded an answer to her question, 'Captain … er.'

'Bott. Hieronymus Bott.'

'Captain Bott,' Marjorie almost spat his name out; he'd called her a crone, 'Captain Bott where are you taking us?'

'Windsor Castle.'

'Oooh, lovely' Marjorie's tone lightened. She turned to Busbeater, 'We haven't been there for donkey's years have we? Since we had tea in the grounds and Loosehorn and that peacock had their contretemps.'

'It was hardly a contretemps,' barked Loosehorn 'that was my 1933 Madeleine Vionnet halter neck evening gown he was trying to …' Loosehorn shuddered at the memory 'eat.'

'That was a rather lovely number' agreed Marjorie.

Bott stood open mouthed at this conversation. What on earth was going on? It had been a long day for all of them after a quite difficult couple of years trying to figure out what their capricious king might do next, but this was without doubt the weirdest collection of individuals he had ever come across - and he'd met many a Frenchman - and what's more he couldn't predict anything they might do or say. It was troubling.

'Windsor Castle is where you will be held prisoner.' he said harshly 'It is not a nice place to stay. It is not as you say …'

And here he tried to impersonate Marjorie. It was late, he was tired and this was his next really big mistake; 'It is not "ooooo, lovely" and will not involve tea!' he went on, ill advisedly.

Before he knew where he was he was on the ground with a furious Marjorie at him with the palm of her hands slapping his chops like he was a cold steak being tenderised before cooking.

'I have had a very long day and I will not be talked to like this by a silly man whose name isn't even a whole bottom!' cried Marjorie in between slaps.

The soldiers pulled Marjorie off just as Busbeater arrived to support and comfort her. Gerald stood in front of Marjorie and announced; 'Captain Bott, you were very rude to my aunt and I demand satisfaction.' He wasn't entirely sure what that meant but he'd seen Errol Flynn do it in a movie which he'd watched with his mum and he thought it rather grand. Unfortunately he'd fallen asleep before it was explained exactly what this entailed.

'I will not duel with a boy' retorted Bott.

Duel? Crikey thought Gerald, so that's what Errol meant. He wasn't so sure he wanted a duel.

'Well, I er ...'

Cornelius stepped in, 'Listen, we all seem to have got off on the wrong foot.'

'I should bleedin' say so' chortled Day; he had enjoyed watching Bott get flattened by the crone.

'Shut UP Day you useless smelly oaf!' fumed Bott.

'So lets all calm down and try and get along,' continued Cornelius, in vain.

'You are all my prisoners let me remind you' said Bott through gritted teeth 'and if it was anyone else in charge by now you'd be in pretty much the same mess as Day is in except he is breathing. Now, get back in the cart and not a word out of any of you until we get to Windsor. Understood?'

Everyone nodded. Bott gasped his exasperation, 'Not you men; just the prisoners.'

'Can I speak?' asked Day.

'No Day. You seem to smell even more when you talk. Bring up the rear. Now if that's all clear. Let's continue on.'

'Bott got beaten up by a crone and Day landed in Poo. This is a great day. A great day' said one of the soldiers with a massive smile across his face as he started pulling the horses toward Windsor Castle.

Gerald glanced back and as The Wardrobe became increasingly obscured by trees and gradually disappeared from view it suddenly struck him; The Wardrobe looked just like the one he thought he saw on TV as he watched the moon landing. That would certainly explain something; but what? What on earth did it mean?

CHAPTER SEVEN

A Chaotic Arrival And Straight To Gaol

The journey to Windsor Castle was a long and very bumpy one. In terms of miles it was barely a handful but the rickety cart and the rough track meant it seemed to last for hours. Marjorie glowered the whole way at Bott, her left eye only just calming down. If she got out of this, whatever the heck was going on, he would pay for the crone gag ... he would pay. Busbeater and Loosehorn were also pondering the situation; that this was almost as big a hoo-hah as when they found themselves arrested by Patriots - or was it the Traitors - after rescuing that booby of a journalist Boot in the Ishmaelia campaign. They glanced at each other and gave knowing winks. They'd been in worse scrapes and escaped; this would be the same. Whatever it was Sheepshanks was thinking, no-one could tell from his expression. With his eyes fixed firmly ahead he seemed to be mumbling something to himself, but he was so inscrutable that it could mean he was hatching a plan or just counting the butterflies as they trundled through the thirteenth century countryside. Cornelius looked the most worried of all; they were separated from the machine, they were in the wrong place and time and heading toward a relatively new fortified castle in which sat the brooding and terminally bad tempered King John. And The Baron might be right behind them, or worse heading for 1216, where they should be. None of this felt good.

Gerald was thinking hard too and he'd noticed that Bott was busy at the front hurrying things along and taking less notice of them all in the cart. Gerald took the opportunity to discretely take out his father's diary. The thick book was bound in leather with a thin leather strap tied to keep it closed. Gerald loosened the strap and opened the book up at random:

22nd January 1533 Hampton Court

Played Real Tennis with Henry. It turns out the king doesn't like losing, so after the ninth game I let him win five-four. There was a worrying moment when I really creamed a half volley which I was certain was a winner. Instead the ball flew right in to his face. There was a lot of royal hollerin' and I thought I must have given him a black eye or something; and only three days before his secret wedding to Anne too. Crikey trousers I thought. What if he cancels the wedding? He's a vain man and might not fancy getting married with a big blue shiner. I may have accidentally changed history, although it was a great shot! Luckily it was above his eye and his face just smarted for a bit. He made a right fuss about nothing. When he finally won, he saw the funny side of it. Afterward he made me and Cornelius sit through a poetry recital; hours and hours and hours of him reading the love poems he'd written for Anne. It was agonising. He didn't half go on. At one point I was worried he was going to club the big baby.

Henry has sworn us to secrecy about his wedding to Anne; it turns out he is still married to Catherine of Aragon. Cornelius says it's Henry's way of forcing the pope to allow him to divorce Catherine. Henry was most insistent we say nothing; he can be a menacing fellow.

Later

We are hearing worrying rumours that a mysterious German nobleman is paying Anne Boleyn a visit in Kent before she travels to London for the wedding. Is it The Baron? We have to get to Anne Boleyn's house and check to make sure The Wardrobe with her wedding dress in isn't the fifth machine and if it is disable it before The Baron gets hold of it. But it's so hard to get away from Henry; he keeps forcing us back in to his blinkin' maze at Hampton Court and it takes us ages to get out each time, which he thinks is hilarious. We must get to Anne's house before The Baron. There's no time to lose.'

Two days later

There has been a terrible and fearsome battle with The Baron just outside Canterbury. He is a frightening man. We won - just. And Anne and Henry can now get married. By the time I am fourteen I want to be stronger to be able to fight The Baron on my own. But between us Cornelius, me and Anne's sister, who is a feisty sort, fought him off. Anne's wardrobe is not the fifth machine. Cornelius brilliantly found out without anyone noticing. I gave The Baron a black eye which took him down; I knew that half volley in real tennis would come in handy! But The Baron is a truly terrifying figure. If ever I have a son, I hope he is braver and stronger than me; I was petrified when he showed up. My son will be heroic and noble.

Gerald closed the diary when he felt one of the soldiers looking at him. He smiled but the soldier seemed pretty disinterested. Gerald was bursting with pride. His dad had met Henry VIII! And was on a mission just like he was - to find the fifth machine. And he fought The Baron. Gerald was determined not to let his dad - Arnold Jones, Hero and Adventurer - down.

After some time Windsor Castle hove in to view with the familiar Round Tower on its mound dominating the landscape. The tower was originally built using timber by William the Conqueror but John's father Henry II had it rebuilt in stone, giving it a more menacing, brooding look. The castle overall was much smaller than it was the last time Marjorie and Busbeater had visited with fewer buildings. Marjorie hoped the Alder Valley Brass Band would be there despite the trouble she had had back in '65 with the rather large chap and his enthusiastic blowing on the euphonium which cost Marjorie her very attractive raffia hat. As they drew closer Marjorie could see that Family Fun Days Out were not a priority at this version of Windsor Castle. It looked very much like it was designed for war. Marjorie gulped; she wish she hadn't been so angry with that Alder Valley Brass Band now and hoped that the euphonium player had been able to extract his instrument reasonably fast and painlessly.

Gerald looked up at the looming castle and shuddered. It was a sunny day but the tower cast a long, dark shadow which enveloped them in their rickety cart as they approached. A chill shivered across them all.

Livestock of one type or another were rambling about the grounds churning the soil in to mud and yikes, the smell - it was so bad you could almost taste it. Gerald shuddered; what a pong. Everywhere soldiers, some of whom were wearing metal helmets, moved urgently about shouting and swearing at one another, ordering peasants around and running hither and thither with earnest intent. They were getting ready in case the barons attacked. It was always likely. Only a week or so before the king had promised the rebel barons safe passage to and from Staines to aid in the negotiations over the details of the final Articles in what would become known as Magna Carta. However, nobody trusted anybody, so Windsor was being fortified as much as possible just in case things turned ugly; they had to be on their guard. And then Gerald and the gang arrived and everyone stopped being on their guard to have a really good gawp at this odd collection of strangers trundling in to the castle. Much hollarin' and shouting ensued as the cart made its way toward the tower.

'What you got there captain? Some kind of freak show?' chortled one bystander.

Pointing at Loosehorn another bellowed through loud guffaws, 'Hey, Day, don't fancy yours much!'

Yet another seeing the forlorn Day bringing up the rear gleefully yelled 'Poo! Is that your new scent? Essence of Dung? Phewee what a stinker.' Which, thought Gerald was a bit rich coming from this lot who would have come a close second in any 'Who Smells the Most?' competition.

'Get back to work peasants!,' screamed Bott, 'These are my prisoners and I have important news for the king.'

'Prisoners?' came the incredulous reply, 'By the looks of them my granny could have caught them; and she had only one leg - when she was alive!'

Bott thought about a witty reply but for all his education he wasn't a naturally witty fellow.

'Get lost the lot of you' was all he could muster.

Gerald pulled his knapsack closer to his chest and thought about his dad and Neil Armstrong. Crikey trousers, what would they do if they were here? Be brave he thought. He felt for the flywheel just to make sure it was there and looked across at Cornelius. It wasn't reassuring for Cornelius looked more worried now than he did when Baron von Achtung was blamming away at Busbeater's front door. Uncle Busbeater and Major General Loosehorn however had a much more steely look in their eyes. After years of failing to blast rabbits Loosehorn was relishing this apparent and completely unexpected opportunity to get his hands dirty in a proper kerfuffle. Busbeater looked similarly determined and discretely energised. Marjorie had spotted it too and she gave a little shudder of excitement. It had been a long time since she'd seen that look. Sheepshanks was still gazing a bit blankly seemingly unaware of the thirteenth century pickle they'd found themselves in. Cornelius however knew what was at stake and how difficult it was going to be to escape.

'Out, come on, all of you, out,' Bott impatiently demanded waving them off the cart, 'Come on.'

One by one they stepped off the cart and in to a crowd of curious soldiers and peasants. One of them tried to touch Loosehorn's outfit, which was a mistake.

'Get OFF peasant,' he spat and with a swing of his arm sent the miscreant flying to the general amusement of the crowd.

Then Sergeant Day arrived and immediately and with a huge amount of caterwauling the crowd rapidly dispersed firing comments as they retreated with fingers clamped over their noses;

'Cor, have a bath at least.'

'Wow it's Sergeant Stinkathon!'

'Look out it's Sergeant Plop!'

And that was the adults.

The peasant's children naturally thought it all hilarious;

'Hey Poo Pants you Smell of Dung; Ring-a-ring of Dung, A pocket full of Poo, atishoo atishoo were all covered in poo' they sang lustily in-between giggles.

'For goodness sake,' hissed Bott, 'get them inside ...'

Inside the Round Tower the door slammed shut and the yelling, guffawing and general hilarity suddenly stopped. Then abruptly it started once more as the door opened and in staggered Bott. Then it stopped again as the door slammed shut for the second time. Bott leant against the door. 'Thank you for waiting for me' he grizzled as sarcastically as he could. 'Did you not notice I wasn't there? Er here ... er, with you? They nearly lynched me largely due to Dungy Day. Where is he by the way?'

The soldiers who had rounded up Gerald and the gang and were keeping them still with their pikes all looked at one another. Eventually one said, 'We thought he was with you sir.'

'Er ... oh' said Bott.

He opened the door a fraction to be greeted by the pleading eyes of Day,

'Let me in Bott, let me in!'

Bott quickly opened the door.

'a pocket full of poo ...'

Day literally fell in to the room and for a moment lay still, face down. 'The mob' he moaned 'oh the mob! It's a good job they don't get to run anything. Imagine the chaos. Oh the chaos.'

'Go and have wash Day,' ordered Bott, 'for goodness sake.'

Gerald looked around him. The Round Tower they had been brought to for the moment was quiet at least. The stone walls were thick and forbidding with only small slits cut deep in to them allowing just a sliver of light to get through. Torches on the walls burned noisily but not very brightly. The whole place smelled of sweat and damp and echoing around the room was the sound of water dripping somewhere. Bott turned to them, 'My plan is to split you all up ...'

Gerald gulped. Cornelius looked anxiously across at Gerald. He was too far away but Busbeater caught his urgent stare and winked back as if to say, 'It's OK I have him,' and moved closer to Gerald. If they were to be split up he would plead for the boy to be with his uncle. Then for the first time today they had a bit of luck.

Bott continued, 'But we don't have enough empty cells, so you'll have to go in pairs. That annoys me as I suspect you'll be in cahoots and try to plan something, like escape. But it would be a futile plan; in all it's 150 odd years, no-one's ever escaped from Windsor Castle. And as we all know once something is set that way, it never, ever changes.'

At that moment a jangling noise heralded the arrival of the gaoler.

'Ahh, gaoler, finally.'

'Yes sire' said a short, wiry and grubby man whom Marjorie suspected hadn't been outside for quite some time and certainly had never combed or washed his hair.

'Take these ... these ...'

'Freaks?' offered one of the soldiers.

'Prisoners,' corrected Bott, 'and put them in the cells; two to each one.'

'Yes sire' said the gaoler.

'I must be off to see the king' announced Bott.

'You certainly must' mumbled Gerald.

'What did you say?' barked Bott.

Everyone remained silent. Bott harrumphed and set off for the Royal Apartments in The Upper Ward of the castle. 'I will be back' he announced, threateningly.

The gaoler gestured with a fling of his arm for the soldiers to get the prisoners to follow him, two by two in to the even darker, windowless interior. Busbeater held Gerald's arm as the boy clutched his knapsack to his chest. Marjorie and Cornelius were next with Loosehorn and Sheepshanks bringing up the rear. Loosehorn whispered to Sheepshanks, 'Remember Ishmaelia.'

Sheepshanks turned to him and gave him a look which said, 'Oh yes, most definitely.'

They were already in what Bott feared most; cahoots.

Marjorie could resist it no longer, 'Have you never washed your hair? Has it ever seen a comb?' she asked in a matronly tone.

The gaoler stopped and turned around. He had, surprisingly, a very cultured voice; 'Are you addressing me madam?'

The gaoler, this small, greasy little man who may well be the last human being any of them ever saw besides themselves had addressed Marjorie as madam. She was slightly nonplussed by the politeness since so far today everyone had been incredibly rude. She stammered in reply, 'I, er ... I was just, well er, wondering because well, you seem a little ...'

'Grubby?' Offered the gaoler.

'Well, I suppose ... I er, yes,' Marjorie's eye began to wobble.

Un-fussed the gaoler continued on, 'It is unfortunately an occupational hazard. I work in the dungeons pretty much twelve hours a day and by the time I get home, well there's barely time to eat before I have to sleep. Then it's up with the lark and back to work. To be honest what with that, learning to play the hurdy-gurdy, which is not easy since it needs two people really and I can never find anyone to help, and writing my book, there is simply no time to wash one's hair. It's a curse, but one day I will escape this life of drudgery and gambol happily in the countryside, maybe as a happy minstrel or poet or a chronicler of Great Men. The Venerable Bede is my inspiration. A fine man with a lovely turn of phrase. And funnier than you might think too.'

'Oi, gaoler, get on with it will you? We've got homes to go to even if you haven't,' barked and sniffed one of the soldiers.

'Philistines' muttered the gaoler. He continued to lead the way.

On the other side of a heavy iron door, the corridor became narrower and darker, more damp and smelly. The screaming and hollering of the prisoners already there became louder. Gerald squeezed his uncle's hand.

'It's OK Gerald. Remember we are Busbeaters. No castle wall can hold us.'

After a few moments the gaoler stopped at a cell door. He jangled his keys and when eventually finding the right one opened the creaky, very thick wooden door and gestured for Gerald and Busbeater to go in. An impatient soldier was harsher and shoved the pair through the door. Loosehorn made for the soldier, but Cornelius stopped him as the other soldiers began to raise their pikes menacingly.

'It's OK Loosehorn … it's alright, leave it.'

'It bally well is NOT OK' snorted Loosehorn.

'I am sorry for the treatment,' remarked the gaoler, 'These oafs are uncultured and rude.' He glared at the soldier who had shoved Gerald and Busbeater. 'You sir are a knave and a mountebank. You disgrace my gaol with your brutish behaviour.'

At that moment a blood thirsty scream came from a distant cell followed by peels of sinister laughter.

'Be gone from my place of work which is tarnished by your mere presence,' the gaoler continued.

To a chorus of further screams and laughter and the grinding, squeaking sound of metal winches, the soldier left the gaol, a bit embarrassed as his colleagues sniggered. Told off by the gaoler of all people …

At the next cell door the gaoler wafted Marjorie and Cornelius in as if ushering them in to a five star hotel bedroom and not a dark, smelly, damp, vermin infested cell. When Loosehorn and Sheepshanks were safely ensconced the gaoler announced, perhaps unexpectedly, the entertainment plans for the evening. He was proud of his generally humane treatment of his charges. He rarely got to know any of them for long since they were usually executed pretty quickly, so he wanted his brief impression to be a good one. His mother had always said a good impression even on a smelly, useless, condemned criminal was the sign of a true gentleman. It was burned on his memory as she'd said it as she was being led away to be executed.

'I shall be playing the Flute but would also like to try out a tune on my hurdy-gurdy if I can recruit a volunteer to help, and read some of the Chronicles of Bede.'

Amongst the screams and begging for mercy one wag from further down cried out, in a heavy European accent, 'I'd rather be put on the rack than listen to you for one more night on that stupid flute and gurgling hurdly or whatever you call it!'

The gaoler sighed and addressed his new charges; 'I am so sorry about him. He is one half of a traveling duo of Hungarian Stunt Archers. There's a chance they might be executed tomorrow so he's in a bit of a bad mood. Anyway, I'll just put dinner on and will be back presently.'

In turn he shut the three cell doors and with a jangle of keys locked them all. He then shuffled away as the chorus of bloodcurdling screams went on unabated. The remaining soldiers left as rapidly as they could. There was ale to be supped and merciless mickey taking to be, er, taken. And besides it was incredibly smelly in the gaol.

In their cell Marjorie turned to Cornelius.

'Cornelius? How serious is the pickle we are in?'

Cornelius paused for a moment, 'We've got a one way ticket to Pickle Town Marjorie and The Branston Boys are waiting for us intent on dishing out a proper pickling.'

'So quite serious then.'

'Yes,' sighed Cornelius, 'quite serious. Up to our pickled necks in it in fact.'

'Is there anything to do?'

'Our best hope is to rely on the curiosity of King John and maybe Bott's powers of persuasion. He fancies himself as some kind of intellectual, maybe he can convince John to see us before ...' Cornelius stopped.

'Before?' ventured Marjorie with a gulp as her eye set off again betraying her rising level of stress

'Before ...' Cornelius wondered how to say this next bit. He decided to just say it, 'before he has us executed.'

Silence fell, broken by Marjorie stoically but slightly trembly saying 'Like those Hungarian Stunt Archers might be tomorrow?'

'Yes, looks like no more archery, stunt or otherwise for the Magyars.'

'The Maggies?' Marjorie was lost, again.

Cornelius could see the cul de sac they were heading for and changed direction, 'It's quite a long shot but we have one ray of hope.'

Marjorie brightened; maybe all was not lost.

'Gerald has The Big Book Of Facts For The Boy Adventurer.'

'That's the one his father game him?' asked Marjorie.

'Yes. Except it has, well, it is more alive than you might think.'

'What, like vivid chapters of purple prose bringing adventures to life? I wish I'd had books like that when I was at school. Mind you I might have; the only books we were allowed to use were balanced on our heads to improve our posture. Couldn't read 'em from there. They just gave me neck ache.'

Cornelius looked at Marjorie. This family's ability, he thought, to ramble on even at times of massive peril was remarkable.

He ploughed on regardless 'The book is actually alive ... well, sort of.'

'Cornelius, what on earth are you trying to say? It's all sounding like nonsense at the moment.'

Cornelius had to admit that the random blurting of information about books being alive did make him sound a little round the bend and probably wasn't helping alleviate the sense of terrible danger. So, he told it like it was; 'The book protects the reader and his comrades from accidentally changing history.'

'How?'

'Wherever in time it is taken it will tell the reader what happened in that period. Right now it will be telling Gerald all about King John, Magna Carta, the barons, the archbishop, Windsor Castle and who did what to whom, how, where and with what blunt instrument.'

'That is innovative,' sighed Marjorie, impressed 'what will they think of next?'

Cornelius staved off his exasperation as Marjorie once more had that far away look in her eyes and sound in her voice suggesting she was off on a reverie.

'The point Marjorie is that it stops you from changing history by telling you about it.'

Marjorie sensed danger, 'What happens if, purely hypothetically, you did, accidentally change history?'

There was quite a long pause as Cornelius considered his reply, 'If anyone interferes with the way history is written, then the time machine that took them there shuts down and will never work again. The travellers will be stranded. Forever.'

'And the book that Gerald has ...'

'If we stick to it, we'll be OK.'

'Does Gerald know this?'

'No.'

'Oh.'

'But he's bright and he knows the book is special. He'll figure it out.'

'He's twelve years old Cornelius. He's just a boy.'

'But he's a Busbeater,' Cornelius looked up at Marjorie.

'He is,' conceded Marjorie knowing that was a Good Thing, 'and so is the Lieutenant Colonel. Even *more* of one. And rather impulsive like his Aunt Sissy …'

'It's all rather riding on Gerald,' sighed Cornelius, 'I didn't mean this to happen.'

'No, well, there we have it,' Marjorie looked at Cornelius. For the first time since he turned up at Busbeater Mansions blabbering on about time machines and barons, Cornelius looked like a man without a plan.

'And what's more, we have no idea where the Machine is. A true pickle.'

Marjorie gulped. C'mon Busbeater, remember Ishmaelia, she thought.

'Uncle?'

'Yes Gerald old son.'

'This book I have.'

'The one your dad gave you?'

'Yes, that one.'

'What about it?'

Busbeater was going over the door and door frame inch by inch trying to see if there was a crack or a weakness or something that might help in the escape. If he could get to Loosehorn and maybe recruit the Hungarian Stunt Archers they could overpower the guards and the strange gaoler find the time machine and escape. The Hungarians, he reasoned, would be up for it since they were under threat of execution tomorrow; so what have they got to lose?

Gerald was speaking, 'Well, it's odd. It keeps changing.'

Busbeater hadn't been listening. What was Gerald on about? Changing? What was changing? Busbeater guessed … 'Well Loosehorn always likes to take a change of clothes in case of an impromptu formal dinner. It happened before for the Coronation of George VI; Loosehorn very nearly turned up in lime green crepe. That would never have done.'

Gerald was stunned for a moment. What did his uncle think he'd just asked him?

'Er, no Uncle, I am talking about the book.'

'Ahh, yes, the book … er, what about it?'

'It keeps changing.'

'Changing? Like Loosehorn?'

'What? er, no. Look …' Gerald thought the best way was to show him. He opened the book randomly at page sixty seven. Before their very eyes it turned in to page 1 and words began to appear on the page describing the history of Windsor Castle and how John's father, Henry II had rebuilt much of it in stone, including the Round Tower and the Royal Apartments.

Busbeater looked puzzled, 'What the flying buttresses is that all about?'

Gerald pondered for a moment. Then rummaged about in his knapsack to retrieve his father's diary. He had a hunch.

Gerald loosened the strap of his father's diary and opened the book up. On the inside next to 'This Book Belongs to Arnold Jones aged twelve and a half' was a neatly written note. It didn't look like a twelve year old's writing. It said:

'*Arnold. With this diary I present you with The Big Book Of Facts For The Boy Adventurer. Take this with you at all times as I did. It will always advise you wisely and prevent you from changing what you must not change. Seek Cornelius' guidance at all times but remember the book will describe what happens. If you try to alter the way things were, you will be stranded. Happy trails. Father.*'

'Leaving aside for a moment that it seems we have a dynasty of time traveling loons in the family' snorted Busbeater 'what the devil's own cutlery does all this mean Gerald?'

Gerald thought for a moment. 'We mustn't change History. Remember the fifth machine? The one we are all looking for? That one *can* change history? The one The Baron wants to rule the world with.'

'We know all that Gerald old son; what has the book got to do with it?'

'It must mean that the other machines aren't allowed to change anything; or at least the travellers aren't. The book is a guide; a time traveller's guide to history. We use it to make sure we never change events.'

'And if we do' said Busbeater, getting it at last 'we'll be stranded. Here. In this awful place with a mad gaoler and sharing our fate with a bunch of Hungarian archers. Lummy Gerald. This is a tight spot. And you old son might be something of a blinkin' genius.'

This made Gerald almost burst with pride. And then instantaneously deflated as he immediately wondered if perhaps his greatest moment made much difference as he could see no way out of the cell, let alone getting a chance to not change history.

'So Sheepshanks,' declared Loosehorn in his cell, 'Lets start "Operation Getting Out Of A Jam" shall we?'

Sheepshanks was less confident, 'The walls must be ten feet thick sir. I don't think this is the same as The Patriots prison camp which was largely made up of reeds, some barbed wire and an Alsatian called Geoff.'

'We can't just sit here Sheepshanks. Where's your vim? Your get up and go? Has it got up and gone? C'mon man, let's think of a plan. We need a plan; a plan to Save The Day.'

They both sat silently. They knew an escape plan was hopeless. Sheepshanks was right, Loosehorn knew that. Geoff had been the biggest obstacle to overcome as he clung on to Loosehorn's hem for the entire escape in Ishmaelia eventually only letting go when he spotted a female Alsatian some fourteen miles from the prison camp. Loosehorn was convinced the dog had planned it; his own escape with the use of Loosehorn's dress.

This predicament was much, much more … troublesome.

'Good evening everyone; have I any volunteers to help me play my hurdy-gurdy?' The gaoler had returned and he was determined to give them a show.

There was a knock on the Royal Apartment's door. Inside the king was annoyed, 'What is it? What on earth could anyone possibly want?'

The door opened slowly and gingerly a guard poked his head around, 'Er. Captain Hieronymus Bott says he has urgent and pertinent news for you sire.'

'What, now!?' The king bellowed.

'He is most insistent sire. He says he has news of the northern barons.'

King John stiffened. He stood from his table where he had been ploughing his way through an afternoon snack of boar with extra pig on the side, threw down a chicken bone and picked up his goblet. He drained it and wiped his mouth with the back of his hand.

Mostly to himself he said 'The barons? The confounded scheming treacherous northern barons eh? It's not enough I have to listen to their endless whining I have to have news of them too. What could this news be? That they've given up and will pay me what I want so I can reclaim my Empire? No, of course not. That outrageous crook Fitzwalter scents some kind of victory. How I wish I'd killed him when I had the chance.' He slammed his goblet on the table. 'He was planning to kill me after all. It would have been fair ...'

At the door the guard stood nervously. King John was a short man with dark hair and complexion betraying his mother's Aquitaine blood. His eyes were ablaze and he flung their gaze at the guard, 'Send Butt in.'

'Bott sire.'

'What?'

'Bott.'

'Bott? What are you talking about man?' bellowed the king 'Do you want to be sent to quell the rebellion in your breeches with only a dead chicken as a weapon?'

'No sire,' the guard was shaking, 'sorry sire, his name is Bott. Captain Hieronymus Bott.'

'Send Bott in you clod,' bellowed John.

Somewhat nervously Captain Hieronymus Bott stepped in to the king's apartment. The king was now sitting again in a huge chair with his feet on the table chewing a lump of meat having poured himself another goblet of wine.

'You have news of the northerners I believe Butt.'

'Bott sire.'

'Bott, butt, botty, potty … Who cares man? What news do you have?'

Bott began, 'Today sire my men and I arrested an odd collection of ne'er-do-wells claiming to be a troupe of actors. Naturally in this current Emergency I took them to be spies.'

'Spies you say?' John leant forward. For whom? The appalling Dauphin Louis? Or Fitzwalter?

'Well' said Bott, feeling rather important as he seemed to be having an actual conversation with the king rather than just being shouted at and ordered about which is what usually happened, 'at first I thought they were dirty perfidious French spies. But then one of the mentioned a German Baron …'

King John butted in 'A German Baron? Odds crackers, Fitzwalter's time in exile was clearly spent recruiting more villains to his cause. Did you get a name?'

'I didn't sire,' Bott gulped. He knew he should have but things had spun so quickly out of control what with the dung, the mad crone and the blasted wardrobe that it slipped his mind. He had to think fast as he saw John's face glowering, 'I er, I er thought you might have preferred to interrogate them yourself. One of them is a mere boy and the rest are ancient. No match for your wiles sire.'

John, like all men of power was a vain man and easily persuaded of his own virtues, few as they were, so this pleased him.

'Thank you Butty, that is extremely astute of you. Why don't you bring them up and I will, ahhh, talk to them.'

'All of them sire?'

'How many?

'Six.'

'Six? These spies hunt in battalions I see. Did each of them speak of the German Baron?'

'No only two. The boy and his uncle'

'Ahh, good. In that case we will interrogate them in front of their friends to concentrate their minds. Get them all here immediately. And good work Batt. There might be a promotion in this for you.'

Bott left the Royal Apartment in a dream like state. He never imagined it would go so smoothly and so well. He walked like some preening peacock toward the gaol. This was even better than the time he was made Captain Of The Year by his men. Which had been soured only by the fact that he was the only captain there; and he didn't win it unanimously.

Bott gathered three or four soldiers standing idly by and set off for the cells.

As he approached them he froze as the non-concentrating soldiers all clattered in to the back of him; 'Get off' retorted Bott.

The sound of blood curdling screams and scraping all suggested a new and terrible form of torture was being inflicted upon the prisoners. Bott shook himself from his frozen state and began to walk fast almost running. He needed to get there before any of his charges were killed or rendered mute by this appallingly new and heinous method of mistreatment. They mustn't die before he delivered them to the king; his promotion depended on them being alive. He rounded the corner and was confronted by a terrible sight. The gaoler was sitting at some kind of diabolical stringed device forcing one of the Hungarian archers to turn a crank handle which apparently caused so much pain even the gaoler was crying out. It was if the monster Grendel himself was abroad tearing the prisoners limb from limb.

'Stop; in the name of all that is holy, stop!' yelled Bott.

The gaoler looked up, 'Ahh, Bott. You are just in time; do you have any requests?'

Bott was confused, 'What?'

'Requests. Do you have any songs you'd like sung?'

'You were singing?'

'Of course. What did you think I was doing?'

'I, er, well I naturally assumed there was torturing going on.'

'Torturing?'

A disembodied voice with a Hungarian accent called out from one of the cells, 'It's worse than torture; it just goes on and on and on … and on …'

'Ignore him' retorted the gaoler 'Genius is rarely recognised in its own time. These …' he paused for effect 'people will never understand that they are witnessing a new dawn in the age of musical entertainment. One day thousands will gather around to hear people like me sing. Mark my words. It's going to be big.'

'It sounded to me like you were doing something unspeakable to a hog.'

'Sir, I am offended, I …'

Before the gaoler could go in to a full defensive rant, Bott cut him off with a dismissive wave of the hand, 'I am not interested in your ridiculous ideas for entertaining what are and will remain prisoners. No doubt one day you'll be saying we shouldn't execute them. Anyway, enough of this, I must take my prisoners to see the king. He has demanded an audience with them.'

In his cell Gerald gulped. Did he mean them? All of them?

The gaoler stood up and after shoving his Stunt Archer assistant back in to the cell he began rifling through his many, many keys.

'All of them?' he asked Bott.

'Yes, all of them'

The gaoler sighed.

After about twenty five minutes of the wrong keys in the wrong locks and Bott exclaiming 'Good grief man; get a system!', Marjorie, Cornelius, Busbeater, Gerald, Loosehorn and Sheepshanks stood outside their cells waiting to be taken to see King John, one of the most notorious and cruel monarchs in history right in the middle of the massive stress of having civil war rage around him. What could possibly go wrong?

'This way' commanded Bott.

'Good bye m'lady' called the gaoler after Marjorie. She turned and waved him a goodbye.

'I wouldn't get too sentimental crone,' barked Bott, 'you'll be back soon; for some torturing and probably a grizzly death. The king is in a very bad mood.'

Given that she was likely to die horribly some time later that day Marjorie felt she had little to lose; she turned to Bott and lamped him one right in the middle of his face.

'You horrid little man' she wailed.

Bott reeled backwards against the wall clutching his bleeding nose 'You wid pay dor dis' he mumbled.

Giggling slightly the soldiers pulled Marjorie back. Busbeater moved forward to protect his wife. Sheepshanks booted Bott in the shins and Loosehorn grabbed Gerald's hand making to run off. One of the soldiers released Marjorie and made for Loosehorn, only succeeding in ripping the hem off the bottom of his dress as Gerald tripped him up. Cornelius went for the door leading from the cells. It was massive and it was locked. The gaoler appeared holding his many keys aloft on a giant ring and with an apologetic expression on his face said a little sadly, 'I am sorry. I have the key to the door. It is always locked when prisoners are out of their cells. I do like you lot, but I am in the pay of the king. Just doing my job.'

Cornelius leant his back against the door as Bott reasserted himself, 'gaoler get dom madacles. Dat is dot happenind again.'

The gaoler stood there for a moment. Everyone was looking at him, 'Oh, what? You are talking to me? What do you want? Madacles?'

Bott almost screamed his reply, 'Madacles mad, madacles!'

'Shouting doesn't help comprehension you know. What are madacles?'

Bott mimed clasping around the ankles as his nose bled and with a beseeching look in his eyes said;

'Madacles.'

'Oh, manacles. You want manacles.'

'Dat's wod I said doo oaf.'

The gaoler, offended by Bott's attitude in general was nevertheless enjoying the silly man's discomfort. He had known what he meant all along, but wanted him to suffer. He may have to lock these people up but he didn't have to like this self-important yahoo.

'Alright but don't get shirty with me just because you were felled by an old lady.'

'A crone apparently' wailed Marjorie as Busbeater comforted her.

As the gaoler passed Marjorie to pick up the manacles he muttered apologetically, 'Sorry I have to do this … I am …'

'Just doing your job, we know' interrupted Busbeater.

After some more key confusion and general grumbling Marjorie, Busbeater, Gerald, Cornelius, Loosehorn and Sheepshanks were manacled together and taken off to the Royal Apartments accompanied by the drip, drip of blood on the stone floor from Bott's battered nose. As they left the gaol Bott made to grab Gerald's knapsack, 'Wod is in here and why do you keep it so close to you? I demand to see it,' Bott asked nasally.

'The book is in there,' replied Gerald, not mentioning for obvious reasons the flywheel or the diary, 'The book you read.'

'Ahh, des de book' Bott didn't want to heap any more humiliation on himself so decided to let it go. He eyed the knapsack suspiciously though; it struck him that the book wasn't the only thing in there. He would bide his time. And anyway, he could barely talk so needed to save what few words he had to pronounce clearly for the king.

CHAPTER EIGHT

Charming A Tyrant And Riling An Enemy

The guard standing outside the king's apartment was relieved that so far today nothing much had happened and that it would soon be over. It was mid-afternoon and the signs were that as his shift came to an end it was to be a quiet day.

Or very not.

At that moment Bott with his bloodied pink nose, six people in extraordinary dress - one of them a man *in* a dress - all manacled together with four soldiers escorting them came clanking around the corner.

'We are here to dee de kig at his request,' blurted Bott incomprehensibly.

'What at his request? D D Kig? Who is that? What are you talking about?' asked the confused guard.

'De Kig … we are here to dee de Kig!' bellowed Bott. The gaoler was right; shouting it didn't make it any clearer.

Gerald stepped in. Clearly and calmly he announced; 'We are here to see the king; he asked to see us.'

'Oh,' said the guard 'I see.'

He looked at Bott and his eyes narrowed, 'The child speaks clearly and importantly. You gibber like a fool.'

One of the solders, a friend of the guard, snorted 'He was clobbered by the crone. Twice.'

The guard guffawed loudly, 'Clobbered by a crone? You are barely a man!'

Bott scowled 'led us id dolt.'

The guard scowled back. 'It is not convenient. The archbishop went in not ten minutes ago on a matter of some urgency. More urgent I would wager than you and this motley crew of old people and children.' He looked at them and more apologetically added 'No offence.'

'You will have to wait,' he continued. 'Stand over there to one side out of the way.'

His only power round here was preventing people from seeing the king and he was determined to exercise it to its full extent. It often extended to being difficult with people who actually had an appointment, let alone riffraff like this lot who just turned up. He'd kept the archbishop waiting for three temple throbbingly irritating minutes just because he could.

Marjorie, Cornelius, Busbeater, Gerald, Loosehorn and Sheepshanks all inched their way to the side of the room shuffling like some kind of imprisoned caterpillar which was suddenly surprised to discover it had so many legs. Slightly chaotically they settled against the wall as a bleeding Bott joined them.

At that moment Stephen Langton, The Archbishop of Canterbury, emerged huffily from the king's chambers muttering something about the impossibility of some people in what Gerald thought might be a French accent.

The Archbishop swept by and out of the Royal Apartments. He hadn't even noticed the six manacled strangers who had lined the wall and the twelve eyes that followed him as he sped by. Bott had his nose in a hanky trying to stem the blood before he saw the king.

The guard then carried on standing doing nothing in as a deliberate way as possible for some minutes.

'Ahem' grunted Bott.

'Yes?' replied the guard.

'Cad we dee de Kig now?'

The guard looked at Bott as contemptuously as possible, huffed as big a huff as he could manage and, as if it was a massive inconvenience, went in to announce their arrival to the king.

Judging by the shouting and general hollering that went on, the meeting with the archbishop hadn't gone well. After a few minutes the guard re-emerged. His eyes were wildly open and he had the battered and blown about demeanour of someone who had been standing in a fierce wind for several hours. Which was what standing in the way of one of John's rants was like. Almost gasping for air he staggered forward and said, breathlessly, 'You can go in,' adding darkly and not just for effect, 'If you dare.'

The manacled sextet looked at one another and gulped. Gerald spoke first, 'Lead the way Captain Bott.'

Bott looked with irritation at this assertive young boy; he was definitely a very big threat indeed.

'Follow me, prisoners' he sniffed as blood continued to splash on the floor.

The guard opened the door and quickly ushered them through. He wanted the door closed and the memory of that rant to be over as quickly as possible. However for Charlie Farnsbarnes the terrifying memory of the king's rant would haunt him for the rest of his life and sadly for him, it was to be a very long life.

Bott and his dripping nose led the manacled six in to see the king. John spun round, 'What! You disturb me again?! Get out before I execute you right now on the spot!'

The king was shaking with fury as he glared at this strange and motley crew in front of him.

Bott, trembling, spoke first. Which was a mistake. 'Dire; we are here doe doo can indeddicate dese spies on the dubject of de Dermad Barod.'

The king looked at Bott open mouthed.

'What?! Are are an idiot? Some kind of boneheaded dolt?! You come in here with your weird friends and insult me? It's enough I have to hear from Langton about justice and fair play and what not without this un-merry band of halfwits and a literally bleeding oaf at their head cluttering up my rooms!' His fury was unbridled and terribly loud.

Marjorie could see a troubled soul and ventured reassuring words, 'sire, I must apologise …' but before she could say much at all the king rounded on her.

'And you crone. What do you have to offer? Some tips on looming no doubt or how to turn dried dung in to a new kind of hat. Get thee to a nunnery and be gone!'

Busbeater started to move forward to defend his wife. No-one talks to his wife like that. However, he'd forgotten he was manacled to everyone else and nearly pulled them all over. Loosehorn grabbed him and held him back whispering 'it's not worth it Busbeater old man.'

Gerald could see this was all getting horribly out of control. He had read a few more lines of The Book so swiftly played his hand.

'Sire' he said as boldly as he could manage.

'And now a boy! What do you want?! A nice biscuit perhaps, or your mother to wet nurse you?'

Gerald swallowed hard, scrunched up his eyes and summoning all the courage he could from Neil Armstrong and his dad he continued, 'sire. We have come to soothe your fevered brow. We may look like a ramshackle lot but we know that you are surrounded by treachery and dishonour and wish to praise you with entertainment; songs, japes and laughter. We are but poor actors. We have no truck with high politics.'

Everyone looked at Gerald open mouthed. All but Bott and the king were bursting with pride. Gerald silently thanked his mum over and over for letting him watch those old movies on a Saturday afternoon and Errol Flynn and Douglas Fairbanks Junior for being in them. And Mrs Carter for loving his stories so. A few lines of the book and the memory of the swashbuckling movies and he'd turned out the performance of his life. So far.

The king stood stock still, silent at last. With a hint of a smile, either sinister or benign it was hard to tell, he walked toward Gerald. He wasn't much taller than Gerald, but nevertheless his dark and brooding demeanour made his presence a looming one.

Gerald's mind fizzed amidst the sudden silence. What would the king do? What would he say? Was this the smile of a sadist as he imagined the torture of Gerald before his grizzly death? Gerald knew, because the book had told him as he read it in his cell while his uncle tried to prise the hinges off the door with his teeth, that King John had probably ordered the murder of Prince Arthur his nephew and rival for the throne and let a mother and her son die of starvation in Corfe castle. So he knew exactly what the king was capable of; he'd probably think nothing of knocking off a twelve year old he'd only just met. The smile gave him some hope but it could go either way. Gerald knew this was a crunch moment and he was partly terrified, although determined not to show it.

The king moved in closer and stopped right in front of Gerald. He felt the warmth of John's breath and smelt a faint whiff of chicken. Marjorie looked on, left eye going crazy, Busbeater and Loosehorn were rigid with frustration at their inability to Save The Day while Cornelius stood silently and grim faced. Sheepshanks had his hand in his inside pocket, ready to strike. Bott meanwhile looked on confident that this was The End For The Boy; he would cause him no more trouble.

Gerald looked King John straight in the eye. His mother's words flooded his brain.

'Whenever you meet a person for the first time Gerald, shake their hand firmly, look them straight in the eye, smile and ask "how do you do?"'

120

'How do you do sire, I am Gerald Jones' said Gerald and he thrust out his hand.

The king's eyes widened to the size of two moons and with a startled expression on his face rocked his head back.

Here it comes, thought Bott gleefully, Whammo.

He knew King John saw this kind of noble behaviour as weakness; so whatever the boy thought he was doing, he had gravely miscalculated. It turned out however that Bott was the one who had miscalculated. For instead of 'whammo' something completely unexpected and extraordinary happened. The king roared with laughter; 'Boy, I commend you' he guffawed 'you have courage about you.'

He took Gerald's hand and shook it firmly.

He turned to Bott and in a light and easy tone said, 'Unshackle these fine people Bottom, I think we might just get along.'

Bott stood there open mouthed; he was horrified, aghast, amazed and, most of all, appalled. His nose had stopped bleeding. He could speak but it was too late, 'But sire, they are spies ... they know of the barons.'

'Yes, yes I know that' said John irritably 'but I would like to talk to them, especially this plucky young fellow, about it. And if they are entertainers, then well I might like to see them in action. I can't remember the last time I had a good laugh unless you include that incident with the impudent Arthur of course.'

Gerald gulped. Presumably the same rather dead Arthur he thought.

'Come on Butt, crack on, release them' commanded John more urgently now.

Crestfallen and distraught Bott crouched at all six pairs of feet and released the manacles. As he got to Sheepshanks a long brown boot collided sharply with Bott's bottom; he tumbled to the ground, striking his nose on the cold hard stone floor causing it to bleed profusely once again. He scrambled to his feet with his helmet askew, his nose red and bleeding and his prisoners now free and in the good humour of the king. His earlier, very confident walk to the gaol to collect them with the promise of promotion suddenly seemed like a lifetime away. He was crestfallen.

Things were about to get worse.

'Thank you Botty. Now close the door would you?'

Bott did so and stood there wondering what to do next.

'With you on the outside' continued the king.

Utterly humiliated Bott opened the door and, with a glowering look over his shoulder toward Gerald he left. I will get my revenge, he thought.

Marjorie waved him goodbye and called happily, 'Cheerio Bottom.'

Bott seethed anew.

CHAPTER NINE

Winning The Battle Of Wits

'Guard!' cried the king.

The door re-opened slowly and Farnsbarnes walked in still trembling and even more afraid after he saw the mess Bott had been in when he left. Adding to his trepidation Farnsbarnes was surprised to see the Mad Six unshackled. Perplexed he awaited his instructions,

'Get me some more mead please and fetch some cushions so I can scatter them across the floor for my guests to sit on' said John.

Farnsbarnes stood motionless for a moment. "Scatter cushions about the floor"? "My new 'guests'"? Who was this man masquerading as the fearsome and cruel King John? he thought, bewildered in to inaction.

'Come on man, lost the use of yer legs?' John guffawed merrily.

Farnsbarnes nearly fainted. The king had just laughed merrily; no-one, absolutely no-one would believe this. He'd keep it to himself. His friends would think him drunk or infirm in the head. He closed the door behind him. He would concentrate on his odd mission and set off to find some mead. And, madly, cushions. Where would he get cushions? Farnsbarnes' quiet day had turned quite peculiar.

The king now alone with everyone turned to Gerald and asked jauntily, 'So Gerald Jones, who are you comrades? Your fellow travellers? Your troupe?'

Gerald introduced them. First he turned to his auntie and holding out an outstretched arm announced; 'This is my Aunt Marjorie.'

'Nice to meet you sire; we've heard such a lot about you' smiled Marjorie winningly. She gave a little curtsy.

'Don't believe everything you hear' chortled the king, impressed with the general fawning that was going on.

Gerald continued, 'This is my Uncle, Gerald Busbeater.'

'Honour to meet you sire' said Busbeater, offering his hand which the king took and shook heartily.

Turning to Loosehorn Gerald began, 'And this is my … er.'

The Major General interrupted with more surprising news, 'Godfather; Pelham Algernon Loosehorn. A pleasure to meet you' he thrust a hand at the king.

'Good to me you er … sir?' stumbled John as he shook his hand eyeing Loosehorn's dress.

Still taking on board that Loosehorn was his Godfather, Gerald moved on and introduced Sheepshanks who bowed, although not too far.

'Ahh, Sheepshanks. A fine sturdy name … What is your role here?'

'He's our aide de camp' said Loosehorn, 'Ow' he said as Marjorie booted him.

John stiffened slightly 'Aid de camp you say? Are you military?'

Marjorie sensed danger. With so much treachery around it would not do to be seen to part of anything potentially powerful and threatening; best be as neutral as possible.

'Only in bearing sire. We are merely players' she offered digging Loosehorn in the ribs for good measure who muffled his agony in to his moustache. Swiftly Gerald moved on, 'And this is our loyal friend Cornelius Golightly.'

The king shook Cornelius' hand firmly with a slightly quizzical look in his eye.

'Oh oh' thought Gerald.

'Have we met before Golightly?' asked the king inspecting Cornelius' face very closely.

'No sire' replied Cornelius firmly but not in Gerald's view especially convincingly.

'You sure? You seem awfully familiar.'

'No sire. To have met a king just once for one as humble as I would be extremely fortunate. Twice would be an honour too far.'

'Hmm, OK, but you do look very familiar' replied John.

Busbeater glared at Cornelius. If he'd met him, why didn't he say? Who was Cornelius Golightly?

At that point Farnsbarnes and a bunch of servants appeared with flagons of ale and loads of cushions.

'Scatter them hither and thither would you?' ordered the king.

'Yes sire' replied a non-plussed Farnsbarnes still unable to recognise this person as his king; the one who shouts and stomps and makes life pretty unpleasant for everyone around him.

King John poured himself a tankard of ale and began to slurp it without offering any to anyone else. As Farnsbarnes left the room he noticed this and thought that at least some things hadn't changed.

With everyone settled on cushions and sitting in a rather large circle, the king, on the biggest and most regal of all the cushions, asked, 'Now then, do tell, what is your troupe called?'

Everyone looked at one another. That was something they'd never thought to determine. In a brilliant moment Marjorie stepped in; 'We travel under the name of "Busbeater's Magnificent Adventures in Time"' she declared triumphantly.

Busbeater sat beaming at his extraordinary wife. What a splendid name that was.

'In time for what?' quizzed the king

'Erm,' Marjorie was knocked slightly for a moment, 'Well, just in time to entertain you at this time of great peril sire.' Marjorie almost gasped with relief having made that up on the spot. Would the king notice? Marjorie held her breath.

'That is most excellent, most excellent. Just in time indeed,' replied the satisfied and impressed king.

Marjorie breathed out a little too noisily.

'Pardon?' said the king.

'Nothing sire, nothing at all.'

'Thought I heard a sort of hooting noise there.'

'No, no hooting here' said Marjorie eager for the conversation to move on.

There was an awkward pause. Busbeater opened his mouth to say something; he wasn't sure what exactly but anything was better than this silence. Before he could, the king with good humour still intact despite the whole hooting thing clapped and rubbed his hands together.

'I might have to discuss with you how I deal with the barons. They are tricky, treacherous, whiny and cowardly souls. They demand more of me than I am prepared to give. But I shall outfox them yet. And you with your acting ways and clever use of words may prove useful beyond mere entertainment. And you young Gerald …'

Gerald jumped slightly; what was this now?

'You share the name of that chronicler in Wales who I can't really, er, control. So you Gerald of, hmm let me think of a title for you.'

There was a moment of silence as the king pondered something or other. Then, 'I have it; let us call you Gerald of Windsor - you can be my chronicler, writing down how great I am in general terms and how mean the barons have been. People will one day understand how unlucky I have been.'

At the word 'unlucky' the king's countenance briefly darkened as if silently cursing fickle fate. Then he brightened and went on, 'I will of course have editorial oversight. I want my side of the story told; it is after all the winners who write history Gerald and I aim to win. And you can write it all down for me.'

Gerald gulped. Crikey, this wasn't in any kind of plan he'd thought of so far. Everything was getting very complicated. The king meanwhile was in full flow, 'There was something else that odious Bottom character said. What was it? Ah yes I know. He said you knew something of a German Baron? Tell me all you know. For if he is in league with that treacherous Lord of Dunmow Fitzwalter and his villainous compatriot Lord of Alnwick Eustace de Vesci then I must find him and have him, er, removed from the equation.' His voice trailed off as his face glowered and darkened. 'They were once loyal to me; then they turn against me. I can trust no-one.'

King John's moods moved from light to pitch black in moments. The mention of the barons and these two in particular left him glowering. As leaders of the rebellion against his rule in 1212, which included a plan to assassinate him, John had particular reasons to despise Fitzwalter and de Vesci. They had fled the country before John could exact his revenge. But now after they had received a pardon from the pope, they were back making trouble; they had plotted to murder him and now he was having to negotiate with them. That griped King John's wagger no end. And now it seemed there was an unexpected and unknown foe to deal with. It was important he find out just who this new villain was.

It was Cornelius' opportunity to step in and he took it, boldly and brilliantly.

'Sire' he began 'The Baron in question is Baron Friedrich

Hohenzollern von Achtung and he is a disreputable fellow indeed.' This, reasoned Cornelius, might be an opportunity to recruit an unlikely ally in their celestial dual with The Baron. Should he turn up he'd have a ready made and unhinged new enemy to fight; King John. Not allowing facts to get much in the way of a good plan, Cornelius ploughed on pushing as many of the king's buttons as he could think of. He continued, gravely. 'He kidnapped and probably murdered Gerald's parents, which is why the boy rides with us. He made Gerald an orphan as a babe-in-arms; there were no loving arms for this infant to take comfort in.'

'Crikey' thought Gerald 'this is pretty convincing. I am almost feeling sorry for me here.'

Cornelius was warming to his theme. He went on, 'Gerald was eventually taken in to an Abbey where he spent a sparse and lonely childhood, never knowing where his parents were or why they had apparently abandoned him. One day The Baron appeared and pretending to be his' Cornelius gave a deliberate and over-the-top shudder ...' uncle took him across lands far and wide fighting wars in remote and cold corners of the earth teaching only the cruel ways of battle and never once showing him any affection or comradely spirit. How the poor young boy missed his mother.'

This was visibly affecting John, just as Cornelius had hoped. He too had been left in an Abbey before he was three years old and never saw his mother, the beautiful, beguiling, strong willed Eleanor of Aquitaine. And then his father, King Henry II, came and carted him off around Northern France and across England fighting never ending battles and resisting the designs of the King of France on the English throne. He squeezed Gerald's hand.

Gerald, completely startled nevertheless stayed still. He reflected on his position; travelling in a wardrobe of all things and being pursued by an arch villain who was probably right now chasing him across space and time, he had landed in the wrong time and place whereupon he'd been immediately arrested and thrown in to prison. And now he was sitting on a scatter cushion in thirteenth century Windsor Castle on the day before Magna Carta was due to be agreed and his hand was being held, nay squeezed, by one of the most murderous, unscrupulous, treacherous, scheming monarchs in English history - which is saying something - and who was being moved to tears by a story being spun by Charlie the Fireman. Gerald's brain whizzed and whirred. This was supposed to be a really boring summer holiday with smelly old folk; instead he found himself knee deep in the Adventure of a Lifetime. Not even Mrs Carter, his patient English teacher, would believe this one.

John turned to Gerald with a knowing and understanding look and squeezed his hand again.

Cornelius went on, 'The Baron spun cruel stories about how Gerald's brother …'

'I have a brother now?' thought Gerald

' … was always his Mother's favourite …'

'Stop, stop …' sniffed the king 'I can hear no more. You have convinced me of this treacherous fellow's nefarious character. Where is he now? I shall send a squad to smoke him out and deal with him.'

'Alas and alack, we don't know now,' admitted Cornelius. The only bit of the tale that was true. 'We found Gerald abandoned by the side of the road on our tour of Northern England and we adopted him. We haven't heard from or of The Baron since.'

The king, somewhat carried away, then filled in the end for Cornelius, 'And you came here knowing the barons were gathering hoping that maybe he was amongst them whereupon you would exact your revenge.'

'I er, yes, precisely' concluded Cornelius.

Everyone looked at Cornelius and everyone, even Loosehorn gave him a discrete smile of approval. That was without doubt, sheer genius.

Somehow through a mixture of charm, courage and improvisation this unlikely gang of time travellers had turned a frothing King John in to a mellower monarch who in a rare and probably unique moment of empathy could see that an injustice was being done to others. It was fitting pondered Gerald that the king had been brought round by a string of highly creative half truths; a king who dealt largely in deception and lies had been defeated by honourable folk with powerful imaginations. He looked at his comrades and his heart swelled once again with pride.

At that moment the door swung open. Gerald half expected to see Bott staggering in with some new confounded reason why they should all be executed but instead he saw a small boy and a lady in her late twenties walk in to the room. John stood up and greeted then both, not especially warmly.

'Ahh, Isabella, Henry, meet … er' he turned to the gang and looked a little bewildered. He'd forgotten their name, understandably. Marjorie saw once more, but for a last and fleeting moment the lost, troubled little boy in him.

'We are a traveling troupe known as "Busbeater's Magnificent Adventures In Time"' declared Marjorie.

Queen Isabella, for it was she, looked at them all with a hint of disgust. Her son, Henry, who in Gerald's reckoning was about seven or eight years old stood slightly alone. He saw Gerald and a small, timid smile begin to flicker across his face. This was quickly extinguished as his mother pulled him away. Gerald felt dizzy suddenly as he remembered how much he missed his mum. She would never have treated him so poorly; indeed if Linda Busbeater had been Queen of England she'd have had Henry joining in with this crazy troupe.

Meanwhile at the other end of the room John and Isabella exchanged brief and not especially friendly words and she quickly left with Henry traipsing out behind her. At the door Isabella turned to John and exclaimed, 'You treat me like the hired help; all I ask is for some dignity and independence. You all but imprison me. Think of your children at least.'

John, temper now rising smashed his fist on the table. After so many years trying to regain the empire of his brother and father John's mood was fragile; more so than usual with rebellion close at hand.

'You hear my lady, all that I have lost for you.' He bellowed.

Isabella stood quite still and paused for a moment before replying, 'And I, my lord, have lost the best knight in the world for you.'

'What? Hugh de Lusignan? I saved you from him.'

'You stole me away from him.'

Henry the boy who would be king in little over a year looked over his shoulder at Gerald as his parents argued so bitterly; his gaze lingered for a moment. Gerald wanted to say 'come over and play' but Henry was gone as his mother, furious with indignation, swept him out of the room. Gerald felt so sad for the boy; but crikey he also missed his mum. He could feel tears welling in his eyes and used his sleeve to try and wipe them away discretely. Marjorie spotted this and moved over to give Gerald a big Marjorie hug.

Busbeater saw danger; the king had returned to his very bad mood of earlier so Busbeater tried to get things moving along. He took a gamble, 'sire, if it would please you we would like to maybe put on a play for you. This evening perhaps before your big day tomorrow.' Busbeater knew that they needed to reunite Gerald and The Wardrobe since Gerald had the flywheel which meant they could escape to 1216 where they were supposed to be. 'And maybe we could use our … er, our …'

Cornelius was immediately in tune with what Busbeater was trying to do. He helped out, 'Our props cabinet …'

Busbeater flashed a grateful look at Cornelius, 'Yes our props cabinet so we could give you our best and most fulsome performance.'

Busbeater's idea hinged on them retrieving The Wardrobe and escaping before any performances were necessary. He had never been an actor and didn't intend to start now. In keeping with so much that had happened since Cornelius first arrived breathless and sopping in Busbeater's hallway several hundred years and yet just a few hours ago, the plan didn't quite work out.

'What!?' retorted the king. His meeting with his wife had riled him. His marriage to Isabella of Angoulême in 1200 had been useful at the time to reduce the power of his enemies but she was already betrothed to Henry de Luisgnan and by stealing her from Hugh, John had made serious enemies of the powerful de Lusignan family. Initially things went well, but despite bearing five children, of which Henry was the eldest, the marriage had not stood the test of time. John was bored with his wife who it seemed to him was always complaining about something or other; usually money. What was a wife's dowery for John reasoned unreasonably, if not for her husband to spend it on glory and conquest? He had the barons to deal with tomorrow, when he would travel to that boggy meadow in Runnymede to shut down negotiations over their ridiculous charter, and what he didn't want or need right now was Isabella wandering in asking for money to buy clothes for the boy for goodness sake. He imagined she had seamstresses - he didn't take much notice of domestic arrangements - surely one of them could knock up a few tunics. And now there was this bunch of crazy lunatics offering to put on some kind of performance for him. John turned toward his guests; his face thunderous. Hmm, wait a moment though; for him eh? John was a selfish and manipulative man and he rather liked the idea of a performance all about him. His mood lightened.

'Alright then' he said to Busbeater sharply, 'off you go.'

'But if it pleases you sire we'd like to have our props to make sure the pl–' Busbeater began.

The king was now irritated and interrupted him. His mood had resorted to suspicion and self-pity,

'It doesn't please me actually. You can't have your precious props cabinet. In fact I am wondering why you want it so much. So get on with it now, as you are already in pretty strange garb and entertain me. Or else it's a trip to Corfe Castle for the lot of you where you can rest amongst the bones of all those others who have got on my nerves!'

Gerald gulped.

'Er, yes, of course sire,' stumbled Busbeater, 'We just need to have a meeting about which would be the best performance.'

With a dismissive wave of the hand King John headed back to his table of food and kicking cushions out of the way agreed moodily, 'OK, get on with it.'

Everyone gathered in a huddle. Busbeater was apologetic, 'Sorry; that didn't quite go to plan.'

'That's okay Busbeater old boy; you've bought us a bit of time' replied his great friend Loosehorn encouragingly.

'But what the great crested grebe are we going to perform?' fretted Busbeater almost spitting the last word out. The last time he performed in front of an audience he had been eight years old and it hadn't gone well; Aunt Sissy didn't talk to him for years afterwards. She never said why exactly but it might have had something to do with the eight year old's singing and the bill for the replacement windows. Her beloved King Charles Spaniel was never the same again either ...

Gerald had an idea, 'A couple of weeks ago my mum and I watched a film with The Marx Brothers.'

'They are very funny,' cooed Marjorie, 'especially the one who doesn't talk but carries an enormous horn around with him.'

Everyone looked at Marjorie a little startled. Ignoring her Gerald tried to continue, but he was interrupted by the king shouting between mouthfuls; 'What's going on in there? Are you plotting against me?! I will have you executed if you are.' The king was becoming increasingly irritated and impatient.

'One moment my lord' called Busbeater 'we will be with you shortly.'

Gerald continued with his idea, 'At the beginning of their film 'Horse Feathers' Groucho Marx sings "Whatever It Is I'm Against It".'

Marjorie, Loosehorn, Busbeater and even Sheepshanks remembered collectively and simultaneously that they had also seen it on their new fangled TV and could probably, with a bit of prompting, remember enough of it to get by. The chances were a hundred percent that the king would have no idea what this was since it wouldn't be made for at least another 700 years. Gerald was confident he could remember the words as he had spent the rest of the day after watching the film singing it loudly at every opportunity; so he would lead the song. Marjorie, Loosehorn and Busbeater would, improbably, be his backing singers, while Cornelius who had no idea about any of it, would be at the back doing miscellaneous but hopefully vaguely rhythmic movements. Sheepshanks suggested he adopt the same pose as when it was on the TV.

'Pose?' asked Gerald puzzled.

'I was on one foot, with my right arm extended whilst leaning out of the window,' said Sheepshanks as if that explained everything.

'Er, why?' asked Gerald none the wiser.

'The reception is terrible at Busbeater Mansions dear,' interrupted Marjorie, 'so Sheepshanks had to hold the aerial in just the right spot. Which turned out to be on the first floor landing approximately four feet out of the window. It worked a treat.'

'But then I fell ...' added Sheepshanks forlornly.

'At exactly the wrong moment Sheepshanks,' grumbled Loosehorn, 'we still don't know if the butler actually did it this time.'

Gerald looked at Loosehorn, Sheepshanks and Marjorie utterly perplexed. What were they talking about? He decided to move things along ... 'Right, well, anyway, er, yes OK Sheepshanks, you do the pose.'

The king was getting really impatient now, 'Look, I don't have to wait for you lot you know. I have to meet with Langton again in a few minutes and I was rather expecting you to cheer me up because it's going to be another miserable meeting. But at the moment you are testing my patience and good humour to breaking point with your mumbling and inaction.' John scowled at them over a huge leg of chicken he was devouring.

Seeing the chicken leg vanishing down the king's gullet suddenly reminded Gerald how hungry he was. They'd not eaten in ages. And who knew when their next meal would be? His tummy grumbled.

'We are ready my lord' cried Busbeater as Sheepshanks began balancing on one foot. Screwing up his courage Gerald ignored his growling tummy and prepared for the performance of his life; very probably *for* his life. For inspiration he remembered singing with his mum and sharing the hairbrush microphone. He hoped his backing singers Busbeater, Loosehorn and Marjorie would remember some of the words at least, that Sheepshanks wouldn't fall over and that Cornelius would make a convincing dancer. He wasn't entirely confident any of this would work; but there was no backing out now and there was no Plan B. So with one last deep breath, Gerald went for it;

'Hit It!' he called and burst in to song;

'I don't know what they have to say

It makes no difference anyway

Whatever it is, I'm against it!'

Gerald began singing heartily and lustily. Behind him Marjorie and Loosehorn clapped rhythmically-ish and repeating the line 'I'm against it' each time after Gerald. Busbeater whose rhythm came less easily was slightly behind his wife and best friend but he hung in there. Behind all of them Cornelius was 'dancing' by moving backwards and forwards like a slightly crazed chicken while Sheepshanks remained as still as a statue. King John sat aghast at this extraordinary sight; a boy singing, aged adults croaking along at the same time, occasionally, a human statue and at the back some kind of out of control bird impression going on. At first it only irritated him, but there was something he found intriguing about the words.

It went on. Gerald was growing in confidence and started moving around as the front man of the group remembering some of the dance steps his mother taught him; 'side, together, side, together, back, side, together, back.' Marjorie and Loosehorn began to develop a rather impressive hand jive as Busbeater tried gamely to keep up. Cornelius' hypnotised chicken impersonation was growing ever more frantic whilst Sheepshanks remained perfectly, impressively still.

The song went on;

'Your proposition may be good

But let's have one thing understood

Whatever it is, I'm against it!'

Marjorie even managed a 'doo wap' as she began to really get in to it; Busbeater threw her a sideways glance just as Loosehorn lifted the hem of his dress and began kicking his legs up one at a time.

'Stop! Stop!' The king stood up holding out his hand, 'Stop, I have heard enough!'

Everyone stopped, including Sheepshanks who hadn't really started, but excluding Cornelius who had lost himself in the moment rather. He continued his crazed hen performance as everyone else stood stock still. Out of the corner of his mouth Loosehorn hissed, 'Stop it man, stop it!'

But Cornelius was gone, solid gone and with his eyes closed and lips pursed he continued the fowl performance. Then suddenly he crumpled to the ground as Sheepshanks stuck out his leg.

'Oh, I er … yes, I erm, I … have we stopped?' the nutty chicken spluttered meekly.

Everyone was staring at Cornelius as he struggled to his feet while dusting himself down.

'I take it we have' he concluded as matter-of-factly as he could manage.

Momentarily nonplussed the king hesitated. But then he gathered himself together. Everyone stood motionless; which way would this go? Would the last thing Cornelius Golightly ever do turn out to be dancing like a bonkers chicken? Would Marjorie's last words as a free woman be 'doo wap'? Was Loosehorn likely only to be remembered for a rather gingerly executed Can-Can? Gerald stood as tall as he could. He wanted his mum to be proud of him if this was to be, gulp, The End. Busbeater squeezed the boy's shoulder in an 'I'm here' kind of way. Sheepshanks, unseen, slipped his hand in to his pocket in readiness to go down fighting.

But apparently even the most capricious zephyr has more design than this king. The trick had worked and the choice of song was inspirational.

'Bravo! That is exactly what I have been thinking!' exclaimed the king.

What was? Wondered Gerald. What had he been thinking?

'I'm against it. By golly I am. No-one else understands.' John went on.

Gerald was none the wiser. Against what? Understand what? He had no idea.

The king sat down, suddenly a bit dejected. For a while he said nothing and just stared at the floor covered in cushions. Everyone else remained standing, not sure what to do.

Eventually, the king looked up and said, full of woe; 'Do you know what my sainted brother's nickname was?'

Everyone mumbled that they didn't. Gerald did know, but guessed, correctly, that this was one of those rhetorical questions his headmaster used when asking if he thought it was safe to run in the corridor. He waited.

John continued, 'Lionheart. Lion. Heart. Bold, noble, heroic. Want to know what mine was?'

Again everyone was, wisely, mute.

'Lackland. Lack. Land. I lacked land. I don't have the heart of a Lion; no, I lacked land because I was the youngest. That was hardly my fault was it? My brothers had it all; Henry, Geoffrey, Richard, the patronising big head. He gave me bits and bobs when it suited him but took it away again. Just because I rebelled against him while he was captured returning from the stupid Holy Land on one of his stupid crusades.' He put on a high pitched voice '"Ooo get me, I'm King Richard The Lionheart and I am a hero". All my life I have fought to regain my land; the land of my forefathers. The land that is mine by right as a Plantagenet King!' He smashed his fist in to the palm of his hand, 'I have fought valiantly while my so called noble citizens have wallowed around complaining about taxes and having to fight all the time and about not wanting to travel. Oh boo hoo. They weren't born being called Lackland and they don't have a brother idolised by everyone whose nickname was Lionheart!'

John was almost screaming by this point. His sense of injustice, largely unwarranted, burned brightly within him. He had been betrayed by everyone and now he was being forced to agree some charter the barons had written tomorrow which will mean he can't just do what he wants when he wants. By jove, he was against it. He continued his fraternal rant, 'Do you know where my brother is buried?'

Again, diplomatic silence reigned.

'Yes, exactly' continued John. It seemed to Gerald that King John was having a conversation with voices in his own head. The gang were merely spectators. But best to remain still and, well, wait. The king continued, 'All over the place that's where. His body lies in Fontevraud Abbey, where I was left as just a little boy; his heart was left to Rouen Cathedral and his entrails to that abbey in Charroux. Yes that's right, all over the place but not in England. Oh no, not good enough for our saintly Dickie boy. Had to be our mother's beloved Aquitaine. He was always her favourite anyway. I loved her too, but I don't think she cared about me.'

Marjorie began to move forward to comfort him. Busbeater took her arm and stopped her. Already it was clear this king had a quick and unpredictable temper and he knew there was at least a fifty per cent chance that Marjorie's natural instincts to comfort and protect would be rebuffed sending them all to the gallows. They weren't out of the woods yet and whilst in the presence of this unreliable man they never would be. They had to stick together, to reunite Gerald and The Wardrobe and get the blue trousers out of there. He looked at his beloved wife and she caught his gaze. She smiled, understood and stopped. The king meanwhile was in full flow. He hadn't been able to talk to anyone about anything very much for ages. His generally scheming and treacherous ways meant he had few friends. Indeed his one really close confidant John de Gray, Bishop of Norwich he had failed to have made Archbishop of Canterbury some ten years earlier after an almighty ruckus with Pope Innocent III and was instead lumbered with the overeducated Stephen Langton whom John didn't really trust.

'Nope it was our Richard this and our Richard that. The 'Great One' according to Mother. Why does no-one go on about the fact that he betrayed father by teaming up against him with Phillip of France? It wasn't just me; he was as bad. I should have been king - he was too busy swanning off fighting crusades. At least I was here all the time and could actually you know, speak the language. Dickie never even bothered to do that. Yet it's me who is painted as the villain.'

John closed his eyes and grimaced. Clenching both fists together he raised his face to the ceiling and almost bellowed; 'I have been traduced! I am surrounded by treachery!'

A little embarrassed and not entirely sure which way to look, Gerald, Marjorie, Busbeater, Loosehorn, Sheepshanks and Cornelius looked at their feet and shuffled about it a bit.

The king looked at them, his eyes still blazing but maybe his face less tense. Cripes thought Gerald, did he mean them?

Things then took another slightly surprising turn.

'But at least I have you, friends. With your song you show you understand. Which I have to say is unusual since I generally can't abide troubadours. And those awful living statues you get everywhere now. They think they are sooooo clever just standing there for hours. How hard can standing still be?'

Quite hard, thought Sheepshanks, slightly offended.

'But you have shown you understand. I am most definitely against it and everyone who crosses my path who want things from me but show no loyalty. You ...' he pointed to Gerald and Busbeater 'shall accompany me tomorrow to Runnymede when we shut down all this blather going on and agree this blasted charter. I want allies at my side, although I warn you, we will have to listen to Langton droning on about rights of the individual and justice for 'free men' the whole way there and back. It'll be very dull. But your arrival is like having birthday and Christmas all at once. Which I have to tell you I am pretty used to. My parents wcrc an odd pair but very scheming; you'd think then that they'd have been able to work out a time to have me that wasn't Christmas Eve.'

Without thinking Gerald suddenly said, 'One present for Christmas and birthday?'

The king roared with laughter 'My boy, you show more wisdom than any of my advisors and you show up their extensive education by putting your finger right on the issue immediately! Do you suffer the same fate?'

'No but Porker Clements does and he's always saying how annoying it is.'

'I agree with you and your friend Porker.' The king scanned the troupe. 'Do you have him with you, we could discuss our star crossed fortune.'

Busbeater looked around him. Which one of them did the king imagine might be Porker Clements? No-one was introduced as Porker Clements. In fact none of them, apart from Gerald, knew who Porker Clements was.

'No sire, I have not seen him in some time' replied Gerald.

'Ahh, poor soul. Well I expect he felt as I did when on my sixth birthday I was given a crummy shield for my birthday and for Christmas. On the same day! But which wasn't even Christmas Day or my birthday. It was December Twenty Eighth! What sort of stupid day is that?!'

'Explains a lot' mumbled Busbeater.

'What?' demanded the king.

'Er, poor you sire. That is cruel indeed,' amended Busbeater.

With a sideways glance at Busbeater the king moved on, 'Yes, quite so, quite so.'

There was a rapping on the door.

'What? What?!' yelled the king.

Farnsbarnes put his nervous face around the door, 'sire, the archbishop is here for your meeting.'

'Well, tell him to wait. I have business to conclude with these fine people. I will call when I am ready.'

Outside the door Bott had waited. Surely, he thought the king would soon tire of that un-merry band and throw them back in gaol. Then he could reclaim his promotion. But when he heard the king describe them as 'these fine people' he growled with blood boiling indignation growing very purple in the process.

The archbishop, waiting his turn to see the king looked at Bott, 'Are you alright?'

'Yes' Bott hissed.

'You're purple' observed the archbishop plainly.

Inside his apartment the king continued addressing the gang genially, 'You shall be housed for the evening in one of my chambers. It's only one room I am afraid so you'll all have to share.'

The king was most apologetic. But separately and simultaneously everyone thanked their lucky stars and sighed a massive, silent, sigh of relief. Altogether, right now – perfect. The escape was on.

'I will get that Botty fellow to bring you your props cabinet' continued

John.

This was getting better than they could have hoped for.

'So you can rehearse for tomorrow night's festivities after we've got tomorrow's nonsense out of the way. Agreed?'

So long as they could escape before they had to perform again, thought Busbeater, then this was a fine, fine plan.

'Thank you sire' replied Cornelius, finally able to speak after the shame of being caught doing chicken dancing, 'That is most agreeable.' *Absolutely blinking marvellous you lunatic* was what he was thinking.

'And you must be weary and hungry. I shall have food and wine sent to your room.'

'Again, sire we are most humbled and grateful' replied Cornelius, while thinking *we haven't eaten for hours having been held prisoner in your castle and we are shattered you tyrant.*

Marjorie, Busbeater and Loosehorn who by this time of the evening would normally have been on the eighth course of something or other and looking forward to dinner suddenly realised how hungry they were. Gerald whose tummy was in danger of grumbling loudly and out of control was delighted. His mother always taught him never to say he was starving because of the poor children around the world who sometimes really *were* starving. And then he remembered Matilda and her son William de Briouze whom the king had actually and cruelly starved to death at Corfe. Gerald felt bad and vowed never to say he was starving again. But it didn't alter the fact that right now he was mind bendingly peckish.

The exertions of the day had taken their toll on everyone and this sudden generosity from this capricious man's dramatic turns and moods pierced their courage and for the first time they wanted to just stop. Gerald missed his mum terribly and began fretting about whether he'd ever see his dad again to tell him how proud of him he was. Marjorie and Busbeater missed their cosy Busbeater Mansions where the only things to worry about were when dinner was and whether today was the day Loosehorn would bag a rabbit. Loosehorn for his part was pretty tired of wearing this same dress and although wearier than a long distance runner wearing a camel costume he was looking forward to seeing his wardrobe again.

'It may be a blinkin' time machine, but it's also still full of my outfits' he mumbled.

Cornelius too was flagging. In all his adventures this one had so far been the least easy to control. At every turn there was someone derailing the plan. He looked at his traveling companions; he knew if it hadn't been for them, this might easily have been The End. He knew he owed them a great deal and if they ever got out of here he would show them, especially Gerald, just how much. He had a plan.

Sheepshanks whose role was to Help Out could see his friends and employers were beginning to struggle and stepped to the fore, much to King John's surprise, 'sire, If I may.'

'He speaks! The king exclaimed 'You aren't Porker Clements are you?'

'Sheepshanks sire. Valet and Sorter-outer' replied the tall, very slim valet.

'Ah of course, the aide de camp. Continue my man.'

'My companions are weary and hungry and are terribly grateful for your hospitality. If we may be permitted to go at once to rest, we would appreciate that very much indeed. And I would like, if I may, to lead the way if you would be so kind as to issue directions to our chamber.'

The king looked at Sheepshanks and was slightly taken aback by the assertive but friendly nature of the request. Directions? Well, OK.

'Out of the door and turn left. It's just there' said the king.

'Thank you sire,' replied Sheepshanks.

CHAPTER TEN

Operation Getting On With It

Sheepshanks opened the door to the king's chamber and lead the weary troupe out to their own room. The king followed and gave his orders, 'Botty, retrieve these fine people's props cabinet and deliver it to their chamber.'

Bott, still purple and beyond indignation was frustrated with rage as he took his order. How on earth had this happened? He glared at Marjorie. He would get his revenge.

Farnsbarnes was issued with very precise instructions for the contents of their dinner and sent away to oversee its preparation and delivery.

Archbishop Stephen Langton who even during his time as President of the Student Union at the Sorbonne during rag week had never seen such an odd collection of crazies looked on bemused. He also saw someone he had never seen before. Sure it looked like the body of the scheming, moody, treacherous dictator King John but who was this smiling, genial and generous man occupying it?

As he turned to Langton the king's glowering, diabolical demeanour returned, almost to the archbishop's relief. Better the devil you know, he thought. And this king if not the devil himself was certainly a member of a family many called The Devil's Brood.

'You'd better come in' John said, levity in his voice now utterly absent.

'Yes sire, thank you' replied the archbishop.

The door slammed behind them and within moments the king's full volume rage had returned. Bott and Farnsbarnes looked at the gang in some astonishment. How had they, this motley crew of so-called actors managed to win over their king? No-one, not even the Hungarian Stunt Archers had managed to bewitch and beguile him in the same way. And they had been by common agreement, pretty impressive. And much better than the Donkey Jugglers of Lower Saxony. That had ended especially nastily with Bott's orders for their execution to please the king.

Marjorie looked at Bott, 'You heard the king, Bott.' She spat his name out. 'Go and get our props cabinet. We'll be in our room.' Marjorie smiled a victory smile and with her last ounce of energy followed Sheepshanks and the others in to their chamber.

Bott fumed and then turned to retrieve The Wardrobe. He thought about smashing it; and then thought about what the king would do to him if he did - smash him most probably. He decided against smashing it. No; his revenge would be more stealthy. He just needed to bide his time. They are bound to slip up and he'll be ready to pounce.

Busbeater closed the door behind them, 'Glory be' he sighed 'that was a series of frankly very close run things. We out of the woods Cornelius?'

Cornelius looked the most cheered he had for a while, 'I think so. Once Bott delivers The Wardrobe we can then turn the flywheel, get to 1216, check out The Wardrobe with the Crown Jewels in it, disable it if it's the fifth machine and get home.'

'That's all?' quizzed Busbeater knowing that was unlikely to be all.

'Home?' cooed Marjorie 'Home would be lovely.'

Gerald, almost unconscious on his feet, stumbled to the bed in the middle of the room, clambered aboard and fell, instantly and deeply asleep.

'Poor Lamb' Marjorie said as she watched the sleeping boy. She moved over to him and gently removed the knapsack Gerald had kept clutched to his side ever since they first entered The Wardrobe in Loosehorn's room. Placing the bag on the floor she stroked his forehead, 'It's safe now; we're here' she cooed.

At the far end of the large room two chairs were arranged as well as a couple of stools. Busbeater guided Marjorie to the comfiest looking chair and offered Loosehorn the other one.

'No old boy, you have it' said a chivalrous Loosehorn.

Cornelius, Loosehorn and Sheepshanks settled on the stools. Cornelius leant forward, 'Right then, is everyone au fait with the plan?'

'Au fait!?' exclaimed Loosehorn. 'If you mean familiar then I think we pretty much are. We wait for The Wardrobe, start it up with Gerald's flywheel and get the heck out of here.'

'Correct.'

'The thing is,' piped up Marjorie, 'I am pretty hungry and I think the lad ought to have something before we set off again.'

'Good thinking,' replied Cornelius, 'OK, we'll wait for the guard to bring us dinner, eat it and then we'll fire up The Wardrobe. Agreed?'

'Tip top' said Busbeater.

Just then a loud rapping noise on the door heralded either their wardrobe or some grub. It was The Wardrobe.

'Where do you want it?' asked Bott severely.

'Hmm', said Marjorie presented with a sudden an unexpected opportunity to furnish a room, how about over there, by the bed?

'All the way over there?' said Bott 'have you any idea how heavy this is?' he added fumingly.

'Well, you haven't' wheezed one of the four soldiers who had been carrying it.

'Just take it over there,' scolded Bott, 'And stop your complaining. This has to be better than listening to the gaoler's hurdy-gurdy playing which if I may remind you, I rescued you from.'

The soldiers grumbled and staggered in to the room. In a purely supervisory manner, Bott followed the men as they manhandled The Wardrobe over to the side of the bed on which Gerald, completely spark out, lay. As the men manoeuvred it to Marjorie's exacting instructions Bott noticed the knapsack on the ground. He glanced around; no-one was looking. He couldn't believe his luck. Now he could find out what was in this bag and find out exactly who this lot are, betray them to the king and get his promotion; his ticket out of here. Stealthily he picked it up.

'Er, that'll do. We aren't decorators.' He swiftly announced. 'Come on men we have affairs of state to attend to.' With the knapsack shoved inside his tunic, Bott wanted to get out now as quickly as possible.

Marjorie looked at The Wardrobe. It was rather a handsome piece of furniture. She wondered why she'd never noticed it before.

'Go on, clear off' barked Loosehorn as he closed the door behind Bott.

'Last we'll see of him' predicted Marjorie happily.

Outside the room Bott withdrew the knapsack from his tunic and hurried to a quiet place to inspect the contents.

As he left Farnsbarnes and an unfeasibly large banquet being carried by several men was going the other way.

'Grub's up!' cried Farnsbarnes cheerily as he flung the door open before leaving them to their feast which had taken a full seven minutes to deliver.

The huge pile of food consisted of roast hog, roast lamb, roast chicken ('this one's for you' guffawed Loosehorn to Cornelius who had the good grace to chortle at his own expense), hocks of ham, potatoes, vegetables; a couple of flagons of wine ('strewth' exclaimed Busbeater after one sip 'this will strip the wallpaper off the spare room Marjorie') and some suspicious looking cheese. Everyone was so hungry they just dived in. Marjorie woke Gerald and he too, eyes like appropriately sized dinner plates almost flung himself at the food.

After a decent amount of time and without a scrap off food left, they all sat back.

'By jingo' declared Busbeater 'these mediaeval types certainly know how to eat.'

Gerald let rip a rather loud burp. Everyone, relaxed for the first time since before The Baron began blasting away at the front door, guffawed merrily. They had survived the court of the unpredictable King John, his prison, that idiot Bott and now were finally able to escape.

'Right' announced Cornelius 'shall we get the very heck out of here?'

'Splendid' replied Loosehorn.

'Where's your knapsack Gerald?' asked Cornelius 'Let's get that flywheel in place.'

'It's er ... it's' Gerald didn't know where it was. He began to panic.

'Don't worry dear' cooed Marjorie 'I took it from you and put it safe as you slept. Make you more comfortable.'

'Where did you put it Marjorie?' asked Cornelius, only slightly anxiously.

Walking over to the bed Marjorie declared 'Why right here ... by ... the ... oh ... oh my.'

'Oh? What do you mean "Oh" Marjorie?' asked Cornelius, now more agitated.

'Don't adopt that tone with my wife please Cornelius' retorted Busbeater, a bit anxious himself but trying not to show it.

Marjorie stood by the side of the bed looking perplexed 'I put it right here. Right here!' she pointed to the stone slab where the knapsack most definitely wasn't.

'Next to The Wardrobe?' queried Cornelius.

'Yes!' Marjorie fell to the floor on her hands and knees and peered under the bed. Nothing. She scanned the room frantically; the knapsack had gone!

'That bounder Bott!' exclaimed Loosehorn and Busbeater at once. 'He's stolen the knapsack!'

'I am so sorry everyone' said Marjorie her voice brittle with anxiety.

Busbeater and Gerald both ran to her side, 'It's not your fault dear. You didn't lose it. Bott stole it' said Busbeater as soothingly as he could.

'Auntie Marjorie, please don't cry. It isn't your fault,' assured Gerald. He was anxious about his auntie - she looked so distressed.

Briefly Cornelius was furious with Marjorie and her ridiculous desire to have The Wardrobe in just the right place, but he had grown so fond of them all that now was not the time to be angry; instead as ever now was the time to stick together. And draw up a new plan.

'Marjorie. It's okay. We are dealing with envious and silly little men. It is my fault. I should have been more vigilant,' said Cornelius calmly and warmly.

Busbeater looked across at Cornelius and smiled a thank you.

'Good man,' mumbled Loosehorn, 'decent form.'

Marjorie walked across and gave Cornelius a very big Marjorie hug.

Slightly muffled and during the prolonged hug Cornelius declared, 'I … mumble … think … humph … we need a new phnnnnnble plan.'

They all regathered around the chairs and stools.

'OK' announced Cornelius, 'lets rustle up our next move.'

'We ought to get some rest before we do anything' said Busbeater. ' We run the risk of Bott getting to the king but from what we have seen today John is too busy to be bothering with Bott and his lame ideas of spies and what not.'

'I agree' replied Cornelius, 'It is risky but probably riskier to try anything when we are all wiped out.'

Loosehorn chipped in, 'Tomorrow Gerald and Busbeater have to go with the king to Runnymede.'

'Oh cripes, I'd forgotten that,' said Gerald.

'It'll be OK old boy, I'll be at your side. We are Busbeaters remember? We shall prevail.'

Loosehorn continued 'So whilst you are doing that Marjorie, Cornelius, Sheepshanks and I will hunt Bott down and retrieve the flywheel. And give him a good pasting whilst we are at it.'

Cornelius thought this all sounded good. 'Maybe we could recruit the gaoler in our quest. It struck me that he didn't feel any particular warmth for Bott.'

'Good thinking' replied Loosehorn who was, reluctantly finally warming to Cornelius. 'And if we could spring the archers too we could form a posse.'

'Are we going to have to, gulp, perform again tomorrow night?' asked Busbeater.

'Maybe; but if we have the flywheel and The Wardrobe we won't have to for long …' replied Cornelius.

'What do you think Gerald, Marjorie?' Cornelius turned to them both only to see them sitting on the chairs and leaning against each other completely asleep.

'I think that shows this is the right plan' remarked Sheepshanks as he gently lifted Gerald taking him to the bed. Gerald was totally spark out but the movement of him being carried jogged a dream into being.

Gerald sat at his massive desk and with a huge quill in his hand was busily scribbling on a large piece of paper;

Dear Mum,

Summer at Busbeater Mansions isn't boring at all! It's mad, crazy and generally round the bend, but boring? Crikey trousers, not even slightly. It's full of adventure. We have all travelled in Loosehorn's wardrobe to 1215 to the day before Magna Carta was agreed. We have had to pretend we are actors to explain our sudden arrival and I suppose our clothes, especially Loosehorn's, and I sang for the king which seemed to please him, although he's a right moody man. Tomorrow is a scary day. Uncle and I have to go with King John to witness Magna Carta being agreed. One false move and it might be curtains for us. While we are doing that Marjorie, Sheepshanks, Loosehorn and Cornelius (remember Charlie the Fireman Mum? It's him! I know, mad isn't it?) have to get The Wardrobe working again so we can escape. I have also discovered that boring, useless farty deadbeat old dad played tennis with Henry VIII! Why didn't he ever say? No-one's ever going to believe any of this Mum, but it's real.

I think of you all the time and wish you were with me Mum. I miss you so very much, but I am trying to make you proud of me by being as brave and as bold as I can. I will be your knight in shining armour and will save the damson in distress.

Sending you big Marjorie hugs (they're whoppers),

Lots of love, your Bold Knight,

Gerald

xx

As he signed off the desk began to float away. The quill slipped out of

Gerald's hand and drifted off toward the stars. His letter folded itself in to the shape of Apollo 11's Saturn V rocket and flew away moon-bound as Gerald floated gently to sleep. Far, far away his mother's voice echoed serenely around the cosmos; 'fly me to the moon, let us play amongst the stars ...'

The dream was over but Gerald smiled as he thought how proud his mum would be of him.

Sheepshanks lowered Gerald gently on to the bed and pulled a blanket over the sleeping, smiling adventurer.

Busbeater woke his wife and guided her to the bed too. The men arranged themselves variously on the floor and chairs and within just a few moments, they were all completely asleep. Tomorrow was 15th June 1215; one of the most significant days in English history and the gang had to survive it and escape. It was going to be busy.

Bott sat in his small room and by torchlight eagerly looked in to Gerald's knapsack. He found The Big Book Of Facts For The Boy Adventurer and some kind of journal both of which he ignored. They had been the source of his near humiliation earlier, which he had only avoided because of his own genius cunning. There was also some paper with a drawing of an eagle across the top and garish sketches beneath and a garment with, strangely, a man's face daubed across it. All very peculiar but not, he thought, worth the secrecy and possessiveness the boy had shown. Bott was starting to feel a bit disappointed. Maybe there was nothing in here after all. That or it was something in one of those confounded books which, while he was alone, he could confess he couldn't read. He pressed on and rummaged a bit further. At the bottom of the knapsack was something hard and heavy; something metallic. Hmm, this was more promising. He retrieved the flywheel and turned it over several times in his hand. 'This must be the thing they were so keen to hang on to and keep from me' thought Bott, 'What could it be for? Is it some kind of key?' He was inching his way toward the answer but then got stuck quite quickly. 'A key from the Gaol? No, they would have been able to escape when the door had locked and the crone clouted me on the nose.' He thought long and hard in to the night before falling asleep clutching the flywheel. His last thought as he dozed off was about The Wardrobe. 'Had it got something to do with that? They seemed just as anxious to get it back as the boy was to keep the knapsack safe …'

Bott fell asleep snoring loudly enough to wake the very dead indeed.

The hammering on the door was loud and prolonged. Busbeater was the first to wake, 'What? What the crikey trousers is going on? Stop yer hollerin' and yer bangin' will you?'

The king's men called out; 'His Royal Highness demands the boy and his uncle be at his side for the ride to Runnymede.'

'Hold your horses, give me a moment,' stumbled Busbeater as he sleepily made for the door, at which the king's men were still beating. Everyone was stirring now as the door creaked open. It wasn't all bad. Behind the rather impressive soldiers stood Farnsbarnes with several trays of breakfast. The soldiers were brief, 'Eat and be at the king's chambers swiftly,' they barked

'Right, I er, yes of course' said Busbeater, gathering himself at last and cheered by the sight of piles of food.

Farnsbarnes stood to one side as the food was brought in. Cornelius went up to him, 'sir, what is your name?' he asked.

'Farnsbarnes; Charlie Farnsbarnes. What's it to you?'

'I am Golightly; Cornelius Golightly and I was wondering if you might be able to help us.'

'Help you? I hardly think you need my help. You have the king eating out of the palm of your hand. You can demand anything you want and probably get it.' Farnsbarnes replied a little sourly.

'True, but the king is busy on matters of great importance today and we have an altogether different matter to, er, arrange; one we're not that keen on him finding out about if you get my meaning' said Cornelius borrowing heavily from Marjorie's cooing tone; it always seemed to work.

Farnsbarnes didn't get Cornelius' meaning at all but was intrigued

'What matter?' asked Farnsbarnes.

'Do you know where Captain Bott is?'

'Bott? Pah, he's an oaf.'

Cornelius smiled; this was exactly what he wanted to hear.

'I agree; a total oaf indeed. Do you know where he might be?'

'His quarters are just outside the castle round the back. But at this hour likely as not he'll be in the gaol. He does a tour there every morning. It's smelly, dark and horrid like him; I think he likes it down there.'

'Thank you Charlie' replied Cornelius.

This was useful. He was forming a plan. It was clear they should head for the gaol where they might recruit the gaoler and even the archers in detaining Bott as the thieving swine did his rounds.

Everyone was scoffing the huge breakfast which bore a remarkable similarity to dinner the night before. Well, almost everyone. Loosehorn emerged from The Wardrobe, 'What do you think of *this*?' he asked triumphantly.

'Oh I say; bright yellow and very full. How Mediaeval,' giggled a slightly startled Marjorie, 'all the rage in the 1200s I believe' she added smilingly.

Loosehorn proudly smoothed the front of his voluminous and very yellow dress, relieved to be wearing something different at last and marched over to the breakfast banquet, his large military boots thumping loudly on the stone floor.

Busbeater turned to Cornelius, 'Gerald and I better go. We mustn't keep the king waiting too long. He'll only go off on one again. Best to keep him on side a bit.'

'Yes, you are right,' replied Cornelius 'Good luck sir. And good luck Gerald. Without the book at your side it will be difficult, but generally stay neutral.' Cornelius glanced a special glance at Busbeater 'don't interfere or else …' before he could finish Gerald piped up;

' …or else we'll change history and get stuck, I know,' said Gerald.

'He worked it out!' exclaimed Marjorie proudly.

'I knew he would' replied Cornelius and gave Gerald a manly hug.

The next few hours would be crucial and everyone was a bit sombre. Anything could happen and it was not inconceivable that if things went wrong this might be the last time they'd be together.

Loosehorn saluted his friend 'Good luck old man. Bring the boy home. Remember Ishmaelia.'

Busbeater saluted in return and smiled warmly.

Marjorie squeezed Gerald and kissed him on the forehead. She hugged Busbeater and wiped a small tear away. 'Come back dear' she said quietly.

Cornelius shook Busbeater's hand firmly. Smiling he said 'remember, don't interfere.'

Sheepshanks stood to attention and said, 'Good luck master Gerald; good luck Lieutenant Colonel sir.'

'Thanks old man.' Busbeater replied. He turned to Gerald, 'time to go young fellow me lad.'

They turned and left the room together. Gerald felt very nervous without his knapsack. The book and flywheel were crucial of course, but he wasn't carrying his dad with him. That felt worse.

Cornelius closed the door behind Busbeater and Gerald. He paused for a moment wondering if that was the last time he'd ever see them.

'Operation Getting On With It?' asked Loosehorn who sensed and shared Cornelius' anxiety.

'Operation Getting On With It begins,' replied Cornelius determinedly.

'Let's get that snivelling little oik and sort him out,' joined in Marjorie. She was very worried too; her beloved husband and nephew were out there alone. Who knows what might happen? She knew how brave and bold Busbeater and Gerald were, but King John was an unreliable and moody cove; he might do anything. Marjorie shook her head. One thing she had learned in life; only manage what you can control. So she turned her mind to that grisly oaf Bott and how she would control him. He would never be forgiven for his rude and oafish behaviour and for calling her a crone. And now he had prevented them from escaping and maybe saving the world. He would pay for all of that. She was very ready for 'Operation Getting On With it.'

Sheepshanks opened the door and the quartet began their mission.

They walked past Farnsbarnes who helpfully pointed them in the direction of the gaol. They had remembered the route after yesterday's ramshackle journey, but thanked him anyway on the grounds that they needed as many allies as they could.

'Thank you Farnsbarnes' said Cornelius. 'If you see Bott, can you get word to us? Or, more importantly if he wants to see the king before he sets off, would you stop him?'

Farnsbarnes was perfectly happy to drop Bott in it, 'Of course. He is such a clod. I remember one time he …'

'That's marvellous, thank you Charlie' replied Cornelius worrying that Farnsbarnes was about to ramble on a bit; they didn't really have the time. The archers might be executed today and if they were to be allies they had better not be dead ones. Of course they may already be too late, but if they hurried …

Cornelius, Loosehorn, Marjorie and Sheepshanks sped off in the direction of the gaol. After just a few minutes they were at the big door that had impeded their first attempted escape. It was shut but not locked. Gingerly Cornelius pushed it open. It creaked with an almighty groan which echoed down through the narrowing corridor toward the cells. They all froze for a moment. Would this bring the clattering of guards and their immediate arrest?

No.

But deep from within the cells drifted terrible screaming and scraping noises. They all looked at each other. They were too late; the archers it seems were being executed at that very moment. Maybe if they ran they might yet save them.

They arrived at the cells where they found the gaoler inflicting his terrible punishment on the archers.

'Ahh, friends, you have returned,' remarked the gaoler cheerily upon seeing them.

'Er, gaoler, we have … er, what are you doing?' asked Cornelius.

'Do you not recognise my hurdy-gurdy?' replied the gaoler a bit hurt they'd forgotten already.

'Well, er yes but …' Cornelius' anxiety was for the safety of their potential allies the archers who seemed to be screaming in agony.

'Imre and Hector here are helping me out' the gaoler continued.

'Imre and Hector?' quizzed Loosehorn. 'Who the heck are they?'

'Archers; we are the archers,' they replied helpfully and in unison.

'OK, but the screaming and wailing …?' continued Cornelius.

'Singing …' replied Hector.

'Singing?' asked Cornelius highly confused

'Yes, we were singing,' said Hector, 'Rather offended you didn't realise actually' he added quietly.

The gaoler's 'singing' as the gang knew only too well was renowned for being unutterably dreadful; enough to curdle yoghurt, turn young men old and make summer winter. But the archers if anything were worse. Like running your nails down a blackboard in Antarctica dressed only in your pants; chilling.

Cornelius dragged the conversation back to the matter in hand, 'Is Bott here?' he asked the gaoler with as much urgency as he could manage.

'Bott?'

'Yes.'

'Here?'

'Yes.'

'No.'

'No?'

'No.'

'Oh.'

'Do you know where he is?' chipped in Marjorie.

'Ahh, madam, nice to see you again,' the gaoler seemed to sparkle on seeing Marjorie.

'Nice to see you too' replied Marjorie remembering what an unexpectedly nice and polite man the gaoler was.

'Do you think you'll have a chance to get out today? Maybe wash your hair perhaps? It looks like a lovely sunny day …' cooed Marjorie.

'Well, I am …'

Before the gaoler could continue he was interrupted by an impatient

Loosehorn; 'Marjorie, please. Let us save the pleasantries until afterwards. We are on 'Operation Getting On With It' if you remember; it's beginning to sound a bit more like Operation Having A Chat And A Cup Of Tea at the moment.'

The gaoler perked up at the notion of tea; beetroot tea, 'My, my where are my manners? Would you like some beetroot tea? I can't believe I didn't ask you,' he blurted apologetically

Cornelius by now close to exploding with frustration blurted, 'No! For pity's sake.'

'Are you sure? It's no trouble,' continued the gaoler warming to his tea theme.

'We have brought our own special brand of Hungarian Tomato Tea with us if you'd like to try it' offered Imre, picking up and running with the whole tea idea.

Cornelius knew he needed them all as allies but his patience was now wafer thin. However, before he could say anything which might ruin Operation Getting On With It and landing them all in gaol again in the process, Sheepshanks piped up; 'Gaoler, Imre, Hector. It is very kind of you but we do not require tea.' And especially not beetroot tea, Sheepshanks thought. He went on 'What we do need however and as a matter of some urgency is to locate Captain Bott. He stole something very precious from us last night and we are eager to …'

'Give him a good hiding' interrupted Marjorie.

' …find him and …' continued Sheepshanks before he was interrupted again.

'Give him a good hiding' repeated Marjorie.

'Give him a good hiding' conceded Sheepshanks.

'Well, why didn't you say so?' said the gaoler exasperating the gang to the point where Marjorie's eye began to go wonky.

Loosehorn made a sort of grumpy blowing noise through his moustache and through gritted teeth remarked, 'We were trying to.'

The gaoler, unperturbed by Loosehorn's muttering explained, 'Bott was here earlier. Come to think of it he was in quite a cheery mood. Whistling and smiling. I thought at first he was ill. He came for his morning inspection before going to see the king.'

'The king?!' retorted Cornelius. This was potentially very serious. If Bott got to the king before he set off for Runnymede the game might well be up.

'Yes, the king' replied the gaoler, slightly annoyed his story had been interrupted.

'Did he get to see the king?' asked Cornelius urgently.

'If you'll let me tell the story sir, I will inform you of all salient facts and a few figures, if you're lucky, as I go along.'

Just get on with it steamed Loosehorn, but luckily only in his head. The gaoler continued 'Where was I?'

'Bott went to see the king' said Marjorie, anxiously.

'Ahh yes. He went to see the king and was gone for ages. I calculated about fifteen minutes but I have no way of telling the time so it was a useless and unprovable guess. Anyway, yes he went to see the king for some miscellaneous amount of time.'

As politely as he could but flexing his hands in to two fists, Cornelius gasped, 'Please, it is terribly important you tell us the story of Bott's whereabouts quickly.'

'Well, if you keep interrupting me, how can I tell you quickly?' said the gaoler, offended.

'Sorry sir. Do continue' seethed Cornelius.

'Where was I this time? Ahh yes. Well he was gone about fifteen minutes, although as I said I don't really know if it was fifteen minutes as I have no way of telling the time. And was never taught how to either. That's the problem with having a mother executed when still only a boy.' The gaoler was rambling madly now.

Even the archers were getting slightly annoyed. 'Gaoler. For all our sakes, get to the point,' barked Hector.

Throwing a glowering glance at Hector the gaoler continued, 'Anyway, after fifteen minutes or so Bott returned and he wasn't whistling any more let me tell you. He looked pretty furious. I said, "Bott, you oaf, you look …purple." Apparently he had rushed to see the king only to be told by Farnsbarnes that the king had left for Runnymede with the archbishop, the boy and his uncle.'

Cornelius, Loosehorn, Marjorie and Sheepshanks all breathed a huge sigh of relief. Bott had got there too late and Farnsbarnes had done his work. The gang must have only just missed him when they set off for the gaol.

The gaoler unaware of the collective phew going on around him, continued, 'I don't know what he was on about but he kept muttering something about waiting until they all get back and then he'd show those tricky spies. It was then that he ordered the archers be executed at noon.'

Imre and Hector looked startled. This was news to them and unwelcome news at that. Their execution had been agreed apparently and it was today.

'What time is it now?'

'Oh who knows?' said the gaoler carelessly. 'Noon-ish?'

'Where is Bott now?' asked Cornelius.

'Erm probably in his quarters.'

'Probably?'

'Well, I am not his keeper you know. I am *your* keeper though, he said to the now fretting archers; I ought to get things ready for your execution.'

'Er, hold on' said Marjorie.

Marjorie had some sympathy with the gaoler. He had been polite and courteous and even though it was a low bar, something of a gentleman. She played her hand, 'Do you really want to take orders from Bott?'

'Well, no. I'd rather eat poo. But I have to; his orders come direct from the king.'

Marjorie tried to banish the picture of the gaoler eating poo. 'Ahh but we are in the king's favour now. Why as you know two of our comrades ride with him on official duty to Runnymede where the king is to meet the barons. And I think Bott only ordered their execution because he was cross he'd missed the king, who couldn't have ordered it because he had left. And anyway, if it comes to it we can tell him that we overruled Bott and ordered you to let Imre and Hector here off so they can help us perform our play this evening to celebrate the momentous events.'

The gaoler didn't need much persuading; Loosehorn thought he might have been a little in love with Marjorie. He looked across at his lifelong friend; she knew it.

'A fine notion. Do you think I may sing and play my hurdy-gurdy at the event too?' said the gaoler, all thoughts of executions banished by the dulcet tones of his new beau.

Yikes thought Marjorie; she imagined the king would probably prefer to have his fingers pulled out one by one than listen to that racket. But still, this was no time to disillusion the man. They needed him on their side.

'Of course. We will see to it as soon as they all return' she said encouragingly. This was enough for the gaoler.

'Right then lads; you're free.' The gaoler told the archers brightly 'And please call me Jeff.' He looked at Marjorie with huge cow eyes.

Marjorie gulped. 'That's splendid news' she said.

Loosehorn looked at Marjorie with admiration. She had at a stroke recruited three more friends to the fight. He smiled to himself. What a fine woman she was; his friend. Slightly bonkers obviously, like all of them, but maybe in a small way, something of a genius.

Cornelius continued a little sharply, 'So you think he's probably in his quarters?' The gaoler was still a bit lost in Marjorie's eyes.

'Hello? Jeff? Hello?' Cornelius waved his hands about in front of Jeff.

'Eh? Oh er, sorry I er, what?' Jeff was bamboozled by Marjorie.

Cornelius repeated the question.

The gaoler recovered.

'Yes he probably is' he said a little sarcastically. 'But he'll definitely be along here in a few minutes to see the archers hanged. So if you want him, I suggest you wait here.' His tone was worryingly bitter.

It was time for Marjorie to soothe the gaoler's brow again, 'Now, now Jeff; I am sorry for my friend's tone. You see he, like me, is anxious that we find Bott as soon as possible to reclaim our stolen property; it has sentimental value to us, but me especially, you see. If you could help us, we … *I'd* be eternally grateful.'

'Of course madam. I will help. *You.*' Jeff The Gaoler was hopelessly smitten. 'I suggest you wait in the cell here. He won't be expecting you there.'

Loosehorn peered in and said darkly 'I'm not surprised he won't; the cell was small enough when me and Sheepshanks were in there yesterday. Now there'd be four of us squashed in …'

There was more surprising news on its way.

'Imre, Hector, you hide in there too' continued Jeff the Gaoler.

'Heck, SIX of us' fretted Loosehorn.

'It'll be a little cramped but it'll only be for a few minutes. I will push the door to; I won't lock it.' Everyone sighed, relieved. The gaoler wasn't finished though. He was starting to enjoy this subterfuge and wanted to impress Marjorie with his tactical prowess and strategic cunning. He stroked his chin and with a faraway look in his eyes mused; 'Or maybe I should lock it - for authenticity's sake.'

'Er, I think your original plan was best Jeff' cooed Marjorie in her best cooing voice.

'What, executing the archers?' Jeff was confused.

'Er no, I meant about locking the door' Marjorie continued quickly.

'Ah, yes, the door. I will do as you suggest and lock it.' It was all unravelling with alarming speed.

'No! Ahem ... ahh, ha ha - I meant do not lock the door' exclaimed Marjorie trying hard not to sound as if she was exclaiming. If he locked the door and Bott discovered them he would have them trapped; he could easily have them all executed there and then. They needed to be able to spring out and capture him. Springing out through a locked door is tremendously and famously difficult.

'So, not locking the door is the preferred plan?' asked the gaoler with quizzical eyes.

'Yes!' came the collective reply.

'Good. Glad that's settled then.' The gaoler raised his eyebrows as if to say 'really, some people.'

CHAPTER ELEVEN

A Resilient Foe And A Hesitant Journey

Cornelius, Marjorie, Loosehorn, Sheepshanks, Imre and Hector all squeezed into the cell with the door slightly ajar and waited for Bott.

'So,' whispered Cornelius, 'the plan is this; as soon as we hear Bott we rush out and grab him and ... Drat.'

'What?' asked Loosehorn.

'We'll need some rope to tie him up with.'

'The gaoler will have some maybe?' offered Marjorie.

'Fear not,' it was Sheepshanks. Despite having his arms pinned to his side by the over eager attentions of Imre, from inside his left jacket pocket Sheepshanks somehow managed to produce an unfeasibly long stretch of rope. 'Will this do?' There was even a flourish as he presented it.

Cornelius looked astonished. 'How?' he asked falteringly.

Loosehorn who'd seen it all before interjected with a deadpan tone, 'That's nothing; whole tribes lived in there for months on end in Ishmaelia.'

'Well, er, OK. That's umm, great. Thank you Sheepshanks' said Cornelius. And then as an afterthought; 'Don't suppose you've got any tribes in there at the moment have you?'

Sheepshanks looked at Cornelius as if he were mad.

'No, I … no. Of course you don't,' Cornelius continued sheepishly.

Cornelius knew he'd never quite fathom his new companions. There was something so completely round the bend yet utterly indefatigable about them.

So all six of them began to wait in the tiny cell. It was like a game of sardines with very fat sardines shoved in to a super titchy cupboard. The wait would be uncomfortable. And as it turned out, longer than Jeff had suggested. A lot longer.

'We need to buy that Gaoler a clock' muttered Loosehorn after about half an hour.

Two hours later and still no Bott. Things were getting tetchy in the cell.

'Will you get your boot out of my ribcage Sheepshanks?' complained Loosehorn.

'It's not my boot sir.'

'No your boot is in my groin' moaned Imre elbowing the offending booted foot.

'Ow!' exclaimed Marjorie 'that is not Sheepshanks' boot.'

'Well, whose boot is in my ribcage then?' asked Loosehorn grabbing it fiercely 'Ouch. Crikey, it's mine. How did that happen?'

'You've always been very lithe Pelham' said Marjorie.

Loosehorn was amazed at his own flexibility 'It's remarkable; I am at right angles to myself.'

'Shh,' cautioned Cornelius who had been putting up with Hector's bottom in his face for two hours, 'I think I can hear something.'

'That'll be the results of the gaoler's cooking. Sorry about that,' explained Hector.

Many more minutes passed until they added up to nearly three hours

167

altogether. Then suddenly everyone heard the same thing at the same time; heavy boots on the flagstone floor.

It was Bott, 'Gaoler. It's noon,' he announced primly.

Finally thought everyone in the cell.

Bott was continuing. 'Where are the archers? I need cheering up; and seeing them executed horribly for their ludicrous stunt archery will do the trick. I have many colleagues in the Elite Ambridge Archery Unit and to see them mocked by these Magyars with their leaping and whooping was offensive; even if their archery was impressive. What's more I am in a very bad mood after that Farnsbarnes idiot stopped me from seeing the king. They hadn't left for Runnymede. I checked. But oh nooooo, Mr More Than My Job's Worth exercised what little power he possesses to stop me. Well, once I get my promotion, as I surely will now, I will post him to somewhere remote and hostile. Lower Saxony perhaps where they throw donkeys about the place ... or Wales where they are continuously fighting.' He looked at the silent gaoler and added impatiently, 'Well, you oaf, where are they? Have you hidden them?'

The gaoler, smirking, said, 'They are behind you.'

And they were. As well as Marjorie, Loosehorn, Sheepshanks and Cornelius.

'Aiiiiiiiiiee' cried one or all of them, it was hard to tell. The last thing Bott remembered immediately after he thought 'what the cheesy wotsits ...?' as he turned around was being entombed in reams of bright yellow material amid a great deal of hollering, some rope and a triumphant whoop in an Eastern European accent. Then suddenly he was tied up in a cold, dark, smelly cell and the door was locked.

'What on earth was that?' he wondered aloud, completely flummoxed.

But he wasn't alone in the cell. Before him stood Loosehorn, resplendent in his yellow ball gown and black boots and Cornelius who was glowering.

Bott began defiantly, 'You can't harm me. I'm one of the king's Captains!'

Cornelius was calm but menacing; 'The door's locked, you're tied up and there are two of us, one of whom is an angry man in a ball gown. I'd co-operate if I were you.'

Bott gulped. Loosehorn had a crazed look in his eyes and his right boot was twitching.

'Give him a bit of the old Loosehorn Shuffle Pelham' called Marjorie from the other side of the door.

Cornelius continued in the same level and menacing tone glaring at Bott, 'Believe me Bott, you don't want to be on the end of that. Not with those boots' he pointed to Loosehorn's twitching feet. 'You'll rarely walk forwards again.'

'It'll be sideways forever Bott. Sideways you hear?' growled Loosehorn.

'What do you want?' asked Bott trying to remain as defiant as he could.

'The boy's knapsack. Where is it?' demanded Cornelius.

'Ahh, So I was right. It is very important to you isn't it?' Bott almost sounded triumphant.

He had planned on taking the knapsack to the king which was bound to lead to their interrogation and inevitable defeat. So Bott remained relatively unflustered; he felt in quite a good position.

Loosehorn and Cornelius began to worry slightly. He might be more difficult to crack than either of them thought. Neither of them had a clue what the Loosehorn Shuffle might be but they were beginning to think that they'd have to invent one. Then at that moment a screeching, screaming racket began on the other side of the cell door. It was as if the very devil himself had risen to the surface bringing with him all his instruments of torture which he was now greedily employing.

Bott looked horrified, 'OK! OK! I will tell you, just stop that terrible diabolical nightmare!'

Jeff stopped playing his hurdy-gurdy and Imre stopped 'singing.' It had worked and the Loosehorn Shuffle, whatever it might have been wasn't required. Loosehorn was actually slightly disappointed and vowed that the next time, if there was to be next time, he would show Bott just what a Loosehorn Shuffle was …

Bott, broken by the diabolical din told Cornelius and Loosehorn where Gerald's knapsack was. He had hidden it in his quarters round the back of the castle. On hearing this Marjorie and Sheepshanks sped off to find it.

'Ready Gerald?' Lieutenant Colonel Busbeater looked at his heroic nephew.

'You bet your boots Uncle' replied the defiant and determined twelve year old. Without his dad's book in his knapsack he knew this was a real test and if he wanted his dad and mum to be proud of him, now was the time to demonstrate just what he was made of; stern stuff.

Busbeater rapped hard on the door.

'Come!' called King John.

Busbeater walked in with Gerald right behind.

'Ahh, Busbeater, young Gerald you are just in time.' The king was just putting on his small golden crown and when he heard Gerald and his uncle come in he turned around to greet them. He was wearing a long purple robe and gold cape. He spread his arms, did a bit of a twirl and asked,

'What do you think? Regal enough to show those barons who's boss?'

Archbishop Stephen Langton who'd been waiting for the king to get ready for what felt like an epoch sighed and raised his eyebrows to the ceiling.

'Very, er kingly' stammered Busbeater.

'Yes, very noble' added Gerald emphatically.

'Splendid, thank you. I do look rather magnificent don't I?'

No-one was sure whether this required an answer. They soon found out.

'Well? Don't I?' the king went on annoyed that no-one had instantly agreed with him.

'Yes, truly magnificent sire' boomed Busbeater.

The king looked momentarily startled at Busbeater's sudden and rather dramatically sonorous tone. 'Crown too much?'

'Er, no sir, it makes you look ...' before Gerald could finish John did so.

'A bit of a berk. I agree, too much.' He took it off and flung it across the room where it clattered to a halt in the corner, 'Never liked it much anyway.'

After one final look in the mirror and a self-satisfied smile he announced, 'Come on then. Let's get this over with. Make sure you remember everything Gerald. I want everyone down the ages to know what a noble king I was and all about the dolts I had to put up with.'

The king led the way out of his chamber and down to the stables where three horses awaited. At the side of the king's horse was a large Irish Wolfhound. The tall shaggy haired blue-grey beast got up wagging its great tail excitedly when he saw his master approach. Busbeater and Gerald looked at each other with surprised expressions as the king ran toward his dog and nose to nose said some very un-kingly things; 'Awwww, woodgy woodgy woo; how's my big fellow den? Awwww woodgy woodgy woo' and then proceeded to roll about on the stable floor for a few minutes. The dog was howling and gurgling with delight.

Gerald thought back to the unpleasant way the king had talked to his wife and ignored his son. Pity, he thought, that he doesn't behave a bit more like this with his family.

The king stood up and the stable lads rushed over to brush away the straw which had accumulated all over the king's cape and robe in the wrestle with the dog.

'See you later woodgy woodgy' said the king to the dog.

The king then turned to his companions who were looking rather askance and said 'What?'

'Er, nothing sire,' spluttered the archbishop, 'But I think we should be going.'

'Yes, alright bishop. Alright,' replied the king irritably, even though all the delays so far had been his fault.

John, an accomplished horseman, leapt on to his fine, tall white steed with alacrity despite the flappiness of his robe. Next came the archbishop who climbed skilfully but more carefully on to his. The king looked at Busbeater and gestured toward the remaining horse, a tall elegant chestnut coloured beast. In the blink of an eye, with one bound and to Gerald's complete surprise Busbeater was in the saddle. He turned to Gerald and carefully lowered himself holding out his right arm, 'Grab hold old son' he instructed Gerald.

Gerald, a little bemused held his uncle's arm and was instantly swept on to the saddle behind him. Gerald, whispered in to Busbeater's ear, 'Ishmaelia?'

Busbeater replied quietly, 'Exactly young Gerald. Remember Ishmaelia!'

Gerald hung on tightly around his uncle's waist. He was glad he had a heroic uncle; a heroic family. He wondered how everyone else was getting on and hoped they had found Bott and given him a good seeing to.

The king watched Busbeater with admiration, 'sir, you are a skilled horseman. When all this is over I shall take you hunting. There's loads of forest about the land. We could do with more men of your formidable talents on the team.'

Busbeater and Gerald followed the king and archbishop out of Windsor Castle and in to the bright June morning. They were joined by a small squad of soldiers who led the way.

The sun was beating warmly on their backs as the horses and their riders walked slowly along a narrow path through the meadow. Gerald clung tightly to his uncle. Inside his tummy it was like his mum's new tumble drier. It turned over and over as if it were drying a mixed bag of washing which included his pants and his favourite big blue woolly jumper. Led by the king's standard which flew in the breeze looking rather dramatic, the convoy moved on slowly, inexorably toward Runnymede and the waiting barons. Gerald felt proud and worried all at once. So much was at stake. He mustn't change history but without his book he had nothing to warn him about what happened; he had to be on his mettle. He knew his uncle, such an honourable fellow, might not be able to keep quiet if something untoward happened and knowing this king that was distinctly likely. And what happened if Cornelius and the gang don't find the flywheel? They'd be stranded here forever. Or worse if Bott, armed with his knapsack, could somehow convince the king they were spies. Gerald shuddered slightly at the thought of being dealt with by a betrayed King John. Everything seemed so dangerous and yet so thrilling. Here he was, in the middle of history that only ever happened in dusty books. Gerald had to admit, that was quite exciting. But would he ever be able to tell his mum and dad about it? Would anyone ever know? He squeezed his uncle even more.

'Alright old son?' asked Busbeater.

'Perfectly alright thank you Uncle' replied Gerald.

'Good man. You are a true Busbeater.'

King John slowed down so that he was alongside Busbeater and Langton joined them. The three horses rode alongside each other with

Busbeater and Gerald in the middle. Nobody said anything for a time and it was starting to get awkward.

Busbeater attempted to break the silence; 'Fine day for it,' he offered vaguely wondering what sort of small talk was appropriate for the journey to meet quite cross barons with a mad mediaeval king on one side and a rather formidable archbishop on the other.

Langton replied, seriously, 'It's a fine day for justice and for free men everywhere.'

King John looked at Busbeater raising his eyebrows as if to say 'I told you so.'

'Justice?' remarked the king '*Justice!?* What sort of justice is it for the king to have to cow tow to a bunch of whining landowners like the treacherous Fitzwalter who you and I both know is only interested in power for himself. I have tried to make this country great and powerful and all I get is whining and whinging and moaning on about taxes and me stealing from them. It's quite tiresome.' The king's tone was volatile. He was pretty cross but was clearly trying to keep his temper in check which he was managing, just.

Gerald gulped. This could easily go horribly wrong.

'Sire, you have indeed tried,' Langton emphasised 'tried' very obviously, 'but it is true that you have been very, shall we say, unlucky with your wars most of which have been lost.'

Langton sighed a heavy sigh. He knew only too well that the barons were heartily fed up to the back teeth of having to pay for and fight in these foreign wars which they didn't feel was part of their duty to the king. King John was as usual massively defensive.

'If,' he said in his most hurt voice, 'You are referring to that siege at Angers ...'

'Many died that day' interrupted Langton a little bitterly.

'Yes, well that wasn't my fault,' said John, fuming.

'Of course not sire,' replied the archbishop a little sarcastically.

'No, precisely' replied John, missing the sarcasm and so mistakenly under the impression Langton was supporting him and his bad luck with incompetent oafs. He continued; 'If the Lusignans hadn't betrayed me by refusing to fight that pipsqueak Dauphin Louis I wouldn't have had to retreat so, er, hastily.'

'Many men died fighting sir as you rode away and many others drowned trying to cross the river sir in a bid to escape.'

John stopped his horse and glared at Langton

'You speak to me this way? I am your king. You must honour me. Men die in battle; that's what they are for. I had no choice but to retreat. I was outnumbered because the Lusignans betrayed me. I should never have trusted them. Holding up his finger and thumb almost together he went on, 'I was this close to securing the great ancestral seat of my forefathers. And you accuse me of cowardice?'

Langton was cross but he knew that there was a bigger picture here, 'sire, forgive me. I spoke out of turn; as a man of God I naturally feel for the poor souls who lost their lives that day in France. You are no coward but a mighty warrior.'

John made wimpy noises taking the mickey out of the archbishop, 'Oh boo hoo.' And then added more sternly 'Yes, a mighty warrior, and your king, a *Plantagenet* king, so let's not forget that shall we?'

Slowly the king moved his horse onwards and in silence the four of them continued on.

Gerald remembered what he'd read in his book before Bott stole his knapsack. The barons had been fed up with the enormous taxes the king just demanded when he felt like it, the ruthless ways of enforcing their collection and the way he denied their sons' rightful inheritance. Not to mention the way he sold women as wives and how almost everywhere was designated a forest regardless of whether it had trees or not just so John could collect fines for breaking rules that his henchmen made up.

The barons felt abused and were increasingly frustrated at having to pay for foreign wars that seemed to be designed just to satisfy John's frantic need to get back the territories his father and brother once owned; they were lost, could he not see that? Gerald could understand that might be a bit annoying. He carefully saved his pocket money, most recently spent on buying Apollo 11 stuff, and had resisted Nicholas Johnson's attempts to steal it from him, usually by cunningly hiding it in his socks. He knew Johnson just wanted to spend it on buying catapults to fire at poor old Clipstone. There and then Gerald made a decision. When, or at least if, he ever got home again he was going to declare his support for Clipstone against the tyrant Johnson and his henchmen the Butcher twins. It was time for a bill of rights at St Cuthbert's and he Gerald Jones would write it. First though, he had to witness the agreement of the original Magna Carta. And the king was still going on …

'And you know perfectly well Archbishop, if that so-called Holy Roman Emperor Otto and my half-brother Salisbury hadn't got caught out and crushed by Phillip at Bouvines last summer while I was fighting the Dauphin in the south.'

Running away thought Gerald.

'I'd have won a massive victory and we would own all of France. I would be a bally hero and certainly not riding here today to listen to a bunch of whiny nobles.'

He looked at Busbeater, 'Maybe your German baron was there with Otto; even more reason for me to duff him up if we see him today.'

'Maybe sir' said Busbeater hoping with every fibre of his being that he wouldn't be. How on earth was he supposed to stop interfering and changing history if The Baron was there? There'd inevitably be fighting. He didn't know his history to any great extent but he was pretty sure that he would have remembered reading about ferocious fisticuffs between a tall menacing German baron and an old Englishman with his twelve year old nephew by his side at Runnymede as Magna Carta was agreed.

'But you didn't win a massive victory sire and all that expense, financial as well as lives, was for nothing.' said Langton flatly.

'Yes, alright. So you've mentioned - many times,' John glowered at Langton.

John suddenly looked in no mood to continue on to Runnymede. He looked at Busbeater, 'What do you say player? What if I don't actually go? I could let the negotiations rumble on until everyone gets bored and then we'll decide what I do or do not give up?'

Langton was horrified, 'But sire, you ...'

The king waved the archbishop's concerns away and continued looking at Busbeater, 'I trust no-one Langton, not even you. I want to hear from fresh voices. Maybe they'll give me a proper insight and advise me wisely. What say you Busbeater?'

Busbeater gulped. If no Magna Carta was agreed, history would be different, the time machine would cease to work and they'd be stranded in Mediaeval England forever, provided they survived the king's general wrath, a fifty-fifty possibility at best. The king must reach Runnymede.

'Sire, you have been undone by treachery and incompetence, but you ride with friends' exclaimed Busbeater brilliantly, flashing a look at Langton whose loyalties were possibly divided. The archbishop looked at the ground. In his impatience with the king he knew he'd maybe gone too far.

Civil war could break out again at any moment especially if the king didn't turn up today. The barons were in an ugly mood and they didn't trust the king at all. Indeed they had brought a company of knights with them in case things didn't turn out as advertised. And now, at the crucial moment it was all in jeopardy; the king had stopped in a fit of pique. Langton had been massively suspicious of this Busbeater fellow and his nephew; but now it looked as if they might be saving the day.

The three horses stood stock still. The king looked intently at Busbeater; Langton looked at Busbeater. Busbeater wished they'd look at someone else. He fidgeted and was about to say something, anything when the silence was broken ...

'Your majesty' said Gerald 'this is the day you will show your heroic side by agreeing to some of the barons demands; they are bound to show their loyalty to you afterwards.'

The king beamed at Langton, 'See, the boy gets it. My chronicler in chief. He gets it. I will be the hero today.'

Langton threw a confused look at Gerald who just shrugged in return. This boy seemed to know more than his years suggested he should. Gerald continued as the king picked up his reins once more.

'Sire you are a noble king and have dealt with many difficulties well. Today will be your Greatest Day and in the future children will learn of your heroic deeds.'

The king looked at Gerald

'Children? They will consider me Great?' John brightened

'Yes sire' said Gerald chirpily. As a child himself he felt he ought to sound childishly optimistic and upbeat.

'Greater than that outlaw Robin Hood who everyone goes on about in those blasted ballads like he's some kind of saint?' asked John emerging from his sulk a bit more.

'Robin who? M'lord' said Gerald brilliantly.

'Precisely. I am not even sure he exists. It's just an excuse to poke fun at me and praise my brother. Believe me if there was an outlaw abroad I'd have captured him by now' said John, pleased everyone was being nice to him again.

'They will praise only you sire for your wisdom and statesmanship that will rival your brother' Langton had joined in now

The king looked at Langton more suspiciously. He never wanted him as his archbishop and only did so because the pope made him. The king suddenly brightened. The pope! Of course.

King John was instantly cheered, 'OK, let's go. What are you all waiting for?' he asked as if the answer wasn't 'well you of course you sulky loon.'

Langton, Busbeater and Gerald all looked at each other. It had taken a nerve-wrackingly long time and much fawning to get the king moving again. But right at the end there it proved to be just a little bit too easy even for this most unpredictable of men making Langton in particular very suspicious. However, he felt he should continue to lavish praise upon this tricky monarch if only to keep him moving toward Runnymede.

'Excellent sire. Our countrymen will be eternally grateful to you,' the archbishop added.

The king looked a bit sideways at Langton, 'Our countrymen Langton? You've barely ever lived here. You've been swanning around in France for most of your life.'

'But born in Lincolnshire sire,' said Langton defensively but accurately.

'Lincolnshire? What's in Lincolnshire?' said John contemptuously.

'Much of my family,' thought Busbeater slightly offended. But he kept quiet. For whatever reason, and it might have been his brilliant intervention or more likely Gerald's genius for flattering John, the king was on the move again and for now their bit of The Plan For Escape was on track.

Meanwhile Langton continued, 'My family are long from Lincolnshire sire.'

Yours too eh? Thought Busbeater.

'He says in a very heavy French accent' retorted the king sarcastically.

'May I remind you, sire, your mother was French' retorted the archbishop.

'She was from Aquitaine Langton. That's not the same thing at all. She was French only briefly when that aged King Louis the Fat married her off to his wet and feeble son Louis – why are so many French kings called Louis by the way? These Frenchies have no imagination – luckily my father rescued her from the terrible and hopeless marriage and took her for his wife.'

Langton could sense he might be on very dodgy ground if he started to talk about John's family. It didn't take much to get him riled but one thing that guaranteed it was talk of Henry and Eleanor and his sainted brother Richard. His fits of rage might last for hours, days even. Langton needed John to stay calm. So he changed the subject, 'Nice day for it' said the Archbishop of Canterbury.

The sun continued to shine brightly as the royal convoy approached the long level stretch of grassland where the negotiations with the barons were being held. Just beyond it was the River Thames. In between them and the river were arranged two camps. One for the barons, one for the king's retinue. It was an impressive sight. The barons' camp was busy and sure enough there was a large party of well-armed knights hanging around at the ready in case the king tried any funny business. At the other end of the meadow the royal camp had much larger, but fewer tents. Standards flew at both camps fluttering gently in the summer breeze. It was an impressive sight.

As they approached the king stopped.

'Oh no' thought Busbeater fearing the worse again. But all was well. The king merely wanted to show off to his more trusted aids.

'See Busbeater, Gerald? See what I can command!' He spread his right arm out, palm upward sweeping across the scene before him.

Gerald knew fully well that the king had been forced to do this. None of it was at his command. It was this or civil war. But the sight of these two great camps with the sun glinting on the clanking armour was indeed an impressive one.

Wow he thought, genuinely in awe. This is amazing; this is one of the greatest moments in English history and I'm here, right in it. He squeaked slightly as his pants and big blue woolly jumper rumbled around inside his tummy.

'You alright old boy?' asked Busbeater quietly.

'Yes thank you Uncle. Sorry, just got a bit excited.'

'I know what you mean' replied Busbeater. The Lieutenant Colonel had seen some sights in his time. He'd fended off battalions of rampaging madmen with just one stick, shot game with Allan Quatermain, fought off the Patriots, or was it the Traitors, in Ishmaelia and survived Loosehorn's heroic if misguided attempts at making crème brûlée but nothing was quite as extraordinary as this. He looked on in awe as some figures began to make their way toward them.

John's half-brother the Earl of Salisbury approached and declared, happily but guardedly, 'sire, you are here.'

'Well of course I am. What did you expect you idiot?' said John, as gracious as ever. 'It's time we stopped negotiating and got on with our lives. So let's just get this agreement sorted out and I'll be off.'

King John alighted from his horse with great deftness but before he went on he asked, 'Salisbury. Is there a German Baron with them today?'

Salisbury looked a little puzzled, 'German? Why no sire. Fitzwalter and Vesci are still here obviously.'

'Well of course' replied the king 'they would be.'

'And Giles de Briouze has turned up.'

'What the Bishop of Hereford? Really? What's his beef?'

'He believes you pursued his brother's family cruelly and unjustly; that you stole his land, his castles and his fortune from him.'

And starved his sister-in-law and nephew to death; thought Gerald a bit surprised that wasn't the main thing.

'Oh does he?' said John as if to deny it. Then brazenly added, 'Well, he could afford it.'

'He didn't think so' said Salisbury dryly.

'Want, want, want with these people' sighed the king exasperated and with no hint of irony. Salisbury flashed a glance at Langton who shared the earl's irritation. Most of the noblemen on the king's side weren't that enamoured of him either but better this, they calculated, than the continued chaos of civil war.

'Come on Busbeater, Gerald. It doesn't sound as if your Baron is here; that's a shame,' the king pretended to but didn't really care that much. This was all about him. 'Anyway, never mind, I want you to see this. Maybe work it in to your play this evening. Certainly record it for posterity eh what?' The king was almost cheerful.

'Thank you sire' said Gerald as he clambered off the horse, followed immediately by Busbeater.

Salisbury looked once again at Langton as if to say 'Who the very heck are these two?'

Langton shrugged his shoulders and as he got off his horse whispered, 'They keep him in a good mood somehow. So just tolerate them. For now.'

Gerald was still on his mettle and knew that everyone he met here would have an agenda of their own. It was like lunchtime break at St Cuthbert's. There was Johnson with the Butcher twins roaming the place beating up and stealing from the little kids; Sharon Good and her enormous personality frightening the teachers, especially the male ones and Clipstone just trying to survive. And all the time Mr Fitzsimmons watched on helplessly from the teacher's staff room.

Courageously Gerald marched over to the Earl of Salisbury and announced, 'Hello. I am Gerald Jones. It is very nice to meet you.'

The Earl of Salisbury, a taller man than the king was dressed in a white robe trimmed with gold. His hair was receding and he was a little portly. But above all he was utterly taken aback by this assertive young fellow, and not a little impressed.

'And a pleasure to meet you young Master Gerald. I am the Earl Of Salisbury.'

'And this is my uncle; Gerald Busbeater' introduced Gerald.

'You are named for your er, uncle' said Salisbury to Gerald but looking up at the tall and slightly fearsome man at his side. Busbeater had decided it wise to adopt his most military bearing for the next few hours. He felt he and Gerald were walking in to the Lion's Den; seizing the initiative was clearly the best way forward. So he stood as tall as he could, which meant he was taller then everyone and projected his most booming of booming voices.

'Pleasure sir I am sure' he indeed boomed.

Gerald was mightily impressed and wondered mischievously what would have happened if Loosehorn had come as well. What on earth would they have made of him?

'Come on Busbeater, Gerald, get a move on. You too Langton' cried the king impatiently. He was walking briskly toward his headquarters. 'I want this over with as quickly as possible.'

Just then a rather grand looking man in his seventies strode forward; it was William Marshal, one of the greatest knights of all time and loyal servant of John's father and brothers. Given the treacherous nature of the family that took some doing and it hadn't been without a few massive disagreements along the way.

'Sire, welcome on this great day. All your work in negotiating with the barons has come to this epic moment. One that will ensure you are enshrined in the chronicles forever as a wise and bold king'

'Yes, yes, thank you Marshal, thank you. I have made sure of that by bringing my own chronicler. Is there any mead about the place? I am thirsty after my ride.'

'Why yes sire' replied Marshal. A couple of servants were dispatched to get some. Marshal then noticed the king's company; unexpected and unusual company at that.

'Who are you?' he asked sharply upon seeing Busbeater and Gerald.

'I am Gerald Jones, the king's chronicler' said Gerald thrusting out his hand and looking Marshal in the eye 'and this is my uncle Gerald Busbeater.'

Marshal had had a glittering career as a tournament champion and had been influential in John being accepted as king after his brother Richard's death. More recently and in his later years he had spent an inordinate amount of time trying to moderate King John's more outrageous behaviour. He was now puzzled and slightly alarmed. No-one had told him about these extra, er, guests. Who the heck were they and what was the king up to? Marshal sighed. King John's intrigues knew no bounds and if this was another one it was only very alarming because he hadn't seen it coming. Busbeater looked at Marshal and was slightly cheered to finally meet someone of a similar vintage as him.

'Pleasure to meet you sire' he announced, boomingly.

'And you too.' Marshal quickly assessed the two and didn't sense any danger. His calm and thoughtful manner always gave him time to work people out. These two looked a little as if they were making it up as they went along. It was irritating to have interlopers at this crucial juncture but the king seemed to be happy to have them; and what they needed right now was a king who was happy. At least as happy as John ever could be. Marshal looked at Langton and whispered, 'These two OK?'

'I think so, yes. The boy is the clever one,' replied Langton.

Marshal suddenly remembered the time when he was a boy and the day he was nearly used as catapult ammunition. Gerald smiled at him and Marshal's heart melted. He'd keep an eye out for the boy; he reminded him of himself.

'This way young man, I expect you're thirsty' Marshal suggested warmly.

'And my uncle too' replied Gerald loyally.

'Of course. Er, Bagbeatle is it?' stammered Marshal.

'Busbeater,' corrected Busbeater boomingly.

'Of course, my apologies' said the aged royal aid who thought he'd seen everything, but by jingo, this was new.

CHAPTER TWELVE

Trousers With A Secret And A Close Run Thing

'Is everything ready?' demanded the king. 'I don't want to hang around and make small talk with anyone. I just want these negotiations ended and we can all go home.'

'Everything is ready' replied Langton.

'No small talk? You promise I don't have to do anything but seal it and clear off.'

William Marshal and archbishop Langton looked at each other, 'sire, it would be politically very astute if you just waited a little while after the seal is set. Maybe say a few thank yous. Ask after their children, that sort of thing,' replied Marshal.

Unless you've murdered them, then maybe don't do that thought Gerald, silently, very silently.

'Really? I have to ask after their children?' asked the king a little aghast.

'It would be ...' began Marshal.

'Politically astute, yes I do know you know' butted in the king a little bitterly, 'But what happens if I ask after little Johnny and it turns out they think I had him murdered or something?'

'Something you'd never do sire' said Langton in a sideways kind of way.

The king looked at Langton and seethed a bit. Marshal flashed Langton a look, 'Now sire, that's pretty unlikely isn't it?'

'Not that unlikely Marshal,' replied the king in a moment of almost refreshing honesty; even if it was honesty which involved some murdering.

Gerald and Busbeater stood to the king's side as a scribe brought in a large parchment.

'This it then? The final version?' asked the king looking at it suspiciously. 'Odds bodkins Marshal, are you sure about this? Will it stop the whining?'

William Marshal bit his tongue before saying, 'The barons are happy with the clauses sir as are Langton and I. It seems to make good their grievances.'

'Alright, alright. Their grievances, what about mine?'

'This charter addresses both sides sir.'

'We'll see about that' said John a little too menacingly for Marshal's liking. It was almost as if the king had another, different kind of plan brewing.

Marshal nonetheless continued on, 'There are a few more amendments to make, dotting the 'i's, crossing the 't's that sort of thing which will take a few more days, and copies will need to be made, but this is it and ready for your approval.' He and Langton were anxious, willing the king to agree. Every moment until he did seemed fraught with danger.

Gerald looked on in awe. He could barely believe he was right here, right now. The document, written on stretched calf skin known as vellum, was a rich cream colour and the ink a deep black. And rather than being 1000 years old, it was brand new; minutes old. It was actually very exciting.

'OK' said the king, 'shall we get this thing done?'

Langton, Marshal and King John along with Busbeater and Gerald made their way over to where the ceremony was to take place.

They walked in to the large tent, where a seal press sat upon a table, Gerald counted nearly thirty men all of whom seemed to be on the king's side. Gerald looked around. He wished he'd paid a bit more attention at school when they had done Magna Carta but he was sure he'd remembered the king signing it surrounded by cross barons with swords at the ready. Turns out none of it was true. All these chaps were on the king's side. And he wasn't signing anything; just then a scribe pushed past with bowl of hot wax and delivered it to the king's side. Here he sealed the vellum and that was it; what was eventually to become known as Magna Carta was sealed. This was it thought Gerald; this was how history was made. And it was all a bit low key.

William Marshal invited the representatives of the barons to come forth. Now assured of their rights under the law, the civil war was declared at an end.

'Here they come' said John to no-one in particular but looking at Gerald and smiling a mysterious and possibly sinister smile.

'Hello Fitz' announced the king contemptuously and settled in to the large golden chair.

'My liege' Fitzwalter bowed as referentially as he could and remained standing. He hated the king's living breathing guts, but he was still the king and no-one sat in his presence unless asked.

'You know Langton and Marshal obviously ...' said King John 'they've been here all week.'

'I do sire. Welcome again lords,' Fitzwalter bowed to both. He then saw Busbeater and Gerald standing slightly sheepishly at the back.

'Who ...?' he glared and made ready to grab the sword at his side. John had brought extra, unannounced aides. This had the whiff of treachery about it.

King John turned around and eagerly beckoned them to the front. 'Out of the way Langton, let them through.' John demanded

'But sire ...' objected Langton pointlessly.

'Let Busbeater and Gerald through. This young man here is my chronicler who will give an impartial account of today's events.'

'Impartial account?' mused Marshal. 'So that's their role, even if they didn't know it; they were John's propaganda writers.'

Gerald did already know this and his brain was whirring madly about their play that evening; it had to be one that praised King John for being true, noble and heroic. Someone who brought peace, justice and democracy to his land. A Great Day for a Great King. Crikey thought Gerald, one way or another they had to escape before they were made to enact this pile of untruths; for if the chroniclers were to record their performance for the ages to come that would most definitely be changing history. This was a tricky and scheming king. Gerald scrunched up his eyes; please let Auntie Marjorie have bopped Bott on the hooter one more time and rescued the flywheel.

'Busbeater, Gerald meet Robert Fitzwalter, Lord of Dunmow'

'Pleased to meet you' asserted Gerald thrusting his hand out straight out in front of him. Before he really knew what he was doing Fitzwalter had shaken it firmly.

'Pleasure I am sure' boomed Busbeater. Fitzwalter still bemused shook his hand too. This may not be treachery he pondered, but it was certainly weird.

The king looked beyond Fitzwalter and saw a figure lurking in the shadow of the tent.

'Ahh, Vesci, thought you'd be here for the Big Moment' he announced.

Eustace de Vesci emerged from the shadows to stand slightly behind Fitzwalter.

'Busbeater, Gerald this is Useless de Vesci' said John smiling widely.

'Eustace' protested Eustace.

'Sorry' said the king, not sorry at all 'Eustace de Vesci, Lord of Alnwick' continued John deliberately pronouncing the 'l'.

'It's a silent 'l' my lord.

'If only you too were silent Eustace' retorted the king, pleased with his joke. 'These two tried to have me killed back in '12' he glared at De Vesci and Fitzwalter 'still, we're all friends now aren't we?' he added with a sneering grin

Gerald ignored the massive animosity between the men and shook Lord of Alnwick's hand as did Busbeater who felt some small talk might help ease things a little.

'Pleasure to meet you. Love your castle. My wife and I have visited it many times' he offered and instantly regretted it.

Gerald closed his eyes. *Oh my good grief,* he thought, *Uncle!*

'Really?' said a startled Eustace 'we've not had any visitors and we'd know since certain people,' he flashed a look at John, 'ordered it to be destroyed. So it's hard to know when you visited us. Was it before its destruction? I am pretty sure I'd have remembered you.' He looked at Busbeater rather up and down. 'Or did you perhaps help destroy it?' Massively suspicious of these two interlopers who seemed to be part of the king's plan that destroyed his home and fortress, he began to unsheathe his sword.

'Er ... er,' Busbeater was struggling.

Gerald rode to the rescue, 'My uncle is a traveling player of some advanced years,' he said rapidly, 'and he can sometimes mix places up. He can get a bit, you know ... ' he caught Eustace's eye, stuck his tongue out, crossed his eyes and twirled his finger round by his temple.

Eustace saw this and laughed, much to everyone's amazement, not least his own.

'Ah, yes I see. Of course,' he winked at Gerald and tapped his nose knowingly and slid his sword back in to its sheathe. 'I have a relative of similarly shall we say, elderly tendencies.'

Strewth thought Gerald, that was a hairy moment. His heart was pounding so hard it was almost leaping out of his chest.

The entire tent breathed a sigh of relief, apart from John who hadn't apparently noticed the ratcheting up of tension after Busbeater's innocent but wholly inappropriate small talk.

'I say what the …?' Busbeater suddenly caught on and was somewhat offended at the idea of being thought of as a bit soft in the head.

Gerald squeezed his uncle's hand and whispered, 'I am sorry Uncle …'

Busbeater understood and squeezed Gerald's hand back and lowly said 'thanks old son.'

Gerald smiled, 'Ishmaelia!' he replied.

'Very amusing Gerald' said the king. Marshal and Langton looked on anxiously. That was a close run thing. De Vesci was ready with his sword. If he had drawn it everything would have been off. But Gerald's charm and quick wit had saved the day.

Meanwhile John, for the first time during this whole sorry business was beginning to enjoy himself a little. He had noticed de Vesci's threatening move and relished every moment of it. Bringing Busbeater and Gerald along had been a masterstroke. It had completely unsettled everyone and put them right off their game. 'Still got it Johnny boy' the king said to himself. Just a bit more fun …

'Saer de Quincy not here then?' The king smiled to himself. He could almost feel Marshal shudder behind him. Marshal hated de Quincy and the king knew it. He liked to have fun even at his loyal allies' expense.

'Sire, no he is not,' answered Fitzwilliam, 'He had to attend to some business at home.'

'Pity,' said the king. What he really meant was, pity his fun was over.

'Sire, there are just a few final i's to dot and t's to cross to make sure all is in order' said Langton.

'Really?' said the king, irritated.

William Marshal whispered in John's ear, 'A few more days sire and we'll have lasting peace.'

'Oh, peace!' John practically spat the word out. 'Alright then, four days from now I want you all to have nice loyal oaths ready to swear to me. But from now on, the war is over yes?'

'Yes sire' said Fitzwilliam and de Vesci at once. They then went down on one knee and bowed their head to their king.

'I don't trust him Fitz,' Vesci whispered to Fitzwilliam, 'There's something not quite right about all of this.'

'I agree Eustace, but let's give this a chance. We'll know soon enough if he is playing us for fools.'

'Again' added Vesci.

'Oi what are you two whispering about?' barked John.

'Nothing sire, just rehearsing our oaths.'

'OK, Fine. War is over,' said John. He stood up to go 'Right, satisfied everyone? Got enough material for your play Busbeater, Gerald?'

They both nodded.

'Everyone else satisfied with the clause about the removal of all the fish-weirs in the Thames are you? Honestly the things I do for you.' The king walked away briskly and dismissively.

For a moment Gerald stood motionless. He didn't expect to be so excited. The Moon Landing, now that was something to behold. To see a man on the moon was staggering and just about the most exciting thing a young chap could imagine. But a bad tempered king sealing a piece of paper? No school lesson ever made him so thrilled. He had seen it happen; actually seen it happen. He could feel his dad's hand on his shoulder and his heart swelled; how proud Arnold Jones would be. Gerald turned around 'Dad …?'

It was his uncle.

'You alright old son? asked Busbeater.

'Oh yes Uncle, fine.'

Busbeater looked at his nephew, 'time to get out of here …'

'To Save the Day eh Uncle?' said Gerald brightening.

'Of course …'

William Marshal shook hands discretely with Langton and then with less enthusiasm Fitzwilliam and Vesci muttering to them 'if I see de Quincy again, I'll make sure I am the last thing he claps eyes on.'

Langton moved across worried that this might escalate. Calmly he said, 'But we have our agreement. We have the Rule of Law.' Langton was quietly triumphant.

'Yes' said Marshal. He shook Fitzwilliam and De Vesci's hands again. 'Forgive me for my petulance. This is indeed a Great Day.'

Marshal went over to Gerald and Busbeater, 'You alright young man?' he asked Gerald.

'Yes thank you sire.'

'Quite a day for you,' Marshal said, pointing out the obvious.

'Yes, quite …' replied Gerald.

Marshal turned to Busbeater, 'Listen, your play tonight. What will you say?'

Before Busbeater could answer Gerald stepped in, 'Do not worry sire. We will tell the truth or we will do nothing.'

'If you don't represent the king as the hero here, he will have you executed,' warned Marshal.

'We don't intend to be around long enough. We have an escape plan.' said Busbeater immediately regretting using the word 'escape.'

'Escape?' Marshal was puzzled. He looked steadily at the pair, assessing their strange outfits and curiously out of touch air 'Exactly where are you from?'

'It's a foreign country sire,' said Busbeater.

'Called …?'

'Ishmaelia' they said together.

'Ishmaelia? I have never heard of it,' replied Marshal, 'But it is clearly a fine and noble place if you two are any guide. I am at the castle tonight. If you need any assistance …'

'Thank you sire. We may hold you to that,' replied Busbeater warming rather to the old codger.

'Count on me if needs be,' said Marshal.

'Well, what are you lot doing? Come on I want to go, which means you lot have to as well,' bellowed the king.

'So much for the post-ceremony small talk,' smiled Marshal, 'You'd better go. Don't want to upset him.'

'Come on' said the never patient king, 'We are all agreed, and I don't want to spend unnecessary time hanging around here now. So chop, chop. Come on.'

Busbeater clambered nimbly on to his horse taking Gerald with him in one fell swoop and they followed the king and Langton back to the castle. William Marshal stood and saluted Gerald off. 'I will see you at the banquet tonight' he called and winked.

'So what do you make of your old king then Gerald? Rather dashed heroic? "Robin who?" they'll be singing fairly soon once your play is out and about. Which by the way I am very much looking forward to.' He smiled, darkly.

Strewth thought Busbeater, this could get very awkward especially if the gang haven't got Gerald's knapsack and silenced Bott.

Langton was smiling too. He had worked tirelessly for years to enshrine some kind of justice in to the relationship between the king and his people. To stop him acting in an arbitrary and brutal way and at least allow the barons the right to pass on their wealth and estates to relatives and not just be gobbled up by the king to fund his wars. This may not be perfect, but he felt as though it might be a start. But just getting John to agree, even under threat of war was a monumental achievement. Now there would be peace and justice between the king and his nobles. And one day someone might remember to include the ordinary people; but that would have to wait. For now it was understood; the king was subject to the law just like everyone else. A Big Day.

With two on his back Busbeater and Gerald's horse, still tired from the journey there was a little slower so they fell a little behind the archbishop and the king who was looking over his shoulder and grinning at them. And not in a cheery way. John slowed his horse down allowing Langton to go on ahead. The archbishop was suspicious, but when working with John that was just an occupational hazard, so he decided to concentrate on the Great Day it had been.

'So Busbeater, Gerald, how's things?' asked the king cheerily.

'Marvellous sire' replied Busbeater wondering why the king was quite so cheerful. Hadn't he just given away much of his power?

The king slowed his horse right down and held the reigns of Busbeater and Gerald's too.

'Don't want Langton to hear this bit ...' he looked about him as if every shrub or tree was a spy.

'That charter; it's a meaningless scrap of paper,' said John quietly.

'Really?' said Gerald,' but I thought ...'

'You thought it was some kind of legal document giving my power away and protecting those whiny barons?' John actually cackled 'Bah, not if I have anything to do with it. At best it has stopped this blasted civil war; at least until I can regroup and get my mercenaries together. Then I will destroy them and that young upstart Alexander in Scotland – I have had it with the Scots. They just won't keep quiet. Also I have an ace up my sleeve' King John held his arm up to illustrate his flappy sleeve as if Gerald didn't know what a sleeve was.

Busbeater however leant forward to peer up the king's sleeve.

The king looked at Busbeater quizzically, 'Not literally you twit.'

Busbeater, a little embarrassed said 'No sire, I was just er, admiring your sleeve in general. A fine sleeve; not seen many better than that. In fact of all the sleeves I have ever ...'

The king interrupted, 'Stop it man. You are going mad.'

'What do you have up your sleeve sire?' asked Gerald as Busbeater coughed his way out of the slightly humiliating episode.

'Innocent of course. He won't stand for any of this nonsense. After our little row a few years ago, he thinks I am the bees knees these days. I am informed by reliable sources that he is about to excommunicate the lot of them.'

'Er, ex comm ... what?' asked Busbeater. Knowing that the king thought him a bit of a twerp after the whole sleeve thing, he could ask all the embarrassing questions to save Gerald's reputation.

'Excommunicate' hissed John so Langton couldn't hear. And pointing to the archbishop added 'him too.'

Busbeater still looked lost, 'Kicked out of the church man; no longer under the protection of the pope. Exiled from the church. You know, doomed. Which means I can get my hands on their cash and the pope will back me.'

'And where does this Innocent chap come in to it? If he is indeed a chap?'

'He's the pope man. The pope! Where have you been these past few years? Good grief. The pope will kick them out. It's their end and my victory.'

'Riiiiight' said Busbeater thinking this a bit of a rum deal.

'Also I know once the pope gets to hear about this, he'll annul it.'

'An Ull ...?'

'Annul! He'll cancel it. By jove Busbeater, your education is worse than the worst kind of illiterate peasants. And that's pretty bad. But the point is that this woolly minded nonsense will be strangled at birth by the pope leaving me free to get on with my plans to rout the barons and their friends. Great Charter? A load of windy nonsense more like. In fact I have heard better wind bursting forth out of the backside of my horse. I have already forgotten most of it already. And I intend for your play to help me by telling how I was duped in to agreeing this ludicrous list of complaints so I can then denounce it. And in a few weeks the pope will back me up.'

Busbeater was going purple with rage; for Lieutenant Colonel Busbeater this was a matter of honour. You word was your bond. If you agreed to something well you bally well had better honour it. But this king was a treacherous fellow and Busbeater was struggling to keep quiet. He wanted to ride up to Langton to tell him what the king had just said and get this thing sorted. He fidgeted in the saddle of his horse.

Behind him Gerald could sense his uncle's fury. 'Uncle,' he whispered, 'Uncle don't ...'

But …

'What?! You are going to do what!?'

Gerald's heart sank a billion miles, 'Oh my goodness' he sighed.

The king however was so pleased with himself and his cunning plan that he mistook Busbeater's furious outburst for a hearty endorsement.

'I know; it's a wizard wheeze isn't it? Makes everyone look pretty foolish I'd say.' He sat upright on his horse and said 'come on, let's catch up old Lanky Langton. He's already looking suspicious, if only he knew what was coming.' The king snorted a suppressed chortle.

Gerald gripped his uncle's waste and in slight desperation whispered 'Uncle, shh please. We know he's a rotten egg but we mustn't interfere for our own and for history's sake. Remember Ishmaelia!'

Busbeater stayed worryingly silent.

As they trotted on the king turned to Busbeater and smiled, 'It's genius isn't it? I know you agree, I can see it in your eyes. After that whole thing with the sleeve it's obvious you aren't educated enough to know the right words to use, but I know you agree. Your eyes; they blaze with admiration.'

Gerald squeezed his uncle tightly. He wanted to clout this nasty cruel king round the chops for being so insulting but knew what was at stake. But would the Lieutenant Colonel?

There was a long pause. Then finally, 'I am appalled.'

'*ohmyverygoodness*' breathed Gerald.

'Appalled?' The king's smile faltered.

'Yes' confirmed Busbeater. 'Appalled … that I didn't think of it. But as you say with my meagre education and you of such noble bearing what chance have I of coming up with such cunning. It is a plan of genius.'

The king's smile returned. 'Isn't it? OK, just so we are straight, tonight's play will be all about poor me, heroic, noble and brave being conned by the scheming, double crossing barons. Then I can begin my propaganda effort to finish them off once and for all.'

'Yes' said Gerald and Busbeater together 'got it.'

'Good,' John's face then darkened a little, 'But no mention of the other bits; the excommunication, the pope annulling it. Save those for me. Or else.' He levelled a look at Busbeater and Gerald and slowly drew his finger across his throat. 'OK?'

'Very OK' said Gerald in between massive gulps. *Please let Cornelius have found the flywheel* he thought desperately.

Eventually they caught Langton up.

'Hello sire. Good day isn't it?'

'Very' said the king.

Langton looked at him hard as the king stared ahead. Langton was suspicious. Something he thought, was very up.

Just as they caught up Langton Busbeater whispered 'Ishmaelia' in Gerald's ear.

Gerald was a very relieved boy. He knew how close his honourable uncle had come to blowing the whole thing wide open. He had always been taught that Doing The Right Thing in All Circumstances was right. But now suddenly everything was more murky. They had had to let a cruel and selfish man believe he was some kind of heroic figure instead of the dirty rotten scoundrel he was to save themselves. Yikes thought Gerald, it was clear that being an adventurer was going to be more complicated than he thought. How could he do the Right Thing to make amends, however small? It was then he hit upon an idea. A brilliant idea if he, Gerald Jones, could be so bold; he felt he could. He leant forward and whispered in to his uncle's ear. Busbeater smiled and replied, 'A splendid idea Gerald. A very, very honourable, bold and brilliant idea.'

Breathless Marjorie and Sheepshanks returned to the cell.

'We've (wheeze) got the (puff) knapsack Cornelius' exhaled Marjorie who hadn't run that fast for that long since the day one of Mrs Bunyon's fire-proof oven gloves had caught fire.

Sheepshanks handed it over. He was of course and yet somehow mysteriously in tip top condition and looked as if he had been merely strolling about a bit.

'Excellent, thank you Sheepshanks' said Loosehorn.

Sheepshanks looked intently at Loosehorn.

'What is it Sheepshanks? What's wrong?'

'Sir, everything is in there ...'

'Great' interrupted Cornelius.

' ... but ...'

'Ah'

' ... the flywheel. The book, diary, tee shirt, comic ... everything but the flywheel.'

Cornelius grabbed the knapsack off Loosehorn.

'I say man, have some manners' retorted Loosehorn.

'Sorry' replied Cornelius as he rummaged frantically through the knapsack.

'It's not that big Cornelius. We've looked and it's not there' said Marjorie a little offended that Cornelius hadn't believed them.

'I am sorry Marjorie. You are right, of course you are ...' He turned to Bott who was grinning.

'I knew it. You are French spies and have come here to overthrow the king. And this device is your way of communicating with the Dauphin Louis. Of all the feeble collection of objects in that bag that looked like the most important, the most useful. And I was right. Look at you all. You are lost, broken and I have won. I have thwarted your plot and saved England!' Bott was very pleased with himself.

'Where is it?' Loosehorn towered over Bott who was still tied up but with a triumphant air about him. 'We can get the gaoler to sing again ...'

'I don't care about that trick now I know I have you. I will just sit tight until the king returns and expose you all as the treacherous, dirty criminals I always knew you were. And we all know how the king feels about traitors don't we? And you don't have the guts to kill me.'

Marjorie gulped. He was right; she trembled with fury but bumping him off was too much. And even if they could then they'd definitely not find out where the flywheel was and they'd be stuck here forever. The king however wouldn't think twice about doing them in. All in all this was a tricky development.

'Yes crone. That's right, he'll kill you all, only very slowly and I'll make sure I am the one who turns the handle. The boy will be done last of course - I want him to see you all suffer.' Bott paused for effect, like it needed any more effect. 'It might take days' he added slowly and gleefully shifting about on the stone floor as if his whole body was getting comfortable in readiness to watch this band of fools' epic downfall.

Impassive, Sheepshanks looked on. Hmm, he thought.

Cornelius crouched on his haunches and pushed his face as close to Bott's as he could, ignoring the paint strippingly bad breath and the body odour which was likely to stun an ox at fifty paces. Slowly and as menacingly as he could muster he said, 'Bott; where is the flywheel?'

'Flywheel. So that's what it's called is it?' replied Bott, apparently utterly unfazed, 'Well, that is interesting. You will have to try and find out. You will never discover where I have hidden it; you will never dare go there. I will not speak again.' Theatrically he shut his mouth tight, which was a partial relief because it reduced the general stench by fifty per cent, and turned his face away.

On the verge of passing out, Cornelius struggled to his feet and looked helplessly at Bott.

'Why you dirty ...' he was about to essentially beat the living daylights out of Bott even though he knew it would not work when Sheepshanks intervened.

'Sir, if I may,' said the valet quietly.

He gently moved the defeated Cornelius out of the way. Standing in front of Bott Sheepshanks signalled to Jeff the Gaoler who began to play soothing incidental music on his hurdy-gurdy as Imre turned the handle. Sheepshanks bowed before Bott and began. From his right sleeve he produced a bunch of very colourful paper flowers. He showed them off to the assembled audience

'Oooo, very good,' said Imre, impressed.

Then from his left sleeve he began to produce the flags of all nations on a very long piece of string. This went on for quite a while.

'I say,' said Hector, 'I wish I knew how these chaps do that.'

Cornelius by now utterly bereft of ideas hoped this might be some kind of crazy plan. He took advantage and sat back against the cold, damp cell wall and tried to think of where Bott may have hidden the flywheel. Meanwhile Sheepshanks' continued on.

After a few minutes the flags of nations ran out and he handed them to his assistant Marjorie who paraded them in front of everyone. Improbably there was a ripple of applause led by Imre and Hector who were just loving it. What would happen next?

Balloon animals happened next; Sheepshanks made several in lightning quick time. A red giraffe, a blue leopard and a green, what was that? A frog? Whatever it was it was affecting Bott.

'A leopard? Our much loved King Richard's insignia! You are very clever spies. But you can't con me; I won't drop my guard … oooo, a frog! A lovely frog.' Sheepshanks handed Bott the balloon frog as if he were giving it to a child. Bott was smiling like a six year old, almost cooing, 'A frog. Like my pet frog Freddie … oh how I miss him,' pined Bott.

As Bott became lost in his reverie about Freddie his much lamented pet frog Sheepshanks made his move. He deftly and imperceptibly unbuckled Bott's belt, and slipped his hand in to his trousers. Cornelius winced while Loosehorn went a very strange colour. They were brave men but even they weren't courageous enough to dive in to another man's trouser, especially a man so rancid as Bott. Cornelius hoped it was part of some plan. Bott though wasn't so far gone in his reverie that he hadn't noticed, 'Wha …? What are you doing man? Get out of my trousers!' he squealed.

Utterly unfazed Sheepshanks produced from inside Bott's pants a small rabbit, unconscious from the whiff. Bott was immediately distracted again.

'Oh I say, that's very well done' said the gaoler as he continued his unmelodic hurdy-gurdering. 'A rabbit from Bott's trousers.'

The archers were impressed too with Hector applauding enthusiastically and Imre nodding approvingly in appreciation of Sheepshanks' skills whilst maintaining his hurdy-gurdy handle duties.

Loosehorn was less impressed however, 'A rabbit Sheepshanks? Really? I thought you were … oh,' Loosehorn stopped suddenly.

Sheepshanks had indeed produced a rabbit which Bott was now cooing at. But he had produced something else too.

'The flywheel! You've got the flywheel!' exclaimed Cornelius.

'It'll probably need a wash,' said Sheepshanks disdainfully who was otherwise pretty matter-of-fact about the whole thing.

Bott suddenly realised what had happened. He had been completely duped.

'The flywheel! But how… when … the rabbit? The frog balloon - you tricked me!'

Loosehorn stood still in shocked amazement, 'It was in his *trousers*?' he whispered awestruck.

'To be precise' said Sheepshanks calmly ' it was in his *pants.* '

Loosehorn remained stock still, reduced to silently mouthing the word 'pants' over and over, his glazed eyes fixed on the middle distance.

'I could see he looked uncomfortable sir as he was shifting about on the floor and there was something about his smugness. He looked and sounded like one of those villains in the James Bond films sir you know how they go on and on instead of just finishing off Mr Bond? So I took a chance,' Sheepshanks explained.

'A mighty big one' said Loosehorn 'You don't know what might have been living, or not, in there. Your arm could easily have dissolved or something. Look at the state of the rabbit.'

'Sheepshanks sir, let me shake your hand … er, no the other one.' Cornelius was massively impressed.

Marjorie walked over to Bott, 'So, not so clever now eh Bott?' she boomed.

Bott was traumatised, 'That man was in my trousers!' he squealed again.

'And lived, which is the surprising part' replied Marjorie.

Bott lay curled up like a baby. It was all over. His big plans for promotion and maybe a castle one day where he could order peasants around the whole time were smashed to smithereens. Forever.

'Don't be so pathetic Bott,' dismissed Marjorie, 'Be a man for once …'

With that everyone left the cell and the gaoler locked Bott in. Imre and Hector were discussing animatedly the magic tricks they saw.

'No Imre, I don't think he had time to grow a rabbit in there' said Hector gently.

'Where did he get all those coloured pennants from? Did he maybe have a trap door beneath him?' Imre was in awe.

'What, in a dungeon?' asked Hector incredulously.

'Well, no I suppose ...' conceded Imre.

Hector paused for a moment. It all seemed miraculous. How do they do it? Surely there was an explanation. He turned to Imre with a suggestion.

'We should form a group, a circle of friends and find out how this is done so we can keep the secrets to ourselves and perform at parties and stuff.'

'Still doing the stunt archery though?' asked Imre.

'Oh yes, of course,' replied Hector firmly, 'We will call it 'The Circle Of Magic Archers'.'

'A magic circle' whispered Imre excitedly.

Marjorie, Sheepshanks, Cornelius and Loosehorn stood together and thanked the gaoler and the archers.

'We couldn't have done any of that without you,' said Marjorie.

'Not a problem,' replied Jeff. He looked at Sheepshanks half in admiration, half in fear and shuddered, 'You were on your own with the pants thing though' he added.

'We must be off. We have a rendezvous with the rest of our troupe' said Cornelius.

'Jeff,' said Marjorie 'get your hurdy-gurdy ready for the performance.'

'I shall spit on it and buff it up be assured' said a smiling gaoler.

Marjorie then paused and turned to the Hungarians 'Hector, Imre?'

'Yes?' they replied as one.

'We might need your help later. Might you be on hand this evening too?'

Imre and Hector had performed for the king before and it hadn't gone terribly well, but this might be their last chance to escape. They agreed readily.

'We would be honoured to help' they replied together.

'Maybe we'll learn more of the startling valet's trouser tricks' said Hector .

'Not sure that's wise actually' said Loosehorn.

Marjorie flashed him a look, 'Thank you; all of you. We will get word to you when we need you.'

Cornelius looked admiringly at Marjorie.

'We'll probably need all the help we can get' she whispered.

'Good thinking; nicely done Marjorie.'

Loosehorn, Marjorie, Sheepshanks and Cornelius made their way back to their quarters. It was probably best if it looked as if they hadn't been wandering the castle in the king's absence.

'Farnsbarnes ...' announced Cornelius

'Ahh, you're back,' interrupted the king's guard, 'You've been gone ages. Did you find what you were looking for?'

'Yes thank you we did. In the end.'

'In Bott's pants,' whispered Loosehorn to himself still not quite over the whole episode.

'Anyway,' continued Cornelius staring at Loosehorn who evidently had said that louder than he meant to 'we were wondering if you wouldn't mind keeping our little, er, trip just between us?'

Farnsbarnes nodded, 'Don't worry sir, so much goes on around here that I am required to take no notice of that I am quite practiced in the art of forgetting.'

'Thank you, you are a decent fellow,' replied Cornelius.

Back in their room they waited.

'Nothing else for it' announced Loosehorn 'we just have to hang around here until Gerald and Busbeater return.'

'They will return won't they?' said Marjorie suddenly worried.

'Of course they will,' replied Loosehorn reassuringly but not entirely convinced himself.

'The king needs them for some reason,' interjected Cornelius, 'so unless someone does something mad like tells the king what he thinks of him or inappropriately engages someone in ill-judged small talk ...' Cornelius looked at Loosehorn. They both knew there was a chance that Busbeater might have done just that, 'then everything will be OK.'

Loosehorn closed his eyes 'remember Ishmaelia old boy' he said to his absent friend.

CHAPTER THIRTEEN

A Reunion And A New Plan

'Right, well I am glad that's over with. Maybe I can get on with grown up, proper things now' said the king as he clambered off his horse.

'There is much work to do sire but yes, now things will be calmer it will be easier to bring peace and prosperity to our land' said archbishop Langton.

'Or something … blah blah' said the king dismissively as he went inside the castle. Langton looked on, slightly worried.

Busbeater and Gerald clambered off their horse.

'What did he say to you earlier?' asked Langton.

'Oh nothing' said Gerald a little nervously 'just you know, how he was glad it was all over and what an idiot everybody is, that sort of thing … the usual.'

'Hmm' muttered Langton, not entirely convinced.

'Come on you lot. I want your new play up and running …' called the king.

'We need to write it first sire' replied Gerald.

'Write it? Crikey, you scribes … OK. You've got an hour. I will arrange for your props cabinet to be in this ante chamber here so it's ready.'

Drat, thought Busbeater, once again they were separated from the time machine. This would delay their escape. But then he remembered Gerald's idea. He looked at the boy who winked at him, 'All going to plan Uncle; all going to plan.'

Busbeater was so proud of his nephew, he wanted to shout it from the roof tops. But he thought he'd wait. That might be a bit weird.

'Oh my goodness, oh my goodness, you are back. Oh my goodness' Marjorie was overwhelmed as Busbeater and Gerald walked in to the room.

'We are' said Gerald from deep within an extra special Marjorie hug.

'Do you have the flywheel?' asked Busbeater urgently.

'We do' replied Loosehorn.

'Thank goodness.'

'But the king has just confiscated our wardrobe. Again,' added Cornelius a little dejectedly.

'We know, but it's OK' said Gerald extracting himself from Marjorie.

It was Busbeater's turn now, 'Come here you silly old booby,' cooed Marjorie.

'What's OK?' asked Loosehorn.

'We have a plan for the play and the escape.'

From Marjorie's heaving bosom Busbeater added, 'It is a splendid plan. One with honour which is not something that I have seen much evidence of today.'

'Why Busbeater? What happened?' asked Loosehorn, curious.

'Let me go for a moment Marjorie,' said Busbeater dragging himself from his wife's attentions 'er, oh nothing Pelham, apart from the general madness.'

'Ahh, OK' said Loosehorn not convinced. He knew his old friend only too well and he could tell something had griped his wagger.

'Did Bott discover the flywheel?'

'Oh very much so. It was in his quarters' replied Cornelius. He handed the knapsack back to Gerald, '. Everything is in there.'

Gerald, relieved, checked his father's diary was there and the book and the tee shirt. It was all there. He had his dad back with him and he wasn't letting the knapsack out of his sight again unless there was a super emergency like saving someone's life or something. Thank the very goodness. But wait, oh where's the flywheel ...?

Cornelius was holding it, 'But at first, this wasn't.'

'Where was it ...?' asked Gerald.

Cornelius blinked hard, Loosehorn shuddered and Marjorie bowed her head and covered her eyes with both hands.

'Well?' Asked Busbeater 'where was it? It can't have been that bad.'

'It was in Bott's pants sir,' said Sheepshanks.

Gerald and Busbeater looked at each other and together they exclaimed, 'In his pants?' It *was* that bad.

'Yes.'

'Oh my very goodness' said an ashen faced Gerald 'how ...?'

' ... did we get it out?' Loosehorn finished the question.

'Yes' said Gerald slightly afraid of the answer.

'Sheepshanks here dived in.'

'Did you do the old Flag Of Nations, Unconscious Rabbit thing?'

asked Busbeater who had apparently seen the routine before.

'I did sir' replied Sheepshanks.

'Good for you. But someone's pants? That was a first eh?'

'Very much so sir' replied Sheepshanks.

'They must have been rancid Busbeater, you've never smelled the like' grimaced Marjorie at the memory of Bott's general uncleanliness.

'They were indeed ripe sir' agreed Sheepshanks calmly.

Sheepshanks, thought Gerald, what a man.

'So, what's this plan of yours Gerald old son?' asked Loosehorn keen to get off the subject of Bott's pants as quickly as possible.

Gerald told them that it didn't matter that the king had The Wardrobe since it would give him time to Do The Right Thing. He and Busbeater told the gang that the king had demanded they show him in a favourable light even though he was a bounder and a cad so that the history books would be nice to him. This they clearly wouldn't and couldn't do; but they had to do *something* to be reunited with the time machine. The king had given them an hour to write their play; enough time to practice their routine and for Gerald to adapt the 'I'm Against It' song with more appropriate lyrics. Marjorie said she had recruited Jeff the Gaoler and Imre and Hector.

'Who the great crested grebe are Imre and Hector?' asked Busbeater not all that thrilled that there were yet more people to have to get to know.

'The Stunt Archers' replied Marjorie.

'Aren't they dead?'

'Marjorie saved their lives,' interrupted Loosehorn.

'Really old girl? How?'

'She asked Jeff the Gaoler.'

'And he just said "yes"?'

'He did,' replied Marjorie.

'Flash the old eyelashes did you?' asked Busbeater.

'I did' she replied coyly.

'That's my girl' beamed Busbeater.

'That's great' said Gerald. 'Right, everyone needs to rehearse like mad. We don't have long. Meanwhile, I have an errand to run.'

'You want to see the king? On your own? Now?' asked Farnsbarnes.

'Yes please,' said Gerald whose level and confident tone was at odds with the tumultuous battle between his pants and big blue woolly jumper going on inside his stomach.

'OK, but, well, you are a brave young man.'

Or really stupid thought Gerald *but its part of Doing The Right Thing.*

Farnsbarnes went in to the king's chambers and came out straightaway 'Er, right, in you go.'

'Thank you Mr Farnsbarnes.'

Farnsbarnes smiled. He couldn't remember the last time anyone called him 'Mister.'

The king was at his table eating as usual 'Ahh, Gerald come on in. Written your play have you? Or are you here asking for an extension? You won't get one. When I said an hour I meant an hour.' The king really was unpleasant. He had managed to turn a cheery greeting in to a threat within two sentences. Gerald ploughed on regardless.

'No sire. All is on track. But I would like a favour.'

'A favour? Why you are bold. What is this favour?'

'Well sire I don't know who the audience for this evening is …'

The king interrupted, 'Marshal, Langton, the Bishop of Norwich - don't think you met him today down at Runnymede. Anyway, he'll be attending. And me obviously …'

Gerald took a deep breath but before he could ask his question the king remembered one more person 'Oh and Stuart of course.'

'Stuart sire?'

'My dog, Stuart. He'll be there.'

'Ahh, right, yes OK, your dog.' Crikey thought Gerald, this might be even harder than he thought if he had invited his dog before his own family.

'Well sire, since we are planning to praise you and your deeds today …'

'And I am very much looking forward to that,' interrupted the king. 'I have brought in my other top chronicler to make notes while you perform. Then afterwards you and I can go over it, polish it a bit, you know like we talked about, and then distribute it about the land.'

'Yes, that's excellent sire,' *that's a terrible idea* thought Gerald, 'I think you'll be pleased.'

'I am expecting to be pleased young Gerald.'

'Ahh, well I was hoping that maybe since we are praising you that you might like to have your son in attendance.'

'My son? Which one?'

'Henry sire. Your heir. We met him yesterday …' Oops, Gerald shouldn't have mentioned that. The king went a bit bonkers after Henry and his mother had left.

Sure enough the king lowered his head looking at Gerald with narrowing eyes.

Gerald thought it best to ignore it and keep going quickly ' … and I was thinking what better way for a son to love his father than to see him praised in song and dance in the re-enactment of the Great Day.'

The king was quiet. Hmm, it hadn't occurred to him but maybe it was a good idea. Henry needed to see how great his old man was. Who knew what poisonous notions Queen Isabella was filling his head with. Warming to the idea the king continued his wagon train of thought which was about to arrive at the village called Claiming This Idea For Himself; he would demand the Queen came too. That would wipe the smug, whiny expression off her face.

'Better idea Gerald I shall invite Henry and his mother. They will see me praised and honoured and maybe I'll get a bit more respect round here. A great idea of mine.'

Gerald, who may have only been twelve but was getting the hang of curious adult ways quite quickly, said, 'A brilliant idea. And we are planning some hurdy-gurdy music and maybe some acrobats.'

This was risky, but Gerald felt he was on a roll.

'Hurdy-gurdy? Really? Acrobats, are you sure?'

'Acrobats to depict your mental agility in coming to an agreement with the barons and the hurdy-gurdy to be able more elegantly to sing your praises sire.' Crikey thought Gerald and not for the first time, where did all that come from?

Utterly flattered by this plucky young man the king agreed.

'Thank you sire. We shall be honoured to play for you, you're wife and Henry.'

'And not forgetting Stuart.'

'No, of course; and Stuart.'

'All set old son?' asked Busbeater as Gerald returned.

'All set Uncle. Henry will be there. And so will Stuart.'

'Stuart?' everyone asked at once.

Gerald raised his eyes to the ceiling 'His dog.'

'His dog is called Stuart?' asked Loosehorn incredulously.

'Yep' said Gerald.

'I doubt that will make it in to the history books.'

'Let's hope not.'

'Oh I don't know' cooed Marjorie, 'it's quite a nice name ...'

Cornelius could see this unravelling and so decided to refocus things.

'Right, OK so everyone's rehearsed? Jeff, Imre and Hector are on their way?'

'Yes, I asked Farnsbarnes to fetch them,' replied Gerald.

'The king was happy with that?'

'He was.'

'Amazing. You are a unique young man' marvelled Cornelius.

'I am the product of my family' said Gerald proudly looking at Busbeater, Marjorie, and also Loosehorn and Sheepshanks. 'Has anyone got any paper? A pen?' Ordinarily and with ordinary people and under these circumstances such a question would be greeted with desultory patting of pockets and blank shrugs; but of course these were not ordinary people and before he knew it Sheepshanks had delivered both.

'Here you are young Gerald.'

Thank you Sheepshanks.

'I just need to adjust the lyrics of the song …' feverishly Gerald set to work. There wasn't much time left.

'What happens now?' asked Marjorie as Gerald finished with a flourish.

'We wait for the king's men to summon us,' replied Gerald.

At that moment came a loud rapping at the door.

'The king demands the presence of his players,' boomed the disembodied voice. Less boomingly and slightly more puzzled it continued, 'And I also have a couple of Hungarians in tights and some bloke called Jeff carrying a peculiar contraption out here saying they are part of the performance.'

Cornelius opened the door, 'Indeed they are, thank you.'

The huge soldier backed away and let Imre, Hector and Jeff in.

'Well done, come over and hear the plan' said Cornelius eagerly.

'We are honoured sirs to be part of such an intrepid band,' said Hector.

'Especially the man with flags up his sleeves,' added Imre.

'That is an impressive thing isn't it?' remarked Busbeater.

'OK gang, focus' said Cornelius not for the first or the last time.

'Come!' cried the king

Gerald led the way in to the king's chamber followed by Cornelius, Busbeater, Marjorie, Sheepshanks, Loosehorn, Imre, Hector and Jeff.

The king was sitting on a large chair inlayed with gold. The upholstery was crimson with yellow trim which matched the king's robe and gown.

'What do you think?' Standing up the king looked down at his clothes and spread his arms wide, 'I changed for the performance. Makes me look even more heroic and noble than this morning, if that's possible, doesn't it?' he announced. It wasn't really a question that begged any answer other than …

'Oh yes sire' said Gerald.

At John's feet was sprawled Stuart who was gently snoring next to a large bone. On a much smaller ordinary chair to John's left sat William Marshal who smiled at Gerald and Busbeater discretely. On the king's other side was archbishop Stephen Langton with Pandulf the Bishop Of Norwich further along. Then came the chronicler who would write up events as Gerald performed and who sat poised with quill and parchment. He looked a very dull man indeed.

Furthest away sat Queen Isabella and Henry.

Gerald stood at the front and introduced them all as:

'Busbeater's Magnificent Adventures In Time!'

He bowed extravagantly. They all bowed extravagantly. Sheepshanks shouldn't have bowed extravagantly. He got stuck. The audience began muttering. Henry began to smile and then giggle at Sheepshanks and the desperate attempts of everyone to get him upright.

'No, ahh, er, no … aiieee, not there … er yes, no … ahh' Marjorie hit the spot and suddenly Sheepshanks pinged upright.

Gerald continued, 'For your pleasure we would like to perform for you today; "The Heroic King John Saves The Day and the Country".'

The audience murmured their vaguely interested approval. All but one. John stood up, clapped loudly and boomed, 'Yes, let's hear it for heroic ME and saving the day. I hope you're getting this down chronicler.'

The chronicler nodded nervously.

With the king's hollering, Stuart woke up with a start and began howling and barking excitedly, his tail wagging like mad smacking Marshal in the face quite a lot.

'Yes, woodgy woodgy woo; yes, it's your heroic master yes' cooed King John to his dog.

Loosehorn, Cornelius, Marjorie and Sheepshanks looked aghast and then at Busbeater and Gerald who shrugged their shoulders in a 'we know' kind of way.

'First' continued Gerald 'we would like to begin with a song.'

Henry looked expectantly at Gerald. This was already more fun than he'd ever had in his seven years 258 days, fifteen hours, twenty three minutes and fourteen, no fifteen, no sixteen seconds before. Queen Isabella looked on nervously. She didn't want her boy upset or disappointed any more.

The king, now getting quite excited yelled out 'Ooooo, is it the "I'm Against It" song? I hope it is. It's a belter,' he nudged Marshal and pointed to the troupe, 'It is; it's a real belter.'

'I am sure it is sire' said Marshal with no enthusiasm.

Gerald began tapping his feet, then started to click his fingers and looking at Jeff The Gaoler counted down;

'A-one, a-two, a-one, two three four; hit it!'

Jeff's hurdy-gurdy sprang in to action with Imre at his side cranking the handle. Sheepshanks struck his pose and stood stock still while at the back Cornelius who had had an hour to practice was dancing more confidently now but still rather like a crazed chicken. Hector was doing somersaults and whooping wildly in time to Jeff's music.

Standing behind Gerald, Busbeater, Marjorie and Loosehorn were all doing hand jives in unison while Marjorie's doo waps were timed to perfection.

At the front of these various performances Gerald stood with his back to the audience clicking the fingers of his left hand rhythmically. Then he spun around on his right heel, pointed to the king and began;

'I don't know what they have to say

It makes no difference anyway

Whatever it is, I'm against it!

No matter what it is

Or who commenced it

I'm against it'

Henry was tapping his foot and clapping wildly. He looked beseechingly at his mum. She looked uncertain until Gerald came over and took Henry by the hand and asked the Queen, 'May I?'

'Oh, go on then' relented Queen Isabella, her eyes welling up and a lump coming to her throat.

Gerald whisked Henry up to Marjorie, Loosehorn and Busbeater who showed him the hand jive which he got instantly.

'And again,' cried Gerald.

Jeff began the refrain once more and the verse was repeated. Young Henry started to copy some of Gerald's dance moves; side, together, side, together, back across, side, together whilst still doing the hand jives. He was a natural. He was laughing so hard his eyes were watering and Gerald was loving it. Queen Isabella's eyes were watering too; she cried and cried with happiness to see her son having so much fun.

Now for Gerald's rewritten verses. This was risky and might spoil everything, but with even the Bishop of Norwich, Langton and Marshal clapping along, Stuart the dog trying to join in and the king loving every minute they might get away with it; it had to be done. The honourable thing to do – to tell the truth.

'Today your proposition may be good

But let's have one thing understood and real

I'll renege on the deal!

As I am against it!

Because whatever it is, just like winning wars, I'm against it!

And though its all agreed I am sure

This charter I shall ignore

As I'm against it!'

No-one seemed to notice. They were going around again. Henry was laughing and chasing Cornelius around while Hector played out his acrobatic stunts to his absolute thrilled delight.

Marjorie, Busbeater and Loosehorn kept going but were anxious. It was time to escape.

The king suddenly called out, 'Stop! Stop I say.'

Everyone stopped. This was it. Henry was standing next to Gerald and squeezed his hand. Gerald leant over and quickly whispered in his ear 'You will be king sooner than you imagine. Be wise, listen to counsel. Marshal and Langton will see you right.'

King John pointed at his son, 'Get back to your mother boy! What do you look like child? You are the son of a king not a tomfool.' Henry returned to his mother. She mouthed 'thank you' to Gerald and Henry put up two thumbs.

John was suspicious, 'That's meant to be funny is it?' he asked

'What's that sire?' asked Gerald as innocently as he could manage.

'The stuff about winning wars?'

Uh oh thought Gerald suddenly going cold with fear; he'd overstepped the mark and put everyone in peril.

'I have been unlucky in my wars - you know that Gerald. I am disappointed.'

'It's a device sire,' chipped in Cornelius.

'A device?' the king asked, puzzled.

'You see in the song at the beginning we suggest for example ...'

Careful Cornelius thought Gerald.

' ... that you don't like winning wars which makes the audience think that you prefer it that way ... '

'But?' said the king both menacingly and encouragingly but generally suspiciously.

'But then in the play we act out how outrageous your fortune has been by being let down by incompetent oafs and general buffoons. That it's not your fault. That you are in fact heroic. We set up the story making you seem even more noble, if sire that is possible.'

Well done Cornelius, well done! muttered Gerald to himself.

'Hmm, OK. Well lets get on to that bit now shall we?'

Gerald was amazed he'd missed the bit about welching on the deal struck today. He hoped the chronicler hadn't. Marshal certainly seemed to have noticed ...

'Interesting lines there Gerald. Is there something I should be aware of?' he asked quietly as the king retreated to his chair to await the bit where everyone says how great he is.

'You know the king better than I sire. You know he doesn't always follow up on promises.'

Marshal looked at Gerald, 'You are wise beyond your years young man. Thank you for the, er tip off.'

Gerald whispered, 'sir, forgive me but I know that soon you will not only save the day, but the country. Be ready to travel to Lincoln sir. And don't forget your helmet.'

'What the ...? Young man, what do you ...?'

The king was getting increasingly impatient for the good bit and before William could interrogate Gerald further John blurted out, 'Come on, come on lets get to the interesting part. Chronicler is your quill at the ready?'

'It is indeed sire,' said the nervous noter.

John went on 'There'll be loads about how brilliant I am. So I hope you have enough ink. Oh and make sure you get the bit in about Robin Who ... that's very funny. By me.'

'Robin, er, who sire?'

'Precisely' answered the king not very helpfully.

Gerald got ready to speak again. He felt they had Done The Right Thing. They had shown Henry what it was like to have a good time in what to Gerald's mind looked like a sad and lonely life and they had very subtly managed to expose the king's true motives and possibly saved themselves. Now the next bit; escape.

'Sire, we now move on to the main attraction. The play called The Heroic King John Saves The Day and Saves The Country.'

'About time' blurted John starting to cheer up now. The best bit was finally coming.

'We will need a moment to change. We will withdraw to our props cabinet and be with you before you know it,' said Gerald.

'OK, but hurry!'

Cornelius, Sheepshanks, Marjorie, Busbeater, Loosehorn and Gerald walked briskly towards the room which lay behind a big, heavy purple curtain where The Wardrobe was waiting.

Cornelius surveyed the room. By jingo it was small. The Wardrobe only just fitted in it in its current size.

'When The Wardrobe expands, it's going to be tight' he worried out loud.

'We have no choice. It's now or never,' said Gerald.

Imre, Hector and Jeff followed them in to the room.

'What should we do? How can we help?' asked Imre.

'You have done enough already, thank you,' replied Gerald, 'You must get away through the back door there' he pointed to their escape route.

'Thank you. You are a noble and heroic young man,' said Hector. He then looked at all of them. 'I don't know who the heck you all are but we owe you a great debt; and you madam,' Hector and Imre looked straight at Marjorie, 'saved our lives.' They both bowed. Standing upright once more Hector addressed the whole gang, 'You are all truly magnificent. We will never forget what you did for us.'

Cornelius looked alarmed 'Do try to forget us Hector. We were never here.'

'As good as forgotten sir,' assured Hector.

'What do I do?' asked Jeff suddenly feeling a bit lost and looking longingly at Marjorie

'Why Gaoler; travel with us,' suggested Imre, 'We need your music as this performance demonstrated.'

Jeff look startled 'You mean travel outside. In daylight and all that? With people? Friends?'

'Indeed. You might even occasionally have a bath' encouraged Marjorie.

Jeff smiled, 'Then count me in.'

'What's going on in there?' bellowed the king, 'Get a move on!'

'We have to go' said Loosehorn, 'come on!'

'One final thing' said Cornelius, 'If you find yourselves in Long Sutton on 12 October next year, we might need your help again.'

Imre and Hector looked at each other and Jeff nodded 'We shall be there.'

'Fantastic. Wait for us,' said Gerald 'Now go …'

Imre, Hector and Jeff fled.

Everyone else was in The Wardrobe.

'Come on Gerald,' beseeched Marjorie.

With a final 'farewell!' Gerald leapt in. He dived in to his knapsack and took out the flywheel placing it in the socket. Cornelius withdrew the panel and with a feverish twiddle of the dials spelt out Long Sutton; October 12th 1216.

Gerald turned the flywheel to the left slowly, agonisingly slowly until he heard and felt it click.

He then turned it quickly to the right.

The Wardrobe's doors slammed shut as it shuddered in to life. It immediately began expanding making a terrific racket crashing in to the wooden beams and stone walls of the small room.

'Yikes Cornelius, is it going to make it?' asked Gerald above the terrible screeching and scraping noises.

Cornelius didn't answer but his worried face said all Gerald needed to know; it might not.

For what felt like a lifetime The Wardrobe groaned and vibrated violently as it struggled to break free. Everyone was hanging on to whatever they could to steady themselves. Gerald found himself swinging from one of Loosehorn's pale blue ball gowns.

'Sorry Loosehorn!' called Gerald.

From somewhere deep amongst the mink stoles at the back Loosehorn bellowed his reply, 'Don't worry old son. Just hang on!'

'Oh Busbeater, are we going to make it?' asked Marjorie clinging on to her husband for dear life.

'Of course old girl' said Busbeater not convinced.

Then suddenly all was silent. The shock of the new quiet sent everyone crashing to the floor. They had made it. They had escaped.

King John was getting impatient, 'What's going on in there? Get a move on!'

He turned to his dog, 'Odds bodkins Stuart, what could be taking so long? All that murmuring and no action - it's very suspicious.'

Then suddenly there was a terrific racket. A sound of splintering wood and crashing stone …

'What the …?'

The king got up and a little afraid of the infernal noises coming from the small room approached the curtain gingerly. Behind him Marshal and Langton stood puzzled and a little scared themselves. Langton was muttering prayers to himself while Marshal wondered if this really was The End Of Days. At the very back stood the chronicler physically shaking with fear. His mother had warned him there'd be days like these.

John didn't fancy going in first, 'Chronicler, see what's making the diabolical din.'

'Me sire?' said the terrified chronicler 'go in there?'

'Do you see any other chroniclers hereabouts?' yelled John.

The chronicler nervously put his quill and parchment down and carefully approached the curtain. With one arm outstretched while standing as far away as he could he grasped the corner of the curtain and yanked it open. He then closed his eyes and threw himself to the floor, landing on the king who was already there.

Silence.

The king stood up, much braver now the racket had stopped and brushing the blubbing chronicler to one side he pulled the curtain fully back. The door at the back of the room was swinging open on its hinges. Otherwise all was quiet and very empty.

'By the great hounds of hell! What sorcery is this? Where are they?'

There was nothing in the room at all. Nowhere to hide.

'They've gone sire' offered Langton.

'Well I can see they've gone Langton you utter idiot,' bellowed the king. 'Gone where and how are the questions. How did they get that wardrobe through this door?' He ran to the door just in time to see Imre, Hector and Jeff the Gaoler vanishing at a gallop out of the castle grounds.

John stood stock still purple with frustrated fury, 'I have been duped by a bunch of players!' He turned to the chronicler, 'If you value your miserable little life chronicler, don't write any of this down.'

The chronicler stamped on his quill to demonstrate his very willing readiness to have nothing to do with any of it.

Standing apart by the open curtain Henry looked on and smiled a very broad smile.

CHAPTER FOURTEEN

Off To The Right Time

Everyone sat still for a moment.

'We made it then' said Marjorie, massively relieved.

'We did' replied Cornelius.

'Now what?' asked Loosehorn.

'Now we have to do what we actually set out to do.'

'Before we went to the wrong place?' asked Gerald.

'Yes, before we accidentally landed in the middle of the Magna Carta negotiations' said Cornelius more than a little aware that much of that was probably his fault. 'Sorry' he added.

'So we aren't out of the woods yet then?' asked Busbeater.

'No. We remain very much in them.'

'What's the plan?' asked Gerald the Adventurer.

'In October 1216 the story goes that King John loses the nation's treasure in The Wash as he fled the civil war and pursuing armies of the Dauphin Louis,' explained Cornelius.

'Is this because he welches on Magna Carta?' asked Gerald.

'What?!' exclaimed Loosehorn 'He what?!'

'Calm down Loosehorn old man,' said Busbeater who was over his fury but knew this moment had to come.

'What a bounder, a cad … a mountebank. He agreed the thing and what he then reneges on the deal? I thought your lyrics were a bit near the mark Gerald old man but it was all true!?' Loosehorn fumed.

'Yes,' replied Gerald, 'he told us he was going to write to Pope Innocent III and give a biased account of what happened so that the pope would then overrule it and annul it.'

'And that actually happened?' asked Loosehorn pink with fury.

'It did,' replied Gerald holding the Boys Book Of Adventures which was confirming all that had happened.

'So the civil war continued?' added Marjorie perceptively.

Gerald consulted the book again just to be sure 'Yes and the barons recruited the French king's son to help them fight John. So by October he is being pursued across The Wash on his way to Lincolnshire after months of fighting.'

'What's this got to do with us Cornelius? What's our job here?' asked Loosehorn already looking forward to the next adventure and determined to clout John round the chops for being a cad.

'The king's treasures are in a wardrobe …' before he could finish Loosehorn finished it for him.

'And that might be the fifth time machine?'

'It is rumoured to be so. Cartwright and Carruthers have information.'

'They aren't terribly reliable though are they?' noted Marjorie.

Cornelius smiled 'They have good days and bad days Marjorie.' He continued 'they have information that this might indeed be the fifth machine. So we have to investigate.'

'Will The Baron be there?'

'Very possibly.'

'And the king?' added Busbeater 'He's going to be pretty cross if he sees us again.'

'He's always cross. Anyway, if he is he might not remember us. It will be over a year since he saw us' added Marjorie hopefully.

'It's seems unlikely,' said Busbeater quietly, 'The last day or two are days not easily forgotten. He will remember sure enough when he claps eyes on us.'

'I jolly well hope he is,' added Loosehorn, 'I want to give him a piece of my mind.'

Gerald was reading the Big Book; 'It says here that the king wasn't with the royal train when it sank.'

'Really?' asked Busbeater brightening.

'Rats' said Loosehorn darkening.

'Wait, hang on there's more …' Gerald read the unfolding pages to himself for a moment.

'It says here that no-one knows for sure if he was with it or not.'

Busbeater was now confused, 'So he still might be there?'

Loosehorn looked slightly more cheery at this latest prospect.

'He might' said Gerald looking up from the Big Book. For the first time the book was being less than helpful. Gerald's brow furrowed further.

Busbeater saw it 'What now?'

'Well the various chroniclers of the event apparently don't agree on what happened or even where it happened.'

'But we are heading somewhere now aren't we?' Busbeater looked at the panel 'Long Sutton?'

'That's one of the possible places ...' read Gerald aloud.

'One ... of ... the ... *possible* ... places?' repeated Busbeater slowly looking at Cornelius.

'So we might actually be going to the wrong place again?' he added.

Cornelius knew what he was about to say wasn't going to help in any way whatsoever, 'Cartwright and Carruthers were pretty sure ...'

'Er Cornelius,' interrupted Busbeater 'they didn't know *when* it happened - they sent us wrongly in to massive peril if you remember. Why do we think they know where?'

'Well, they must get it right occasionally' said Marjorie brightly.

'Let's hope this is one of those times' said Loosehorn not convinced it would be.

Gerald was reading more, 'There seem to be three options ...'

Loosehorn interrupted, 'It strikes me we should just use the book to find our way around.'

'It doesn't know where the machines might be' corrected Cornelius 'it can only tell us about what happened in the places where we land.'

'Or are going to ...' said Marjorie 'How does it do that?'

Cornelius wondered if this next bit would make any sense, but he gave it a go anyway. 'It picks up a signal from the panel, processes it and generates the history of the time.'

'Er ...' said Marjorie.

'What?!' burst Busbeater.

'Picks it up? You mean like gives it a lift?' wondered Loosehorn desperately.

Sheepshanks kept quiet. When out of one's depth it doesn't do to flail around.

'Gives it a lift?' flailed Busbeater 'What does that mean Loosehorn?'

'No idea old man. Just trying to make sense of Cornelius' gobbledegook.'

Cornelius gave it one more go. 'It intercepts the signal on radio waves generated by the panel and using the stated date and destination, searches its files and generates the right history.'

'Like a wireless?' asked Marjorie picking up on the only bit of that sentence she understood which was 'radio.'

'Yes, it's wire-less' replied Cornelius not quite getting what Marjorie meant.

'Ahh' said Marjorie, none the wiser.

'Hmm, OK' said Loosehorn not OK with it at all.

Gerald meanwhile had been reading the book; 'Anyway,' he said dragging things back to the point, 'it happened - probably - either in an area between Tydd Gote and Walpole.'

'Are you just making these places up Gerald?' chortled Busbeater.

'Just readin' em Uncle,' replied Gerald smiling, 'or Walsokes or Wisbech.'

'Ahh, now I know Wisbech,' said Busbeater.

'Or across the estuary from Cross Keys to Long Sutton.'

'The place where we are going?' asked Marjorie.

'Yes' said Cornelius.

'Fingers crossed then.'

Just then the machine landed with a gentle thunk.

'Well, we are here, if here is the right place,' said Marjorie.

Loosehorn was relieved. 'Thank Auntie Cecilia's trousers for that' he said oddly 'now we can get on with this mission and stop talking about wire-less-ness and related flummery.'

'Agreed' said Busbeater ' Let's sort this thing out.'

Marjorie looked at her husband and old friend. The two were fired up, no doubt about it and her heart swelled with pride and not a little fear. They had the scent of battle in their nostrils for the first time since Ishmaelia and were raring to go. She hoped they remembered they weren't twenty five any more. But it was rather marvellous to see them so eager for something other than shooting rabbits, the Test Match or what was for breakfast. They seemed so much more alive.

The doors of The Wardrobe flung open. And unlike last time there were no guards with long pikes ready to arrest them. Instead they ventured out on to a deserted and very different landscape from the luscious meadows and verdant woods of Runnymede.

'This doesn't look awfully promising Cornelius,' observed Busbeater looking out across a bleak and empty landscape.

The area known as The Wash in Eastern England had been reclaimed from the sea by the Romans but after they left and up until William The Conquerer's time the sea had been allowed to take it back. Then about 100 years before the intrepid band arrived in their time machine to save the day, landowners and peasants began the process again. And now as Busbeater looked out to the north east from near the village of Long Sutton where they had landed, the sea was slowly being driven back. The coast was still a little close for comfort for some of the villages so they built walls as protection along which watchman kept an eye out for the oncoming tides. Beyond the walls the land looked generally very muddy. Behind him in contrast the peaty fenlands were gradually being drained to be replaced by grassland upon which sheep were wandering and grazing about the place.

Cornelius was more positive

'Actually Busbeater old man I think this might be exactly the right kind of place.'

'What makes you say that?' Asked Busbeater 'It seems to me no-one in their right minds would cut across … ahh, maybe I see your point.'

'Well,' continued Cornelius 'it's not quite so much that King John was likely to think carting the national treasure across such unstable land was a good idea …'

'Quite likely though' said Loosehorn.

'Yes, probably' agreed Cornelius ' but this is exactly the kind of place where if you were mad enough to do that a whacking great wardrobe full of jewels and the like would sink pretty quickly.'

Gerald held the book and was reading, 'It says here that one of the most likely causes of the accident was quicksand.'

Standing next to Busbeater he looked out seaward and it indeed seemed very boggy indeed.

'Where is Cross Keys?' asked Loosehorn starting to look a bit military-ish.

'Hold on' said Gerald 'the book is producing a map.'

'That's quite a thing' admired Marjorie.

Gerald stood with the book flat out in front of him, 'OK, well, the map has a dot saying where we are.'

'How does it know?' asked Marjorie.

Loosehorn interjected before Cornelius could start one of his lunatic explanations. He was determined to keep any more distracting wire-less gobbledegook out of the equation.

'The book is a clever device Marjorie and so long as it continues to work, I am not all that bothered knowing how it does it.'

Marjorie looked a little crestfallen, but agreed, 'Sorry Loosehorn.'

Major General Loosehorn went on 'Nothing to be sorry about Marjorie old girl. Your natural curiosity does you credit but right now, if we are to intercept the king's train we need to know the lie of the land.'

Everyone looked at Loosehorn. Busbeater, Marjorie and Sheepshanks could see the warrior of old re-emerging. Gerald could only think of the man he first saw in a dress shooting wildly at rabbits from the roof, and missing, and wondering where he'd gone. And Cornelius looked on most admiringly of all. He had developed a great deal of respect for Busbeater and Marjorie especially and puzzled admiration for Sheepshanks while Gerald simply grew in stature with each passing moment. But Loosehorn and he hadn't quite seen eye to eye and if he was being honest Cornelius thought him the true booby of the group. But now he could begin to see the value of the man who looked alarmingly like General Custer in a dress.

'Right' said Loosehorn 'where in relation to us is Cross Keys Gerald?'

Gerald pointed to the right 'So, south east?'

'er ... ' Gerald wished he'd paid more attention in geography lessons now; 'yes?' he answered gingerly,

'Spiffing. And Long Sutton?'

Gerald pointed to his left slightly behind him,

'So north west from here. So where are we, precisely Gerald old son?'

Gerald studied the map to be extra sure. He wanted to impress his godfather, 'Sutton Bridge' he said assertively.

'Splendid. Does that thing do distances?'

It did. It revealed that they were standing three miles from Long Sutton in one direction and just over two miles to Cross Keys in the other.

'As the crow flies I take it Gerald?'

234

'As the crow flies sir.' Gerald just called Loosehorn 'sir'; he had suddenly become that impressive.

'Splendid. So we are pretty much smack in the middle so if the king's train comes along these parts, we'll definitely see it.'

'We should do,' replied Gerald, 'it was pretty big. There were a lot of men and horses and pack animals.'

Busbeater joined Loosehorn who was scanning the horizon, 'Ready? You look ready Loosehorn old chap. Not looked readier since the old days.'

'I AM ready Busbeater. You?'

'Readier than ever.' They turned to the rest of the gang.

Busbeater suggested the plan.

'So we know the king's wardrobe is part of a very large train making its way to …?'

He looked to Gerald 'Somewhere called Swineshead. There's an Abbey there.'

'And come from?'

'King's Lynn,' read Gerald 'Although it was called Bishop's Lynn then. King John was ill there apparently but pressed on regardless.'

'So he was in a hurry. That might explain the harebrained scheme to drive through the mud' mused Busbeater.

'Although it's likely he went separately in a different way' added Gerald .

'We'll soon find out I suppose,' said Cornelius.

'Those other places you mentioned Gerald …' Loosehorn wondered, figuring that the more information they had, the better off they'd be.

'Walsokes, Wisbech, Walpole and Tydd Gote?' repeated Gerald.

'That's them. Are they far?'

'Walpole and Tydd Gote are the closest, just over two miles that way' he pointed behind him over his left shoulder. 'Wisbech and Walsokes six miles thataway' he pointed over his right.

Loosehorn looked about him, 'OK, well we are in a reasonable position for all but Wisbech and Walsokes. There are quite a few big drawbacks; first there are six of us and likely to be thousands of them; second even though two miles isn't much we really could do with horses and thirdly we have no weapons to speak off save for what's likely to be in Sheepshanks pockets. This is going to be awkward.'

Cornelius added a further perhaps much bigger drawback, 'And of course The Baron may well be here somewhere,' he quickly scanned around, 'and if the king's wardrobe really is the fifth machine we'll need to get to it before The Baron and if it isn't we need to protect ours from him.'

Everyone murmured their agreement. The Baron - of course; in all the adventuring they'd almost forgotten about him. This was another hefty challenge indeed.

'Sir, If I may?'

'What is it Sheepshanks?' asked Loosehorn.

'We have company.'

Sheepshanks was standing on a small mound and with his telescope had been peering in a westerly direction across the grassland.

Loosehorn and Busbeater joined him. The mound was not big enough for all three of them and they wobbled for a few moments before clinging on to each other which made it worse.

'Maybe one at a time would be better' suggested Busbeater in a wobbly way.

'Oooooof.' With a thump Sheepshanks fell off first before Loosehorn retreated in an ungainly way.

'Hand me the telescope Sheepshanks will you old man?' asked Busbeater.

He peered through the lens, 'I say' he said 'Oh, I say, I say, I say.'

'Is it The Baron?' asked Cornelius anxiously.

'Let me see Busbeater' demanded Loosehorn trying to scramble up the mound, grabbing hold of Busbeater as he did so.

'Get off! ... no wait, you have a look I'll ... ooooof, ouch,' Busbeater tumbled to the ground as Loosehorn peered to look through the telescope.

'Oh, I say. I say, I say, I say.'

'What!' exclaimed Cornelius, then more calmly added 'do you see gentlemen?'

'Imre, Hector and Jeff.'

'Three of them? That's great but not worth getting that excited about' replied Cornelius at least relieved it wasn't The Baron.

'Well they are here. They said they would be and they are' butted in Marjorie a little defensively.

Loosehorn beckoned Cornelius over, 'Take a look through this. Rather more than three I think.'

Cornelius scrambled to the top of the mound with the help of Loosehorn's gown and peered out, 'Oh, I say. I say, I say, I say.'

'What?' asked Gerald and Marjorie together.

'There are hundreds of them Marjorie,' said Busbeater proudly, 'Imre, Hector and Jeff are at the head of hundreds of men on foot and horseback.'

At that moment Gerald could see with his naked eye what looked at first like a sort of dark mist drifting across the fens but soon discernible figures emerged. Figures of men and horses, dozens, no hundreds of them.

'Oh I say. I say, I say, I say' cooed Marjorie.

'Sorry we are a bit late,' began Hector apologetically 'we camped in and around Long Sutton for the night and were expecting you there. But our scout here,' Hector revealed a scruffy dark haired boy of roughly Gerald's age, 'said he saw you lot arrive here.'

'Out of nowhere sir. It was like magic' said the boy still a little afraid of the odd people standing in front of him.

Cornelius spoke first, 'No need to apologise Hector. It is damned fine to see you and ...' he looked at the gathering horde, 'Your impressive battalion. Our, er, ship deposited us at Bishop's Lynn a little late and this was as far as we got before nightfall, so made camp here.'

Cornelius wondered to himself why they hadn't landed at Long Sutton. He glanced at The Wardrobe sitting incongruously in the flat fenland. He pondered for a moment; sometimes it's as if that machine knows more than it lets on.

'A rough and ready place to make camp for sure' said Hector looking about him at the bleak landscape. 'Never mind, we are together now.'

'Who is everyone?' asked Busbeater still slightly amazed.

Hector sat on his horse looking very proud. He said he would help and help he would. He explained what had happened after they all left Windsor Castle.

He, Imre and Jeff had escaped Windsor and after some time laying low had gone on the road. They told their story of the brave Gerald, noble Busbeater, fearless Loosehorn, mysterious Sheepshanks, determined Cornelius and graceful and heroic Marjorie as they moved about the country.

'Not your real names obviously' said Hector spotting Cornelius' alarmed expression. 'We used pseudonyms.'

'Was one of them Robin by any chance?' asked Gerald as innocently as he could.

'Why yes. We named your character Robin of the Hood. How did you guess?'

'Oh just a stab in the dark.' He replied. He wondered, but didn't ask, which one of them they'd named Maid Marion.

'And Mr Loosehorn's character we named Maid Marion' added Imre helpfully. Everyone looked rather startled.

Hector continued telling his story.

It transpired that as the months passed their reputation grew and soon crowds of some thousands waited for them in towns and villages across the land. The stunt archery was going well and Jeff's hurdy-gurdy playing was now extremely skilful. He had even learnt a couple of stunt archery moves. As they went along they picked up more and more players and acrobats who wanted to be part of the troupe. Soldiers who had fought in King Richard's Crusades as well as sons of those who had fallen at the king's side joined as security. Before they knew where they were they had dozens and dozens of men and women ready willing and able to help the people who had saved Hector, Imre and Jeff's lives. Three days before they had left Nottingham heading for Long Sutton to rendezvous with their friends.

'We were a bit worried that maybe you had been recaptured and killed. For it was as if you vanished.'

'We ran very quickly,' said Gerald quickly.

'But with your props cabinet still? It's a miracle how you carry that with you and with no pack animals. Where have you been all this time? It is odd that we have not come across you on our travels,' continued Hector.

'Er, ahh, we spent a of lot of time abroad. Spain mostly' guessed Loosehorn.

'Ahh, of course. With the Moors' replied Hector.

'The Moores? Who might Mr and Mrs Moore be?' wondered Loosehorn.

'Yes, er that's right' Cornelius picked up the thread. 'We spent a year with the Moors in Spain. A truly remarkable time.'

'And lovely beaches' added Marjorie, not terribly helpfully.

There was a long pause. That was a true conversation stopper. Breaking the slightly awkward silence Hector said, 'But now we are together, what is your plan?'

Loosehorn walked to the front, 'This is an impressive gathering. Thank you Hector, Imre, Jeff. But we need to get organised and we haven't much time. Have you any military men with you?'

'Many of the crusaders had to leave us to defend their lands in this interminable civil war, but there are two men at arms here. You may recognise them.'

Charlie Farnsbarnes and Sergeant Day climbed down from their horses and moved to the front.

'Farnsbarnes!' exclaimed Gerald.

'At Windsor Castle you called me Mister. You bravely stood up to the king and are polite and noble. When I heard Hector and Imre were raising a horde to aid you, I felt honour-bound to help. I am at your service.'

'Welcome, welcome' said Cornelius and shook him warmly by the hand. Everyone joined in welcoming Farnsbarnes, making Day feel a little lost. No-one was quite so pleased to see him. Least of all Marjorie.

But he was here and seemed willing to help. Marjorie looked over to him and said,

'Sergeant Day. Forgive us for not being so fulsome in our welcome. But we didn't get off on the right foot.'

'No' replied Day. Looking at Sheepshanks he said 'but that man is a dead eye with the catapult and even though he put me right in the poo with his deadly aim, I thought a man like that is a good man to have on your side. And after years of listening to that thundering oaf Bott and marching hither and thither in one stupid military misadventure after another and then on hearing how he treated you … well I felt I should try and help if I could. And I am sorry I called you a crone.'

Marjorie moved toward him. Day cowered slightly fearful of what she might do. He was right to be fearful. She employed a full-on Marjorie hug.

'Welcome Day. Welcome.' She said.

'Hmmmmph' Day replied.

'What's your first name Day? We should know now we are on the same side,' asked Marjorie.

'Dmmmph' he replied.

'Pardon?' cooed Marjorie.

'Dmmmph!' he said more desperately this time.

'Er, let him breathe Marjorie' suggested Busbeater.

'Oh, sorry of course …'

Day retreated, a little pale and gasping for air. Raspingly he said, 'Dave. My name's Dave.'

'Dave?' said Gerald. 'Dave Day?'

'My parents weren't great, er, thinkers' said Dave Day.

'Apparently not' replied Gerald.

Imre muttered something to Jeff who in turn muttered something to his cohorts and before long after a bit of murmuring, three riderless horses were brought to the fore. A little apologetically Imre said, 'We only have three spare horses. We know that is not enough for all of you.'

Busbeater replied, 'This is dashed decent of you. I think three will suffice. Loosehorn, Cornelius and I should take one each. If necessary Gerald can ride with me, Marjorie with Loosehorn and Sheepshanks with Cornelius.'

Busbeater leapt on his horse and in much the same way Loosehorn did likewise. Cornelius also expertly and with equal élan mounted his.

From his tall chestnut coloured steed Busbeater addressed the assembled forces before him.

'Welcome,' he boomed 'We are all honoured that you have come here today to help.'

There was much whooping and hollering and arm waving in response to this. And at the back a donkey was flung in to the air.

Busbeater looked startled.

'Donkey Jugglers from Lower Saxony. Here to avenge their fallen comrades, executed on Bott's orders,' whispered Imre.

'Of course' whispered Busbeater in reply. More sonorously he continued on to the massed ranks, 'Today we form a new group. We are now Oddfellows of the 1st Foot and Horse Brigade of Ishmaelia!'

More hollering and whooping and general excitement.

'I am Lieutenant Colonel Busbeater, your Commander In Chief and this' Busbeater gestured to his right 'is Major General Loosehorn, my second in command. To my left is …'

He looked at Cornelius and quietly asked 'how should I announce you.

Have you rank?'

Cornelius looked straight in to Busbeater's eyes, 'Captain. Captain Cornelius Golightly of the 21st Lancers'

'The Empress of India's Lancers? From the Battle of Omdurman?'

'Yes sir.'

'By jove' replied Busbeater 'Churchill was there wasn't he?'

'Yes sir'

'We must talk …'

'Another time sir' said Cornelius nodding to the crowd.

'Ahh yes.'

After one last lingering glance at the increasingly mysterious Cornelius, Busbeater cranked up the booming again.

'To my left is Captain Cornelius Golightly.'

More general whooping. Loosehorn looked at Cornelius. Captain eh? he thought, impressed. Who is he?

Busbeater turned to Imre, Hector and Jeff.

'Would sergeant be OK?' he asked.

They all nodded enthusiastically.

'And here are Sergeants Imre er …'

'Nagy' prompted Imre Nagy 'and Hector is …'

'Hector Biro' said Hector.

'Biro? Really?' asked Busbeater.

'It's a fine and noble Magyar name sire' said Hector a little wounded.

'Yes it is, it's a splendid name' said Busbeater enthusiastically. Must try not to call him felt tip pen or something awful he thought. He began again.

'Sergeants Imre Nagy, Hector Biro,' he paused 'Jeff T Gaoler ...' Busbeater looked at Jeff with a quizzical expression as if to say 'that OK?'

Jeff nodded. It was as good as any. He'd never needed a surname before and in fact wasn't even sure he actually had one. Come to that Jeff had barely ever been used, so Jeff T Gaoler would do just fine.

Busbeater recapped and continued, 'These are my Sergeants' Imre Nagy, Hector Biro, Jeff T Gaoler, Dave Day and Charlie Farnsbarnes.'

Much more cheering and hollering and general excitement went on.

Busbeater continued; 'Our mission today is to intercept the king's train. Captain Golightly must, and this is very important, must be able to seize the king's wardrobe. It is our sole mission to make sure he gets to it and escapes. If you wish to mete out punishment ...'

At the word 'punishment' there was much cheering at the back and donkeys flung in to the air

'...on a particular foe, then do so, but only after Captain Golightly is clear of The Wardrobe. Is that perfectly understood?'

The Oddfellows Of The 1st Foot and Horse Brigade of Ishmaelia clattered their swords and shields together and hurled donkeys in the air and generally whooped their understanding and approval.

Busbeater sat tall with a straight back upon his horse and felt good. It was a long time since he had rallied the troops. Marjorie came up to his side, 'Proud of you Busbeater you old devil,' she said devotedly.

Busbeater looked down at his wife, 'Proud of you too Marjorie,' he said, eyes sparkling.

'Well done old man' called Loosehorn.

'Brilliant work' said Gerald proudly.

Cornelius was about to add his praise when from behind them, a familiar voice sent a chill through to his very core.

'Zo Golightly. Ve meet again.'

Yikes, thought Gerald, it's The Baron!

CHAPTER FIFTEEN

A Courageous Hero Saves The Day

Baron von Achtung sat nonchalantly upon his large white horse about fifty yards from them. He was leaning forwards against his saddle.

He travels with his horse, thought Gerald. *It's a time traveling horse!*

The Baron surveyed the general scene contemptuously and then revealed his surprise. Sitting upright he raised his arm and with an amused grin dancing across his face he said, 'Zis is my Captain. I zink maybe you haff met before.'

Marjorie gave a scream of horror, 'Bott!'

'Yes, crone. It is I. Thought you'd leave me alone to rot in that cell did you?' Captain Hieronymus Bott emerged from behind The Baron and began to move toward them.

'Yess,' hissed The Baron, 'Bott and I met some time ago. Just after you left ze castle in my machine' his voiced screeched the last few words.

Busbeater made a move toward The Baron. But Bott was too quick and suddenly seized Gerald.

'Nobody move or the boy gets it!' Bott yelled.

'Oh mercy me!' wailed Marjorie. 'If you harm a single hair on that boy's head I swear I will …' she stopped.

'Will what crone? Give me one of your hugs?' Bott sneered. 'I am ready for you now and you won't find it so easy to thwack me on the nose.'

Busbeater walked his horse slowly toward Bott, 'No. I will deal with you …' said the Lieutenant Colonel.

Bott gulped.

And pointing to the Oddfellows, Hector added, 'And then this lot will.'

Cornelius saw this was getting very dangerous. He knew The Baron best and knew more than anything he wanted some time to show off just how clever he was. He was also perfectly capable of hurting Gerald and not caring at jot about it.

'OK, OK. Calm down everyone. Bott, let Gerald go, we won't attack you,' said Cornelius as soothingly as he could.

The Baron guffawed, 'Har har har. You are very funny Golightly. I give up ze boy and vot, we all play tiddlyvinks or something? I don't zink zo. No, he stays vis us until I retrieve the king's vardrobe and zen take my vardrobe back from you, now zat I have ze boy and ze flyvheel in his bag. But first, I must show you how much cleverer zan you I am.'

He turned to his fawning Captain and asked 'Vere vas I Bott?'

'Rescuing me, sire from the cell in Windsor Castle, sire' said Bott simperingly.

Marjorie looked beseechingly at Gerald.

Gerald was clinging on to his knapsack. He knew The Baron and Bott wanted this more than they wanted him. But he also knew he had hundreds of allies. His plan was to stay very still and give his comrades a chance. He needed to give them as much time as possible.

Cornelius was thinking along similar lines. If he could keep The Baron talking, they'd have time to think of a plan.

'So Baron. How did you find us?' he asked.

'Ah vell, zat iss a most interesting story …'

Cornelius smiled to himself. The Baron had taken the bait. He'd probably talk for ages and ages now, keen to show off how clever he was. Sure enough, The Baron was continuing; 'I vos struggling a bit I admit ven I came upon your very own Mrs Bunyon who vos was very helpful.'

'Our cook!' interrupted Marjorie horrified at what she imagined was to come 'What have you done? Have you hurt her?' This was all too much.

The Baron laughed a very long and villainous laugh.

Gerald with Bott's arm around his neck thought to himself that maybe the cook wasn't the priority right there and then.

The Baron eventually stopped guffawing and said; 'Hurt her? Hurt her? My vord you don't know your staff very vell do you? Mrs Bunyon vos my spy. How else did you zink I found grubby old Busbeater Mansions? I had tracked the fourth machine down to somevhere near ze town of Oakham, but vos losing patience and vos running out of ideas. Von day I vas in ze pub vondering vot to do next ven I start talking to zis chap. He vos a little drunk I zink, and irritating at first. Vos I going to a fancy dress party dressed like zis he asked repeatedly – I mean, I ask you do I look like I am going to ze fancy dress party?' throwing his arms out in a grand rhetorical gesture he looked around him quizzically.

Amongst The Oddfellows Of The 1st Foot and Horse Brigade of Ishmaelia there was much murmuring along the lines of actually yes, he did rather.

'Silence!' screamed Bott.

'What a creep' thought Gerald.

Bott squeezed Gerald's neck still tighter and whispered menacingly, 'Don't get any ideas boy. Or it'll be curtains for you …'

Yeah, yeah thought Gerald. He wasn't scared of Bott, but he did think what an old windbag The Baron was. Baron von Achtung Arch Villain? Baron von Windbag Arch Droner Onner more like. He just sounded like one of his teachers prattling on about how dangerous bunsen burners can be when you wave them about. Nobody ever listened, even after the chemistry lab was nearly burned down by someone waving a bunsen burner about. Gerald was all the time waiting for the moment that would surely come. When Cornelius and his uncle would enact a plan which would force Bott to loosen his grip.

Meanwhile Baron von Vindbag was droning on; 'Anyvay it seems zis drunk vos none ozzer zan Mr Nigel Bunyon. Ze 'usband of your very own Mrs Bunyon. Soon he vos telling me how 'is vife had been promised money by zese old codgers for some vardrobe or ozzer and zay had run off without handing over ze cash. You vill vell imagine ven he mentioned 'codgers' and 'vardobe' my ears pricked upvards. Vardobe? Codgers? Zen Mrs Bunyon came in to rescue her pitiful husband und soon started to tell me ze whole zorry story.'

Gerald wriggled under Bott's ever closer attentions. Bott struggled but clung on getting very irritated with his recalcitrant charge.

'What did I say boy? Don't try anything funny ...' he hissed.

'Pah, you wouldn't know something funny if it turned up with pipers and drummers playing a tune and announcing in loud voices how funny it was' retorted Gerald a little squeakily.

'Why you ...' Bott was fuming and close to losing control.

'Bott, Bott' said The Baron soothingly and yet menacingly 'Zere is no need. Ve vill soon haff vot ve require.'

Just then Marjorie felt a soft nudge in her back. She swiftly turned around expecting an enemy and was ready to lamp him when she saw a donkey, 'Oh' she whispered.

From behind the donkey emerged a donkey thrower from Lower Saxony.

'Oh' she whispered again followed by 'hello.'

'Madam Busbeater,' hissed the man ,'forgive me for bothering you.'

'Not at all, what is it?'

'The Baron' continued the man quietly.

'He is an old windbag isn't he?'

The donkey now nuzzled up close to Marjorie, 'Hello boy,' she cooed.

'It's a girl' corrected the Saxon.

'Oh, sorry.'

'Anyway, The Baron.'

'Ah yes, The Baron. What about him?'

'He isn't German.'

'What do you mean? He certainly sounds it.'

'That is the trouble; he sounds like a made up version. He is an impostor. No true born German would speak like this. It is ridiculous. He dishonours us with his tomfoolery. I wanted to tell you Madam as you and your troupe seem honourable fellows. But we want to be first in the queue to biff him around the noggin when it comes to it.'

'If, surely' said Marjorie.

'It will happen. Soon. We want to bring him down.'

Marjorie thought for a moment, 'I will make sure the boys know the plan.'

'Thank you madam' and with that he and the donkey retreated; the donkey looking resigned to its fate of being hurled about the place like so many donkeys before him and quite a few to come.

Marjorie pondered for a moment; Cornelius was pretty mysterious – in a mostly good way – but now its becoming apparent that even their new arch enemy isn't all he seems either. And he seems quite threatening. It's a rum do. What is going on? Where are these people from? Who on earth are they?

Meanwhile The Baron was, obviously, still droning on. Cornelius really was right; he really loved the sound of his own voice.

'Ven I arrived just too late Mrs Bunyon was hiding under ze bed. After much sobbing - not by me just to be clear, Mrs Bunyon said she thought she heard vone of you mention zis Magna Carta zing, or Magnum Catweazle as she called it; dimvit. Zo vonce I got back to my machine I zet ze course for Runnymede. I arrived just after ze agreement on zat piece of toilet paper you English get all zo vorked up about und discovered Bott languishing in his cell. He tells me everyzink as you vill be imagining. Zat you were here viz the barons, zat you performed for ze king, zat you annoyed him greatly and zen' he put his hand to his mouth and blowing in to it said 'you vanished. After vorking vis Bott for a few months and following ze king on his mad course charging through England fighting his civil var I learn of his vardrobe vis the treasures in it and I zink, like you, zat maybe zis is ze fifth machine! I should have known zose dummkopf detectives of yours vud get it wrong again - remember ze Austin Seven incident, har har har, zat vos very funny. Your face - it vos a picture. An Austin Seven!'

The Baron paused for a moment. Then recovering, continued 'zey zent you to ze wrong place a year early! Idiots. But anyvay, ve are here togezzer. It is such a pity Golightly zat you vill finally and fatally lose!'

Imre asked Cornelius what he was talking about. A fifth machine? Mrs Bunyon?

'It's complicated Imre. Best you don't know. Stick to the plan.'

'What's an Austin Seven?' piped up Hector innocently.

Cornelius looked pained.

'It's an old type of car ...'

'Car, what's a car?' Hector was confused.

Cornelius suddenly remembered he was in the thirteenth century, ' ...

er I mean a siege engine … that doesn't look anything like a wardrobe.'

'Of course not. A siege engine doesn't look anything like a wardrobe' added Hector with a snort.

'Quite' reflected Cornelius ruefully, remembering the whole Austin Seven catastrophe all over again. He shuddered at the thought.

Then at that very moment Hector's confusion and Cornelius' discomfort was diverted.

There was a small commotion from amongst The Oddfellows and through them came the same small boy from earlier. He whispered in Day's ear.

'Captain Cornelius sir' said Day very quietly

'Yes Day?'

'The watchmen on the seawalls report massive activity across the estuary between Cross Keys and Long Sutton. It is the royal train and its headed our way.'

'Thank you Day. Is the king with them?'

'No sire. His Standard is not flying.'

'Good.'

The Baron was still going on and on.

Cornelius whispered urgently in Busbeater's ear, 'The royal train, without the king, is heading right for us. We are in the right place. I await your orders.'

Busbeater nodded his understanding discretely looking at Loosehorn as he did so.

Loosehorn winked by reply. The game was a foot.

'Day, get everyone ready. We are about to go' ordered Cornelius softly but firmly.

'But the boy sir.'

'We'll take care of that. He'll be OK. Once the Lieutenant Colonel gives me the word I will order the charge.'

Busbeater looked behind him and smiled.

Cornelius decided enough was enough.

He interrupted the bombastic Baron in full flow.

'Von Achtung!'

'Ah yess Golightly. Are you vanting to hear more stories about how great I am? Or do you just vant to vatch me utterly defeat you?'

'No sir. Rather I wanted to help you. The royal train. Word has reached us that it is apparently traveling between Walpole and Wisbech six miles that way.' He pointed to his right.

'Vott!' The Baron turned furiously to his sidekick.

'You said it vos definitely coming through here Bott!'

'But sire, I was told … ' protested Bott.

'You idiot Bott, you idiot' snarled The Baron.

Gerald gulped. The Baron's expression as he bore his teeth was like a vicious attack dog and it made him suddenly look like the Arch Villain of Cornelius' description and not the crazy old windbag of just now. Gerald now knew The Baron was a terrifying foe. His stomach mixed up his pants and big blue woolly jumper again. Being an adventurer was exciting and terribly nerve wracking all at the same time. But Gerald knew that something was afoot. The gang were about to act …

Busbeater nodded to Sheepshanks who from his rear guard grassy knoll produced his super size catapult and with extraordinary accuracy sent a large stone from a nearby wall clattering in to Bott's helmet sending him flying straight in to a cow pat. Gerald gleefully escaped from Bott's attentions and in to the arms of Marjorie.

That Baron fellow has never watched any James Bond films thought Sheepshanks as he continued to rain stones down on Bott and The Baron with fearsome accuracy.

The Baron, realising he'd been tricked and that the train was actually coming through behind him – he was furious that he had been duped so easily – turned and rode as fast as he could toward it. Stones ricocheted off his coat, his helmet, his back.

'Gott in himmel, zat smartz!' he bellowed as he accelerated away. A donkey landed with a thud beside him briefly causing his horse to rear up, 'Woah zere Copenhagen, woah!'

The Baron and his horse quickly recovered their poise and continued on at lightning speed. Bott struggled to his feet only to be felled again immediately this time by another flying donkey.

It was raining donkeys on Bott's head, 'Ow, oof, ow, I ,er, aiee … OW!'

Cornelius turned to Busbeater

'We must protect our rear; to protect our machine. But I must get to the king's wardrobe before The Baron and disable it if its the fifth machine I must overtake him.' He set off at a fearsome gallop.

Busbeater called his Oddfellows. They must protect their Wardrobe.

'Men! Men! The Sergeants only will ride with us to support Captain Cornelius. You must stay here and build a barricade around our Cabinet!' He couldn't tell them the real reason for that would be impossible to explain and really dangerous from a changing history and getting stuck in this scary place point of view. Inspired he carried on, 'It has vital state documents inside that The Baron must not get his hands on!'

The Oddfellows were disappointed for they wanted to charge, but they obeyed and began preparing the Defence of The Wardrobe.

Now the chase was on.

In hot pursuit of Cornelius and The Baron, Busbeater's steed ran past Gerald. Gerald answered the unasked question, 'You bet I do Uncle' and was swept up on to Busbeater's horse at full tilt.

'Oh be careful' wailed Marjorie, her left eye wildly out of control.

Next Loosehorn raced by, yellow ball gown flowing impressively behind him and was followed by the array of sergeants. Sheepshanks on foot also swept past Marjorie.

Meanwhile Bott was still staggering about, very dazed and surrounded by angry donkeys. Marjorie rubbed her hands together and with the Lower Saxony Donkey Jugglers marched toward him, encouraged by the braying of the revenge-seeking beasts of burden.

'Hurt my nephew and call me crone … again will you?' Marjorie said menacingly as she approached the disoriented Bott.

'Execute our cousins after they performed for the king eh?' cried the lead Donkey Juggler.

Bott smiled weakly, 'er … er …' he spluttered.

Busbeater and Gerald's horse was almost flying across the ground just behind Cornelius who in turn was just behind The Baron. Suddenly there was an almighty scream.

'Ahh. I think Marjorie has found Bott' said Busbeater, grimacing slightly.

Loosehorn's horse caught up and was soon alongside Busbeater. Gerald was slightly surprised to see Sheepshanks riding tandem with the Major General since he had last seen him on the grassy knoll at the back of everything catapulting very accurate stoney missiles. How had he caught up? Sheepshanks saluted Gerald. Gerald gave the thumbs up to

Sheepshanks, only just staying on the horse in the meantime.

'Hold on Gerald old son' said Busbeater spurring the horse on again.

'I can see the train. Looks like it's already going wrong for them' called Loosehorn.

Indeed it was. As they rode swiftly ever closer toward the royal train they could see it was already getting bogged down in quicksand. And it was massively long. Gerald thought it must be at least the length of four cricket grounds. 'Three if one of them is The Oval' suggested Busbeater.

The royal train consisted of pack animals laden with heavy looking bags, horses carrying men and pulling carts piled high with boxes and sacks while hundreds of soldiers walked briskly behind. They were clearly in a hurry and being reckless about it.

Busbeater and Loosehorn had nearly caught Cornelius and all three horses were spurred on for one last effort. The sergeants were a few yards behind.

Busbeater turned around, 'Sergeants! Stay with Captain Golightly. Make sure he gets to The Wardrobe safely and before The Baron!'

The sergeants whooped and pushed their horses on, speeding past Busbeater and Loosehorn catching up with Cornelius with each thunderous hoof.

As they approached the noise was fearful. Donkeys and horses whinnied and whined as they were pulled in to the quicksand. Men were shouting and screaming trying to save themselves, the royal treasure, the animals; anything. But they had travelled too fast across unstable ground. The momentum of this huge train was pushing animals, men and treasure in to the Wash. It was a frightening scene.

In the middle section stood The Wardrobe taller than any other item. Slowly, inexorably it was being dragged in to the mud.

The Baron arrived first pushing drowning men out of the way as he scrambled for The Wardrobe.

'Out of my vay!' he snarled.

Some fifty yards short Cornelius turned around to Loosehorn and Busbeater and shouted back at them.

'You stay; the sergeants and I will take it from here.'

'Carry on Cornelius. We are counting on you!' cried Busbeater above the infernal racket of this terrifying scene.

'We need you Captain Golightly!' called Loosehorn.

Cornelius accelerated heading directly for The Wardrobe with the sergeants right behind.

'Sheepshanks. You know what to do' said Loosehorn.

'Very much so' said a determined Sheepshanks. Steadily he dismounted, stood with his legs two feet apart and from his inside jacket pocket produced the biggest catapult Gerald had ever seen.

The Baron callously ignoring pleas for help from the doomed soldiers was within touching distance of The Wardrobe. Above the frightening din of terrified men and beasts came a faint whistle. It grew louder. The Baron turned and saw a very large stone heading straight for him.

'Aieeeee' he yelled as it clonked him squarely on the head stunning him for a few moments. Just long enough for Cornelius and the sergeants to gain the advantage. Sergeants Day, Farnsbarnes and Jeff T Gaoler, leapt from their horses while The Hungarians performed impressive somersaults landing directly on the prone Baron wrestling him on to firmer ground and crucially away from The Wardrobe.

'Go Captain!" cried Imre Nagy aboard The Baron's huge back.

The Baron was immensely strong; they wouldn't be able to hold him for long.

Cornelius leapt across the quicksand on to the listing wardrobe. He scrambled on, pulled the doors open and dived in.

Inside were crates of jewels and crowns and all manner of royal regalia. They were sliding about crashing heavily in to each other and The Wardrobe. One false move and Cornelius would be squashed. He had to get to the back of The Wardrobe. If it had a socket and/or a flywheel it was the legendary fifth machine. If not, it wasn't. At that moment the largest of all the crates began sliding inexorably toward him. With his back against the side of The Wardrobe, there seemed no escape. He would surely be crushed …

'Quickly Captain! We'll hold it for you' announced Hector and Imre who had left The Baron to Day, Farnsbarnes and Jeff T Gaoler.

'Thank you' said Cornelius very relieved. He scrambled over the crates and quickly inspected the back of The Wardrobe. He could see nothing. He pressed the palm of his hands against all the panels. Again, nothing. He thumped it as hard as his knuckles could bear. Again, nothing. It was just a wardrobe. Full of King John's treasures, but nonetheless just a wardrobe.

'Sir, we can't hold it much longer' Hector and Imre were struggling with the crate.

'Go men! Go. We are done here. Get back to the Oddfellows. The Baron will switch his attentions there.'

Meanwhile Loosehorn, Busbeater Gerald and Sheepshanks were looking on at the carnage of the accident happening before them.

'We can't let them die!' exclaimed Gerald.

'We can't change history Gerald' agonised Loosehorn.

'But no-one even knows where this happened or how many people and animals died!' beseeched Gerald.

He had a point.

'Come on Loosehorn. Let's Save The Day!' said Busbeater triumphantly.

Loosehorn, Busbeater, Gerald and Sheepshanks ran toward the unfolding disaster and spread out, pulling distraught men and petrified animals out of the mire.

After a few minutes of general saving, Gerald was pulling out a soldier who was even younger than himself when he heard a cry. He looked up. It was Cornelius.

'Come on Gerald. It's not the fifth machine.'

'But, no wait!' called Gerald, 'I must save ...'

'We've no time Gerald! The Baron is coming and we must get back to our machine.'

Busbeater, Loosehorn and Sheepshanks mounted their horses and on Cornelius' signal began to head off back to defend The Wardrobe.

'Gerald?!' cried Busbeater 'Come on, we must escape!'

The boy in Gerald's grasp was slipping back in to the quicksand.

'Don't let me drown sir' cried the boy.

'Cornelius, take the knapsack ... I will catch you up!' said Gerald, slightly scared but very determined.

Cornelius leant over and took the knapsack, 'Gerald. Come with me!' he pleaded.

'I must do the right thing' said Gerald, calmly 'and you must defend our Wardrobe. Don't let The Baron get the flywheel! We both need to do the right thing.'

Cornelius was utterly torn. Saving Gerald or stopping The Baron from seizing The Wardrobe; it truly was the Devil's alternative.

'Cornelius, Go! You need to save ... everyone' Gerald understood what was at stake. But he couldn't let the boy go, 'and you are wasting time.'

Cornelius set off; what a man Gerald was. What a man! he thought to himself ...

Gerald looked up at his vanishing comrades and then at the boy whose face was covered in grimy, slimy mud.

'Of course I won't let you drown you clot' he said and kept on pulling him. The quicksand was strong and wasn't giving up its prize easily. But Gerald kept pulling and pulling and suddenly, the boy was free ...

Just then charging after Cornelius The Baron leapt over the chaos, picked up Gerald with one hand and hurled him in to the quicksand without breaking stride.

'You pitiful little dolt!' he screamed.

Gerald's landing was soft but firm; he had been lucky and landed on some harder ground. But before he could get to his feet a flailing mule struggling to escape sent Gerald sprawling in to the quicksand.

'Oh, yikes and crikey' thought Gerald as he saw his uncle, Loosehorn, Cornelius, Sheepshanks and the Sergeants all vanishing with The Baron in wild pursuit.

Swiftly he began sinking. He'd read somewhere that it made it worse if you struggle. But lying still didn't seem to be making it much better. He was sinking faster and faster. He began to sniffle. 'Don't blub Gerald. Be brave ... be brave' he ordered himself.

He wanted his mum more than anything in the world right now, right now. The quicksand closed over the top of his sandy coloured hair.

He was gone.

'I don't think so Master Gerald' said Sheepshanks as he and Cornelius hauled him out of the mud. 'I very much do not think so!'

Gerald blinked and spluttered spitting mud and all sorts out of his mouth. 'Sheepshanks, Cornelius ... I thought you'd gone back with the rest.'

'We don't leave people behind Gerald,' said Sheepshanks matter-of-factly.

'And this chap helped' added Cornelius turning to the boy Gerald had saved.

Gerald prepared to thank him with an outstretched hand.

'Thank you' said the boy as he wiped the mud from his face.

Gerald was startled. He recognised him, 'Henry!'

'The thanks is all mine Gerald. Your Baron friend trampled me in to the mud in his villainous haste. You saved me. And England. Now, go. You must flee from this place.'

Cornelius said urgently, 'Henry, it is important we weren't here …'

Henry was puzzled for a moment. But they had saved his life and he remembered only too well the hilarious performance they had given for him over a year ago, although it was forbidden to talk of it in the royal household. He owed them a very great deal; there was no need for explanations.

'I will make sure none of you were here. I will tell a confusing story when we join the royal party in Swineshead. I am only nine, I can be vague and get away with it. But I am also the heir to the throne, so they will believe me. I'll say it happened at Wisbech or Tydd Gote. That will confuse everyone.'

'Come on sir. We must go.' said Sheepshanks

Gerald waved the future king of England goodbye.

'Be safe friends!' called Henry.

Cornelius grabbed his horse, 'Come on you two, on you get!'

'Sir, it will be quicker if you ride alone. I can carry Gerald.'

'No, come on Sheepshanks, the horse will be faster.'

'Not with three of us on his back. Cornelius, sir, I must insist!'

Cornelius, not entirely convinced nonetheless decided to trust Sheepshanks' judgement and agreed with one proviso.

'Then go! But I will linger behind and have your back.'

Sheepshanks picked up Gerald and began running unfeasibly fast leaving Cornelius behind.

'It really is quicker this way Master Gerald and you've had a nasty scare,' Gerald didn't argue.

As Sheepshanks sped like a gazelle across the soggy but increasingly firm ground Gerald asked him, 'Sheepshanks. Have I just changed history? Have I broken the machine?'

Gerald had saved King Henry; should he have let him die?

Belying the fact that he was going like the clappers Sheepshanks calmly replied, 'The way I see it Master Gerald . .allez ooop!'

He leapt a small wall and then continued ... 'The way I see it Master Gerald, it was The Baron who nearly changed history ... allez loop ... By saving the future king you made sure everything happened ... allez loop ... like it was supposed to. If The Baron had trampled Henry in to the mud and killed him, then he would not be king ... allez loop ... and everything would be different.'

'And The Wardrobe wouldn't work.'

'Exactly sir.'

Gerald closed his eyes and hoped against hope that Sheepshanks was right and that The Wardrobe was still working when they arrived.

'allez ooop ...'

As they closed in on The Wardrobe they saw The Baron fuming madly in front of a mighty barricade built of stone and pikes and mud by the Oddfellows with Marjorie standing on top brandishing - what was that - a donkey? Alongside her the whole horde hurled everything they had at him. But nothing seemed to hurt him for long; he fended off all that came his way. He was a frightening foe.

'Let me through. Zat vardobe is mine I tell you. It's mine!'

From atop the barricade Imre could see Sheepshanks hurtling at an unfeasible speed across the fens toward them. He knew he would never clear the barrier carrying Gerald. He looked at Hector, 'The old flip back switcheroo?' he suggested.

'There has never been a finer time for the old flip back switcheroo Imre' replied Hector.

'Cover me,' Imre got ready.

'Hey Mr So-Called Baron - you're flies are undone!' cried Hector.

Always the mature one thought Imre. It worked though.

'Vot? My flies ... I am sure I ...' he looked at his trousers puzzled and embarrassed.

'Har har! The gate is open but the lion is asleep!' cried the Oddfellows gleefully and as one.

Imre leapt down from the twenty foot high barricade and was in position. It was almost as if Sheepshanks knew exactly what to do. Sprinting toward Imre he crouched and with his right leg outstretched placed it straight in to the Hungarian's strong cupped hands.

'allez oooooop ...'

Imre lifted Sheepshanks high in to the air with the aid of a turbo charged back flip somersault. Still upright Sheepshanks passed serenely over the barricade and landed perfectly on his feet. Imre's standing start somersault also propelled him back over the barricade but he landed with less aplomb. He clattered in to the Lower Saxons' reserve donkeys.

The Baron looked up 'My flies, zay are not undone ... you svine, you tricked me!' The Baron had been duped. Again.

Marjorie ran to Gerald, 'Oh my look at you. You are back, thank the very goodness. You are all covered in mud … where have you been?'

'All is fine Marjorie, don't worry. Sheepshanks, Cornelius and I helped out one last person. All is well.'

Busbeater and Loosehorn were mightily relieved the rescue had worked, but as they stood behind Marjorie they silently beseeched him not to mention any sort of rescue that involved peril. Which it had. Lots and lots and very lots of peril.

Ten minutes earlier

As Busbeater, Loosehorn and Sheepshanks were racing back to The Wardrobe from the disaster of the sinking royal train, a desperate Cornelius had caught them up. He gave Busbeater the knapsack and flywheel and said, 'For all our sakes Busbeater, keep this safe.'

'Of course old man' Busbeater replied.

'Now all of you speed back to The Wardrobe! The Baron is close behind …' he cried.

Immediately Cornelius turned around and set off for Gerald; Sheepshanks instantly volunteered to go with him and help in the rescue.

Until they all flew serenely over the Oddfellow's barrier, neither Busbeater or Loosehorn were sure any of it had worked.

At that moment Cornelius and his horse hurdled the barricade and landed with a slight skittering motion. Cornelius leapt from the horse.

'How fast can you run?' he marvelled at Sheepshanks. 'I have never seen anything like it.'

'Should have seen him in '36. Now that was fast' added Loosehorn matter-of-factly but cryptically.

Cornelius slapped Sheepshanks on his shoulder, 'Well done man. Although it was touch and go!'

Busbeater and Loosehorn put their head in their hands.

'Touch and go!?' exclaimed Marjorie 'What happened Gerald!? Where were you? Why weren't you with the rest? Why are you covered in mud? What happened!?' Marjorie's eye was going wild as she imagined all manner of horrors.

'I'll explain later Auntie ... We have to go now ... er ... who's that up in the tree?'

'Oh, that's Bott dear' said a suddenly icy calm Marjorie.

'He seems to be wrapped in something' Gerald observed.

'Leaves and raw meat' replied Marjorie proudly.

'Oh right. Been there long?' asked Gerald.

'Since you left. The Oddfellows and I have been busy.'

She certainly had what with trussing up Bott and building a twenty foot tall barricade.

'Is Bott likely to come down at any point?' wondered Gerald.

'Not until the hungry birds have pecked him a few thousand times I'd say' replied Marjorie.

'Right oh' said Gerald for the first time properly scared of his Auntie.

'Let me through it iz mine I tell you, mine you svines!' came an unmistakable German accent from the other side of the barricade.

'The Baron still going on is he?' asked Cornelius.

' 'fraid so' said Imre from atop the barricade.

'Why don't we steal and break his machine Cornelius?' asked Loosehorn.

'He always hides it. I have never been able to track it down. And I have tried. It's as if he is in league with someone …' Cornelius knew that time was up 'We'd better go' he added urgently.

'Yes, we ought. But first …' Busbeater went over to the barricade

'Oddfellows!' he announced. 'Today you have done a great thing. It will never be recorded in the annals of history, at least not sensibly. You are amongst the many unknown warriors who shape our destiny. I salute you The Oddfellows Of The 1st Foot and Horse Brigade of Ishmaelia with our battle cry "Remember Ishmaelia!"'

'Remember Ishmaelia!' they cried in return and a few donkeys flew through the air, several of them hitting Bott. This new game would amuse the Lower Saxons no end for weeks to come.

'Come on chaps, quickly' said Cornelius anxious to get everyone away as fast as possible.

Imre, Hector, Jeff T, Dave and Charlie stood to attention, 'On behalf of us all, it was an honour to serve you sirs and madam' said Hector.

'The honour was all ours' said Busbeater.

Jeff T broke ranks and kissed Marjorie's hand.

'Ooo, you've had a bath sometime in the last year' she observed.

Jeff T winked, 'Thank you ma'am.'

'Come on will you, good gracious what a lot of goodbyes you lot insist on … er, doing' said Cornelius with a huge grin across his face.

Gerald looked urgently at Hector.

Hector understood and tapped the side of his nose.

'Mum's the word,' said Hector knowingly and smiling broadly, 'You are a magnificent young chap.'

'Thank you Hector. Thank all of you,' said Gerald.

'Come on young fellow m'lad' called Busbeater.

Gerald clambered aboard.

Busbeater gave the knapsack back to Gerald who took out the flywheel and placed it firmly in to the socket.

Cornelius dialled in the next destination.

Without looking at the panel Gerald turned the flywheel slowly to the left until it clicked and then swiftly to the right. The Wardrobe shuddered and then, 'It's mine I tell you … you svine … it's mine!'

'Odds crackers Golightly, it's The Baron!' exclaimed Busbeater.

The Baron had one foot in the door. Behind him The Oddfellows were grabbing and pulling. The Baron was immensely strong and seemed to be winning the tug of war.

Calmly Sheepshanks stood up, went over to the leg of The Baron which had followed his boot further in to The Wardrobe, produced the biggest metal rod you have ever seen hiding in someone's trouser leg and cracked it across The Baron's shin.

'Aiiieeeeeeee!' curdled The Baron and he fell out backwards in to the crowd of Oddfellows.

The Wardrobe doors slammed shut and it began expanding. Suddenly, all was quiet.

'Is that the end of The Baron Cornelius?' asked Gerald hopefully.

'I doubt it. He's survived worse I am afraid.'

'That is quite a shame' said Gerald.

'I say Cornelius,' said Busbeater, 'we off home now? Back home in time for the Test Match?'

'Not straightaway' said Cornelius.

'Oh bother' said Busbeater, but less disappointed than he sounded as he was rather enjoying this adventuring lark. 'Where to then?' he said wearing a distinct smirk; he was quite excited at the prospect of more derring-doing.

Cornelius revealed the panel.

'July 20 1969; the moon – the far side.'

CHAPTER SIXTEEN

Fly Me To The Moon And Then Home Please ...

Gerald looked at Cornelius.

'The far side of the Moon? July 20th 1969? The moon landing?'

Gerald was exhausted; he had out witted a tyrannical king, acted in an improvised musical, briefly been taken hostage, nearly drowned in quicksand, saved the future king and was covered in mud. Any ordinary young chap would just want to go home. But this was no ordinary young chap. This was Gerald Jones, The Boy Adventurer and son of Arnold Jones; and boy adventurers do not get tired. Not when they can land on the moon! Amongst quite a few exciting things that had happened lately, the prospect of his very own moon landing was the *most* exciting thing in the world ever. Until the next one.

Marjorie looked at mud drenched Gerald, 'Can't we just take the boy home? He needs a bath at the very least.'

Cornelius didn't disagree, but ...

'It's a promise I made to his dad' he said quietly.

Gerald summoned up all his energy and courage and made a big effort to do some super perking up, 'I am OK Auntie. I promise. If it was a promise for my dad then I am most definitely up for it. And it's our very own moon landing. How corkingly exciting is that?'

To prove that he was indeed up for it he bounced up on to his feet and said, 'ta-dah!'

Busbeater put his hand on his shoulder, 'You are most definitely a Busbeater Master Gerald.'

'Here! Here!' cried everyone.

Gerald suddenly remembered something, 'Cornelius.'

'Yes?'

'When I watched the moon landing with my mum and then again at school I noticed something on the picture that no-one else saw.'

'Oh yes' said Cornelius 'What was that?'

'Us.'

'Us?' asked Marjorie perplexed.

'Yes what do you mean Gerald old son?' asked Loosehorn who had been glowing after the derring-do in the skirmish of Sutton Bridge but was now confused again.

'Us,' repeated Gerald. 'When I was watching Apollo 11 closing in on the surface of the moon I saw a wardrobe fly past. At first I didn't know what it was and my mum didn't see it so I thought I'd dreamt it. After all I'd been up for hours and might have been a bit round the bend with excitement. But then the next day at school as we watched it again, I saw it again. A Wardrobe. This Wardrobe.'

'That's right,' said Cornelius, 'you saw yourself. You saw us. But you were the only one who could have seen it Gerald. In effect you were in two places at once. But only you can see that; only the time traveller themselves can see that – otherwise there'd be chaos.'

'Because its all very normal otherwise' observed Busbeater a little sarcastically.

'Wow' thought Gerald not entirely sure he understood. 'Wow, that's sort of epic.'

'We didn't see it though' said Loosehorn 'and we would have wouldn't

270

we?'

'Don't you remember?' said Marjorie joggingly 'Sheepshanks fell out of the window just as they were landing …'

'Oh yes. And we lost the picture …' Loosehorn remembered.

'Sorry sir' said Sheepshanks.

'After everything you've done Sheepshanks, I hardly think 'sorry' is necessary. But you know, next time, try to hang on a bit more tightly.'

'Cornelius?' began Marjorie 'the moon …'

'What about it?'

'Well, it doesn't have any air does it?'

'Not so much' agreed Cornelius.

'So much?' asked Marjorie.

'None. You are right. It has no atmosphere' Cornelius conceded.

'Bit like that bar in Simla Marjorie. That place had no atmosphere either.' Everyone guffawed at Busbeater's joke except Gerald who had no idea what they were on about. Adults, he thought. What a confusing bunch they are; brave, ridiculous and occasionally very slow on the uptake. But he loved his new friends. What a life he had. What an absolutely magnificent life he had.

Marjorie had a point he thought. How would they breathe?

'We need space suits Cornelius' said Gerald puncturing the laughter.

At that moment The Wardrobe began to creak and groan. Everyone was alarmed.

'What's that Cornelius?' asked Busbeater in a worried kind of way.

'Erm …' said Cornelius.

The creaking and groaning carried on for a few alarming seconds and then suddenly stopped. At the back of The Wardrobe a panel flung open and out fell what looked, a little improbably, like six spacesuits. Exactly like the one Gerald saw James Burke demonstrating on the television.

'Well, there's a thing' said Marjorie in wonder.

'If we asked for a comfy car would a Rolls Royce pop out from somewhere?' asked Busbeater peering in to the panel.

'The machine supplies only what we need. Gerald asked very specifically and very correctly for spacesuits and since the machine is taking us to the air-free moon, it supplied them. What we probably don't need on the moon is a luxury car. So, no Rolls Royce I am afraid' said Cornelius.

'Pity …' mumbled Busbeater.

'By jove' said Loosehorn 'is this something to do with that wire-less nonsense you were going on about before?'

'Probably Loosehorn,' replied Cornelius scratching his head, 'one thing I have learnt is that these machines are fiendishly inscrutable. Sometimes its best not to ask too many questions.'

Loosehorn sat down with a thump suddenly worn out, 'I bought this thing in Casablanca thinking it was just a wardrobe full of Lady Spankhandle's expensive and rather marvellous gowns and accessories. I am not sure I would have if I had known all this. It's all just been one frankly alarming revelation after another.'

Cornelius sat next to Loosehorn, 'I am glad you bought it Loosehorn. There is no-one I'd rather share adventures with than you and your friends.' He looked up, 'All of you are remarkable. Your courage and sense of honour and doing the right thing is extraordinary. You are brave, noble and completely round the bend. You are all truly Magnificent.'

Marjorie sat down too and gave Cornelius a hug, 'You aren't so bad yourself. You are part of us now. We are your friends.'

'Yes, Captain Golightly and we look after our own. You are a decent cove,' added Busbeater

Gerald sat down next to Marjorie and fell asleep instantly as if someone had flicked the off switch inside the exhausted Boy Adventurer.

They all looked at him; the pluckiest, bravest, muddiest and most noble of them all.

Sheepshanks recovered one of Loosehorn's stoles and formed a pillow for Gerald's head as Marjorie covered him in long ball gown. Gerald was smiling in his sleep; dreaming of The Greatest Adventure of All; landing on the Moon. And for some more mysterious reason, his mum's cooking.

'It's a bit of a way to the moon in 1969. So lets try and get some rest' said Cornelius.

'Agreed' said Busbeater. And they all settled down.

'Gerald, Gerald' whispered Cornelius as he shook the young chap's shoulder 'wake up Gerald, I want to show you something.'

Gerald rubbed his eyes and looked blinkingly at Cornelius, 'Charlie? Has my mum set the kitchen on fire again?' he asked sleepily.

'Not that I know of' said Cornelius gently.

'Oh, crikey, sorry Cornelius. I was dreaming.'

'Come this way Gerald.'

Cornelius took Gerald's hand and pulled him carefully to his feet. They stepped over the sleeping gang and toward The Wardrobe doors where, just to the right of them, Cornelius slid open a panel which revealed a large window.

'Have a look.'

Gerald looked out in to the inky blackness. He blinked a few times as

273

his eyes adjusted. He saw a blue-ish glow to his right.

'Oh my very goodness!' he squeaked 'Is that Earth?'

'It is indeed' replied Cornelius.

Gerald looked at the beautiful blue and white marble suspended there in space, half in sunlight half in shade making it look as if it was nestling in a starry blanket. It was his home. Their home. Everyone's home, where everyone lived, ate, argued, fought and studied boring old physics. Down there somewhere was his mum and dad. He put his hand to the glass as if trying to touch it, touch them.

Linda Jones shuddered and looked around. What was that? She felt something on her shoulder. Probably nothing.

Upstairs Arnold Jones scratched his shoulder 'what the ...?'

'And look over there Gerald' Cornelius was pointing to the left.

'Apollo 11!' Gerald squeaked again.

By now everyone was awake and peering over Gerald and Cornelius' shoulder in awe. Cornelius stood aside so Marjorie could get to the front for a better look. Loosehorn was happy at the back behind Gerald with Busbeater and Sheepshanks.

The Wardrobe was racing through starry space, catching the small silver landing module as it headed for the moon. The moon was right there; right in front of them. A huge, grey but shining ball in the sky. They were close enough that they could see craters large and small.

'That's the Sea of Tranquility, where they are going to land' said Gerald pointing expertly to what in Busbeater's eyes was a crater just like all the others. How could the boy tell?

Gerald had studied the map of the moon for days on end so he knew exactly where Neil and Buzz would be when they landed.

'That's The Sea of Storms' he added knowledgeably 'and right over there' he pointed to the middle 'is the Sea of Vapours.'

'Oh I say' said Marjorie.

The Wardrobe was catching Apollo 11 up rapidly. Then as it was making its landing approach they were suddenly alongside.

Gerald stared out of the window and straight in to the cockpit of the lunar module. Without thinking he waved.

Neil Armstrong looked up at exactly the same time and waved back as he guided the machine in.

'Go for landing, 3,000 feet'

'You're looking great' beep ...

The Wardrobe veered away just as a massive dust cloud revealed what Gerald already knew

'Contact light? OK engine stopped.'

beep

'we copy you down Eagle'

beep

'Houston er, Tranquility Base here. The Eagle has landed.'

With a thwump The Wardrobe landed over on the far side of the moon.

Gerald looked out of the window, 'It's just the moon, but at night' he said like an excited little boy upstairs on the landing looking down at all the presents under the tree on Christmas morning.

'That's right' said Cornelius 'according to your Book Of Adventures this side of the moon always faces away and can sometimes be night and sometimes day.'

Busbeater said rather excitedly 'Shall we get out there then? On the night side of the moon?'

Gerald was well ahead, already pulling on his suit.

'It's a bit big' he echoed from somewhere inside the enormous suit.

'Is that the smallest there is?' asked Marjorie.

'No, but this one might be' squeaked Busbeater standing up to his tummy in half a space suit.

'You two should swap I think' giggled Marjorie.

Sheepshanks was already, miraculously but no longer surprisingly in his suit and helping Marjorie on with hers.

'Not quite so … ooo … tight Sheepshanks' wailed Marjorie.

'Sorry Mrs Lieutenant Colonel Ma'am' he apologised.

From inside his suit Cornelius called, 'Is everyone ready?'

They were.

'Everyone got their communicators on?'

'Communicators?! What the blue cheese is that now Cornelius?' bellowed Busbeater.

'It's so we can talk to each other with our helmets on.'

They all looked blank.

Cornelius sighed.

'Show them all would you Sheepshanks?'

Sheepshanks showed each of them the button marked 'Communication Button' on their suits and pressed each of them.

'OK. Now is everyone ready?' sighed Cornelius.

'Yes Cornelius' they all said in unison a bit like naughty schoolchildren after having been told off by their teacher.

'Right. Helmets on everyone.'

Lieutenant Colonel Busbeater, Major General Loosehorn, Marjorie Busbeater, Sheepshanks, Captain Cornelius Golightly and most of all Gerald Jones stood ready in their space suits.

Gerald then removed the flywheel and the doors flung open.

The Wardrobe shrank with a swift shudder. Everyone was still inside only much closer together now.

'It's awfully dark' said Marjorie.

'It's not called the Big Broad Daylight side of the Moon now is it?' replied Busbeater.

'How are we going to see was my point' said Marjorie.

'Press this Ma'am' offered Sheepshanks and pushed a panel on Marjorie's suit. A light on the top of her helmet illuminated everything brilliantly around her.

'After you Gerald' said Cornelius.

Gerald was barely able to contain his excitement. He was just about to step out when he suddenly stopped.

'Everything alright Gerald?' asked Cornelius, concerned, 'Is the suit OK?'

'Oh yes, that's all tickety-boo. But Cornelius, this thing about changing history. Are we about to be the third and fourth and so on people on the moon? There are going to be other Apollo missions after this one. They are even launching an Apollo 13 …'

'Lummy,' said Loosehorn 'Unlucky thirteen? That's asking for trouble.'

'Is this allowed? We don't want to be stranded here!' said Gerald.

'Oooo, no thank you' said Loosehorn.

'Good point Gerald but we are OK. This far side of the moon always faces away from the earth so no-one will be able to see. So long as we tidy up after ourselves no-one will know we were ever here.'

'Can I do the commentary?' Gerald asked no-one in particular and before anyone could answer did anyway.

'Beep. Houston, this is Commander Gerald Jones descending from The Wardrobe - beep. We copy you Commander - beep - One small step from a muddy child, one giant leap for the troupe known as Busbeater's Magnificent Adventures In Time - beep - !'

And with that Gerald leapt out on to the surface of the far side of the moon. It was just as he imagined it, only dark. He turned on his light and began to explore.

After Gerald came Marjorie followed by Busbeater, Sheepshanks, Cornelius and finally Loosehorn.

Gerald watched everyone blunder about. Marjorie walked like she was climbing imaginary stairs while Busbeater discovered very quickly that you could jump quite a long way with minimal effort. Cornelius was practicing the somersaults the Hungarians did with such style. On the moon with very little gravity it turned out they were very easy to do.

'Don't know what all the fuss is about' he said on his seventh consecutive somersault.

Sheepshanks on the other hand was strolling about like it was a Sunday afternoon in the park,

Meanwhile, Loosehorn stood with his back pressed up to The Wardrobe.

'You sure this is safe?' he called out.

Gerald looked startled. Safe? This from the man he first saw blasting away at rabbits from the rooftop?

'What's the matter old man?' called Busbeater after seeing his chum in some distress.

'Er, nothing' replied Loosehorn.

'It's clearly not nothing. You are clinging on to The Wardrobe like a starfish. Come on, spill the beans.'

'Well alright, if you must know ever since childhood I've had a fear of floating away.'

'What?!' spluttered Busbeater.

'Floating away ...'

'A childhood fear of floating away?' repeated Gerald wondering what sort of childhood you had to have where floating away was a worry.

'Believe me' replied Loosehorn 'watching your Nanny float away when holding only an umbrella is enough to traumatise even the most stout hearted of children.'

'Why have you never said?' asked Busbeater.

'It's hardly the best way to introduce yourself is it? "Hello, I am Major General Pelham Loosehorn and I have a fear of floating away." People would think me mad.'

'Well, it is a bit mad,' said Busbeater not very sympathetically.

'Its not particularly been a problem up until now. I never imagined I'd be in a place where there'd be hardly any gravity,' Loosehorn added reasonably.

Busbeater was keen to reassure his friend, 'We're all OK – look,' he said before bouncing up and down a little too vigorously, 'Whoa ...wahay ... whoa ...'

'Thanks old man, that has really not helped. I'll just stay here if that's alright with everyone' said Loosehorn gingerly.

It was. Everyone, apart from Loosehorn who clung on to The

Wardrobe for dear life, went off exploring.

Gerald stood still. He was on the moon. Slowly he bent down on one knee and with his giant space gloves shovelled up some moon dust which glistened slightly from his headlight and let it run through his fingers. He marvelled at it; 'moon dust' he whispered to himself in awe. He then looked up to the sky and turned his light off to see the stars better. Here on the far side of the moon where it was night a billion stars sparkled like diamonds strewn across a black velvet carpet.

'It's beautiful isn't it?' said Busbeater who appeared next to him.

'I wish I could describe how beautiful Uncle.'

'You will Gerald old boy. One day you will find the words and everyone will read them. And they will understand.'

'Thank you Uncle.'

'Now, I think maybe ...'

'We should be getting home?' Gerald finished his sentence.

'Shall we?'

'I'd like to see mum and dad.'

'I think they'd probably like to see you too. We'll take you home when we get back to Busbeater Mansions.'

Gerald didn't want to leave Busbeater Mansions, but he did want to see his mum and dad.

'Come on Gerald me old china, lets go,' encouraged his uncle.

Busbeater put a gentle hand on Gerald's shoulder, switched on his light and they headed back to The Wardrobe.

'Weeeeeeeeeeeeeeeeeeeeee ...' it was Marjorie bouncing around with Cornelius ' ... eeeeeeeeeeeeeeeeeeeeee. I say Busbeater, this is a lot of fun!'

Loosehorn was still pressed up against The Wardrobe trying not to look down … or anywhere.

'Come on gang. Time to get this boy home' said Busbeater.

'Awwwwwwww' said Marjorie and Cornelius together.

'One more bounce?' Gerald asked his uncle.

'Oh come on then' said Busbeater, 'Loosehorn, will you join us?'

'er …'

'Please Loosehorn!' beseeched Gerald.

'er … er … Wooooooooooooooooooah!' He ran for Marjorie and clung on. He shut his eyes tightly.

Busbeater, Gerald, Sheepshanks, Cornelius and Marjorie with Loosehorn attached like a limpet all danced around the far side of the moon. Gerald began singing and everyone joined in;

'Fly me to the moon,

Let me sing among those stars,

Let me see what spring is like on Jupiter and Mars …!'

Inside The Wardrobe Gerald placed the flywheel in to the socket which with space gloves on was a slower and more awkward procedure than normal.

Cornelius slid back the destination panel and dialled in: 'Busbeater Mansions, Little Piddlington, Rutland, England, Saturday 26th July 1969.'

Gerald turned the flywheel left – click – then to the right. The doors slammed shut and The Wardrobe shuddered in to life once more. A smooth take off meant they could start taking their space suits off immediately.

'By jolly blinking jove' said Busbeater as he removed his helmet 'that was absolutely, completely and utterly amazingly, thunderingly spiffing.'

'I agree' said Marjorie.

'Is it over?' asked Loosehorn, his eyes camped shut

Gerald sat on his own taking his suit off slowly.

'You alright Master Gerald?' asked Sheepshanks, looking out for him as he always did.

'Oh yes thank you' sniffed Gerald.

'You seem a bit upset if you don't mind me saying.'

Gerald felt a tear tumble down his cheek, 'I wish my mum could have been here that's all. That's her song and we sang it on the moon and she would have loved that.'

'She'll be very proud when you tell her.' He put his arm around Gerald who bravely didn't blub. He was looking forward to seeing his mum and dad so much. What tales he would tell.

The journey home was made in silence largely to play a prank on Loosehorn who was still occasionally and increasingly frantically asking 'is it over?'

No-one had answered him since they left the moon and he hadn't opened his eyes. Eventually Cornelius could stand it no longer

'It is Loosehorn, it is over. You can open your eyes now' he said kindly and with a broad grin.

Loosehorn, still in his spacesuit looked to see everyone dressed in their ordinary clothes and Gerald proudly wearing his dad's Dan Dare tee-shirt.

'Well, thanks a lot you could have told me' he barked with the beginning of a smile flickering across his face.

'More fun this way we thought Loosehorn old man' guffawed Busbeater.

'Bounders the lot of you,' beamed Loosehorn.

The Wardrobe landed with a loud-ish crunch on the remnants of the bits of the room it shattered when they left.

Gerald withdrew the flywheel and the doors flung open to reveal Loosehorn's room. 'Home!' he cried and leapt out as The Wardrobe shrank to its normal size.

Everyone followed eagerly.

'I am off to find our cook' said Marjorie and marched off to find Mrs Bunyon.

Sheepshanks was at the window looking out on to the gravel drive, 'We have visitors' he announced plainly.

'Oh cripes' said Gerald, 'not The Baron again.'

Gerald went over to the window. He squeaked, 'Mum! Dad!'

From the driveway Linda and Arnold Jones looked up and waved at their son.

Gerald skittered his way out of Loosehorn's room, down the stairs and out of the front door which the Baron had so eagerly smashed.

'Mum!' he ran in to his mum's arms nearly knocking her over.

'Hello Gerald sweetheart' she sobbed 'you're so muddy! What on earth happened?'

'I'll explain later Mum.' Gerald turned to his dad.

'Son I ...' before Arnold Jones could say any more Gerald threw him an enormous hug ' … oh, I er, crikey you are muddy' he said, taken aback.

'Cornelius explained everything,' spluttered Gerald 'I know how brave you are and what an adventurer you are and how you played tennis with Henry VIII and beat The Baron with Anne Boleyn's sister …'

'Did you read my message?' Arnold asked.

' I did Dad, I did. I am so proud of you. You're an Adventurer!'

Arnold Jones was wiping tears from his eyes as Cornelius came out 'So are you Gerald' he said just loudly enough for Gerald to hear.

'Well, it was an elaborate plan but it seems to have worked' Cornelius grinned and shook Arnold warmly by the hand.

'Hello Cornelius,' said Linda quietly, 'Arnold told me everything. And I mean everything. It's why I …' she looked fondly at Arnold 'why we are here. We were going to wait for as long as it took. But in the end we waited fifteen minutes and then you all showed up … from wherever the heck it is you've been.'

There was a moment as Gerald stood still wondering how Cornelius meeting his mum again would would work out.

'I'm sorry Linda I …' stammered Cornelius.

Linda went up to him, gave him a peck on the cheek and said, 'Thank you for looking after my son.'

'He needs no looking after Linda. He is plucky, courageous, noble and strong. Like you,' he paused and looked at Arnold, 'Like both of you.'

Just then Lieutenant Colonel Busbeater and Major General Loosehorn arrived.

'Linda m'dear,' said Busbeater giving her a big hug

'And Loosehorn.' said Linda 'My that's a fine summer outfit in er … er …'

'Aquamarine is the word your searching for Linda. I've just put it on. My yellow ball gown was - well lets just say it's seen better days. Now come here.'

Loosehorn hugged Linda Busbeater tightly.

All the hugging reminded Linda,

'Where's Marjorie?'

'Get out and stay out! You are fired!' It was Marjorie shouting from the hallway.

Mrs Bunyon came hurtling out of the front doors followed by her half shut suitcase. After scrabbling around picking up her meagre belongings and shoving them back in her case she sped off on foot down the drive.

'Booooooooooooooo' called Loosehorn as she went.

'Shame!' cried Cornelius.

'Clear off traitor!' cried Busbeater.

'Ouch' exclaimed Mrs Bunyon rubbing the back of her leg as she fled.

Everyone looked for Sheepshanks.

'Just a little memento to send her on her way' he announced innocently, putting his catapult away.

'Still got it then Sheepshanks?' observed Linda.

'Ms Linda, lovely to see you again.'

Marjorie fresh from firing Mrs Bunyon hurtled over to Linda.

'Linda my dear. Are you well?'

'Mmmmph mmmm phphphphmm' replied Linda from inside a massive Marjorie hug.

'Tea for everyone?' asked Sheepshanks.

'I'd rather have something luminous Sheepshanks. And make it a large one,' replied Marjorie.

'Wonder what the Test Match score is?' Busbeater asked Loosehorn as they began to wander inside.

'How in the great crested, blue trousered grebe would I know Busbeater? In case you hadn't noticed I've been with you the whole time.'

'Always Mr Picky with the details ...' smiled Busbeater.

'That was fun wasn't it?' said Loosehorn.

'Oh very much so' replied Busbeater 'I felt like alive again.'

'We showed those so called young men a thing or two though eh?'

'Rather!'

'301 for 9' announced Loosehorn suddenly.

'What?'

'England are 301 for 9 at the end of the third day. That is now.'

'You did know you old devil you. How?'

'I read The Big Book of Adventure too you know ...'

Busbeater turned to face Loosehorn, paused and saluted his friend.

Loosehorn returned the salute. They then shook each other's hands warmly.

'Back in the game for adventure Busbeater old man?' said Loosehorn.

'Definitely back in the game,' replied Busbeater.

'Just less of the floating away next time maybe' added Loosehorn.

'Never fear. I'll look out for you old boy' said Busbeater.

Gerald held his mum and dad's hands as they all went inside. He wanted to tell them everything about his great adventure, immediately.

'Charlie, well Cornelius showed up in a bit of a flap and then The Baron drove his tank on uncle's lawn and we escaped just in time to the wrong time and then we got arrested lost The Wardrobe and were put in prison but auntie Marjorie was nice to the gaoler who helped us but first we had to perform a song and then see Magna Carta being agreed and King John is a rat because he reneged on the deal and then we went to the right time and I saved Henry's life and the Hungarian Stunt Archers formed a brigade and Uncle Busbeater and Loosehorn remembered Ishmaelia a lot and you know what its like Dad what with you clonking Henry VIII in the eye and then oh yeah there was the hurdy-gurdy playing and Bott in a tree and then we went to the moon and sang your song Mum it was incredible but it turns out Loosehorn is scared of floating away can you believe and what a time to find that out and I waved to Neil Armstrong …'

While Gerald rattled breathlessly on Linda and Arnold Jones looked at each other smiling broadly as they went inside. That's their boy alright.

As everyone trouped in, Cornelius found a piece of paper under the empty milk bottles by the front door. He read it and smiled, 'Hey everyone. Cartwright and Carruthers have news … but, crikey, apparently you order one hundred and thirty two pints of milk a day?'

'We like milk', called Marjorie.

'Well, clearly, but one hundred and thirty two pints? That is a quite lot by anyone's standards. I am a bit surprised you lot don't moo or something all the time.' Still shaking his head in disbelief Cornelius then read the other bit of the note, 'Anyhow, Cartwright and Carruthers think the fifth machine might be in Paris in 1793.'

Gerald who had barely breathed for several minutes gulped, 'Oh wow Cornelius, lets go!'

'After you've had a bath and I've had a large creme de menthe' announced Marjorie.

'Oh alright,' said Gerald, 'I knew this place would be boring' he grinned.

Everyone headed for the drawing room.

'Does anyone know how to cook?' asked Marjorie.

'I do ...' offered Linda.

'Nooooooo Mum ...' guffawed Gerald Jones, a True Adventurer now just like his dad. Oh and Neil Armstrong.

THE END

until next time ...

Lieutenant Colonel Busbeater writes:

Hello fellow Adventurers. If you enjoyed this barnstormingly magnificent adventure please drop a nice note on the Amazon thingy. (No, Marjorie, not the Rainforest, the review page on the jolly old website). It would be spiffing to know if you liked it and told others about it. Your reward will be a Big Marjorie Hug.

No Marjorie I have no idea what I just said either, but the youngsters do. Is it time for tea and buns yet?

Made in the USA
Charleston, SC
16 April 2016